# Bou...

## (Born in Blood Mafia Chronicles, #1)

## Cora Reilly

Subscribe to Cora's newsletter to find out about her next books, bonus content and giveaways! ( http://corareillyauthor.blogspot.de/p/newsletter.html )

Cover design by Romantic Book Affairs Design

## Prologue

My fingers shook like leaves in the breeze as I raised them, my heartbeat hummingbird quick. Luca's strong hand was firm and steady as he took mine and slipped the ring onto my finger.

White gold with twenty small diamonds.

What was meant as a sign of love and devotion for other couples was nothing but a testament of his ownership of me. A daily reminder of the golden cage I'd be trapped in for the rest of my life. Until death do us part wasn't an empty promise as with so many other couples that entered the holy bond of marriage. There was no way out of this union for me. I was Luca's until the bitter end. The last few words of the oath that men swore when they were inducted into the mafia could just as well have been the closing of my wedding vow:

"I enter alive and I will have to get out dead."

I should have run when I still had the chance. Now, as hundreds of faces from the Chicago and New York Familias stared back at us, flight was no longer an option. Nor was divorce. Death was the only acceptable end to a marriage in our world. Even if I still managed to escape Luca's watchful eyes and that of his henchmen, my breach of our agreement would mean war. Nothing my father could say would prevent Luca's Familia from exercising vengeance for making them lose face.

My feelings didn't matter, never had. I'd been growing up in a world where no choices were given, especially to women.

3

This wedding wasn't about love or trust or choice. It was about duty and honor, about doing what was expected.

A bond to ensure peace.

I wasn't an idiot. I knew what else this was about: money and power. Both were dwindling since the Russian Mob 'The Bratva', the Taiwanese Triad, and other crime organizations had been trying to expand their influence into our territories. The Italian Familias across the US needed to lay their feuds to rest and work together to beat down their enemies. I should be honored to marry the oldest son of the New York Familia. That's what my father and every other male relative had tried to tell me since my betrothal to Luca. I knew that, and it wasn't as if I hadn't had time to prepare for this exact moment, and yet fear corseted my body in a relentless grip.

"You may kiss the bride," the priest said.

I raised my head. Every pair of eyes in the pavilion scrutinized me, waiting for a flicker of weakness. Father would be furious if I let my terror show, and Luca's Familia would use it against us. But I had grown up in a world where a perfect mask was the only protection afforded to women and had no trouble forcing my face into a placid expression. Nobody would know how much I wanted to escape. Nobody but Luca. I couldn't hide from him, no matter how much I tried. My body wouldn't stop shaking. As my gaze met Luca's cold gray eyes, I could tell that he knew. How often had he instilled fear in others? Recognizing it was probably second nature to him.

He bent down to bridge the ten inches he towered over me. There was no sign of hesitation, fear or doubt on his face. My lips trembled against his mouth as his eyes bored into me. Their message was clear: *You are mine.*

# CHAPTER ONE

*Three years prior*

I was curled up on the chaise longue in our library, reading, when a knock sounded. Liliana's head rested in my lap and she didn't even stir when the dark wooden door opened and our mother stepped in, her dark blond hair pulled back tightly and fasted in a bun at the back of her head. Mother was pale, her face drawn with worry.

"Did something happen?" I asked.

She smiled, but it was her fake smile. "Your father wants to talk to you in his office."

I carefully moved out from under Lily's head and put it down on the chaise. She drew her legs up against her body. She was small for an eleven year old, but I wasn't exactly tall either with five foot four. None of the women in our family were. Mother avoided my eyes as I walked toward her.

"Am I in trouble?" I didn't know what I could have done wrong. Usually Lily and I were the obedient ones; Gianna was the one who always broke the rules and got punished.

"Hurry. Don't let your father wait," Mother said simply.

My stomach was in knots when I arrived in front of Father's office. After a moment to stifle my nerves, I knocked.

"Come in."

I entered, forcing my face to be carefully guarded. Father sat behind his mahogany desk in a wide black leather armchair; behind him rose the mahogany shelves filled with books that Father had never read, but they hid a secret entrance to the basement and a corridor leading off the premises.

He looked up from a pile of sheets, grey hair slicked back. "Sit."

I sank down on one of the chairs across from his desk and folded my hands in my lap, trying not to gnaw on my lower lip. Father hated that. I waited for him to start talking. He had a strange expression on his face as he scrutinized me. "The Bratva and the Triad are trying to claim our territories. They are getting bolder by the day. We're luckier than the Las Vegas familia who also has to deal with the Mexicans but we can't ignore the threat the Russians and the Taiwanese pose any longer."

Confusion filled me. Father never talked about business to us. Girls didn't need to know about the finer details of the mob business. I knew better than to interrupt him.

"We have to lay our feud with the New York Familia to rest and combine forces if we want to fight back the Bratva and the Triad." Peace with the Familia? Father and every other member of the Chicago Outfit hated the Familia. They had been killing each other for decades and only recently decided on ignoring each other in favor of killing off the members of other crime organizations, like the Bratva and the Triad. "There is no stronger bond than blood. At least the Familia got that right."

I frowned.

"Born in blood. Sworn in blood. That's their motto."

I nodded but my confusion only grew.

"I met with Salvatore Vitiello yesterday." Father met with the Capo dei Capi, the head of the New York mob? A meeting between New York and Chicago hadn't taken place in a decade and the last time hadn't ended well. It was still referred to as the Bloody Thursday. And Father wasn't even the Boss. He was only the Consigliere, the adviser to Fiore Cavallaro who ruled over the Outfit and with it the crime in the Midwest.

"We agreed that for peace to be an option we had to become family." Father's eyes bored into me and suddenly I didn't want to hear what else he had to say. "Cavallaro and I agreed that you would marry his oldest son Luca, the future Capo dei Capi of the Familia."

I felt like I was falling. "Why me?"

"Vitiello and Fiore have been talking on the phone several times in the last few weeks, and Vitiello wanted the most beautiful girl for his son. Of course, we couldn't give him the daughter of one of our soldiers. Fiore doesn't have daughters, so he said you were the most beautiful girl available." Gianna was just as beautiful, but she was younger. That probably saved her.

"There are so many beautiful girls," I choked. I couldn't breathe. Father looked at me as if I was his most prized possession.

"There aren't many Italian girls with hair like yours. Fiore described it as golden." Father guffawed. "You are our door into the New York Familia."

"But, Father, I'm fifteen. I can't marry."

Father made a dismissive gesture. "If I were to agree, you could. What do we care for laws?"

I gripped the armrests so tightly, my knuckles were turning white, but I didn't feel pain. Numbness was working its way through my body.

"But I told Salvatore that the wedding would have to wait until you turn eighteen. Your mother was adamant you be of age and finish school. Fiore let her begging get to him."

So the Boss had told my father the wedding had to wait. My own father would have thrown me into the arms of my future husband now. My *husband*. A wave of sickness crashed over me. I knew only two things about Luca Vitiello; he would become the head of the New York mob once his father retired or died, and he got his nickname 'The Vice' for crushing a man's throat with his bare hands. I didn't know how old he was. My cousin Bibiana had to marry a man thirty years her senior. Luca couldn't be that old, if his father hadn't retired yet. At least, that's what I hoped. Was he cruel?

*He'd crushed a man's throat. He'll be the head of the New York mob.*

"Father," I whispered. "Please don't force me to marry that man."

Father's expression tightened. "You will marry Luca Vitiello. I shook hands on it with his father Salvatore. You will be a good wife to Luca, and when you meet him for the Engagement celebrations, you'll act like an obedient lady."

"Engagement party?" I echoed. My voice sounded distant, as if a veil of fog covered my ears.

"Of course. It's a good way to establish bonds between our families, and it'll give Luca the chance to see what he's getting out of the deal. We don't want to disappoint him."

"When?" I cleared my throat but the lump remained. "When is the engagement party?"

"August. We haven't set a date yet."

That was in two months. I nodded numbly. I loved reading romance novels and whenever the couples in them married, I'd imagined how my wedding would be. I'd always imagined it would be filled with excitement and love. Empty dreams of a stupid girl.

"So I'm allowed to keep attending school?" What did it even matter if I graduated? I would never go to college, never work. All I'd be allowed to do was to warm my husband's bed. My throat tightened further and tears prickled in my eyes, but I willed them not to fall. Father hated it when we lost control.

"Yes. I told Vitiello that you attend an all-girls Catholic school, which seemed to please him." Of course, it did. Couldn't risk that I got anywhere near boys.

"Is that all?"

"For now."

I walked out of the office as if in trance. I'd turned fifteen four months ago. My birthday had felt like a huge step toward my future, and I'd been excited. Silly me. My life was already over before it even began. Everything was decided for me.

I couldn't stop crying. Gianna stroked my hair as my head lay in her lap. She was thirteen, only eighteen months younger than me, but today those eighteen months meant the difference between freedom and a life in a loveless prison. I tried very hard not to resent her for it. It wasn't her fault.

"You could try to talk to Father again. Maybe he'll change his mind," Gianna said in a soft voice.

"He won't."

"Maybe Mama will be able to convince him."

As if Father would ever let a woman make a decision for him. "Nothing anyone could say or do will make a difference," I said miserably. I hadn't seen Mother since she'd sent me into Father's office. She probably couldn't face me, knowing what she'd condemned me to.

"But Aria—"

I lifted my head and wiped the tears from my face. Gianna stared at me with pitiful blue eyes, the same cloudless summer sky blue as my own. But where my hair was light blond hers was red. Father sometimes called her witch; it wasn't an endearment. "He shook hands on it with Luca's father."

"They met?"

That's what I'd wondered as well. Why had he found time to meet with the head of the New York Familia but not to tell me about his plans to sell me off like a better whore? I shook off the frustration and despair trying to claw their way out of my body.

"That's what Father told me."

"There has to be something we can do," Gianna said.

"There isn't."

"But you haven't even met the guy. You don't even know how he looks! He could be ugly, fat and old."

Ugly, fat and old. I wished that were the only features of Luca I had to worry about. "Let's google him. There have to be photos of him on the internet."

Gianna jumped up and took my laptop from my desk, then she sat down beside me, our sides pressed against each other.

We found several photos and articles about Luca. He had the coldest gray eyes I'd ever seen. I could imagine only too well how those eyes looked down at his victims before he put a bullet in their heads.

"He's taller than everyone," Gianna said in amazement. He was; in all the photos he was several inches taller than whoever stood beside him, and he was muscled. That probably explained why some people called him the Bull behind his back. That was the nickname the articles used and they called him the heir of businessman and club owner Salvatore Vitiello. *Businessman*. Maybe on the outside. Everybody knew what Salvatore Vitiello really was, but of course nobody was stupid enough to write about it.

"He's with a new girl in every photo."

I stared down at the emotionless face of my future husband. The newspaper called him the most sought after bachelor in New York, heir to hundreds of millions of dollars. *Heir to an imperium of death and blood,* that's what it should say.

Gianna huffed. "God, girls are throwing themselves at him. I suppose he's good looking."

"They can have him," I said bitterly. In our world a handsome exterior often hid the monster within. The society girls saw his good looks and wealth. They thought the bad boy aura was a game. They fawned over his predator-like charisma because it radiated power. But what they didn't know was that blood and death lurked beneath the arrogant smile.

I stood abruptly. "I need to talk to Umberto."

Umberto was almost fifty and my father's loyal soldier. He was also Gianna's and my bodyguard. He knew everything about everyone. Mother called him a scandalmonger. But if anyone knew more about Luca, it was Umberto.

***

"He became a Made Man at eleven," Umberto said, sharpening his knife on a grinder as he did every day. The smell of tomato and oregano filled the kitchen, but it didn't give me a sense of comfort as it usually did.

"At eleven?" I asked, trying to keep my voice even. Most people didn't become fully initiated members of the Mafia until they were sixteen. "Because of his father?"

Umberto grinned, revealing a gold incisor, and paused in his movements. "You think he got it easy because he's the Boss's son? He *killed* his first man at eleven, that's why it was decided to initiate him early."

Gianna gasped. "He's a monster."

Umberto shrugged. "He's what he needs to be. Ruling over New York, you can't be a pussy." He gave an apologetic smile. "A wuss."

"What happened?" I wasn't sure I really wanted to know. If Luca had killed his first man at eleven, then how many more had he killed in the nine years since?

Umberto shook his shaved head, and scratched the long scar that ran from his temple down to his chin. He was thin, and didn't look like much, but Mother told me few were faster with a knife than him. I'd never seen him fight. "Can't say. I'm not that familiar with New York."

I watched our cook as she prepared dinner, trying to focus on something that wasn't my churning stomach and my overwhelming fear. Umberto scanned my face. "He's a good catch. He'll be the most powerful man on the East coast soon enough. He'll protect you."

"And who will protect me from him?" I hissed.

Umberto didn't say anything because the answer was clear: nobody could protect me from Luca after our wedding. Not Umberto, and not my father if he felt so inclined. Women in our world belonged to their husband. They were his property to deal with however he pleased.

# CHAPTER TWO

The last couple of months had gone by too fast no matter how much I wanted time to slow, to give me more time to prepare. Only two days until my engagement party. Mother was busy ordering the servants around, making sure the house was spotless and nothing went wrong. It wasn't even a big celebration. Only our family, Luca's family and the families of the respective heads of New York and Chicago were invited. Umberto said it was for safety reasons. The truce was still too fresh to risk a gathering of hundreds of guests.

I wished they'd cancel it altogether. For all I cared, I didn't have to meet Luca until the day of our wedding. Fabiano jumped up and down on my bed, a pout on his face. He was only five and had entirely too much energy. "I want to play!"

"Mother doesn't want you to race through the house. Everything needs to be perfect for the guests."

"But they aren't even here!" Thank God. Luca and the rest of the New York guests would arrive tomorrow. Only one more night until I'd be meeting my future husband, a man who killed with his bare hands. I closed my eyes.

"Are you crying again?" Fabiano hopped off the bed and walked up to me, slipping his hand into mine. His dark blonde hair was a mess. I tried to smooth it down but Fabiano jerked his head away.

"What do you mean?" I'd tried to hide my tears from him. Mostly I cried at night when I was protected by darkness.

"Lily says you cry all the time because Luca has bought you."

I froze. I'd have to tell Liliana to stop saying such things. It would only get me in trouble. "He didn't buy me." Liar. Liar.

"Same difference," Gianna said from the doorway, startling me.

"Shhh. What if Father hears us?"

Gianna shrugged. "He knows that I hate how he sold you like a cow."

"Gianna," I warned, nodding toward Fabiano. He peered up at me. "I don't want you to leave," he whispered.

"I'm not leaving for a long time, Fabi." He seemed satisfied with my answer and the worry disappeared from his face and was replaced by his up-to-no good expression. "Catch me!" he screamed and stormed off, pushing Gianna aside as he darted past her.

Gianna tore after him. "I'll kick your ass, you little monster!"

I rushed into the corridor. Liliana poked her head out of her door and then she too ran after my brother and sister. Mother would have my head if they smashed another family heirloom. I flew down the stairs. Fabiano was still in the lead. He was fast, but Liliana had almost caught him while Gianna and I were too slow in the high heels my mother forced us to wear for practice. Fabiano dashed into the corridor leading into the west wing of the house and the rest of us followed. I wanted to shout at him to stop. Father's office was in this part of the house. We'd be in so much trouble if he caught us playing around. Fabiano was supposed to act like a man. What five-year-old acted like a man?

We passed Father's door and relief washed over me, but then three men rounded the corner at the end of the corridor. I parted my lips to shout a warning, but it was too late. Fabiano skidded to a halt but Liliana ran into the man in the middle with full force. Most people would have lost their balance. Most people weren't six foot five and built like a bull.

I jerked to a halt as time seemed to grind to a stop around me. Gianna gasped beside me, but my gaze was frozen on my future husband. He was looking down at the blond head of my little sister, steadying her with his strong hands. Hands he'd used to crush a man's throat.

"Liliana," I said, my voice shrill with fear. I never called my sister by her full name unless she was in trouble or something was seriously wrong. I wished I was better at hiding my terror. Now everyone was staring at me, including Luca. His cold gray eyes scanned me from head to toe, lingering on my hair.

God, he was tall. The men beside him were both over six feet but he dwarfed them. His hands were still on Lily's shoulders. "Liliana, come here," I said firmly, holding out a hand. I wanted her far away from Luca. She stumbled backward, then flew into my arms, burying her face against my shoulder. Luca raised one black eyebrow.

"That's Luca Vitiello!" Gianna said helpfully, not even bothering to hide her disgust. Fabiano made a sound like an enraged wildcat and stormed toward Luca, and started pummeling his legs and stomach with his small fists. "Leave Aria alone! You don't get her!"

My heart stopped right then. The man to Luca's side took a step forward. The outline of a gun was visible under his vest. He had to be Luca's bodyguard, though I really couldn't see why he needed one.

"No, Cesare," Luca said simply and the man stilled. Luca caught my brother's hands in one of his, stopping the assault. I doubted he'd even felt the blows. I pushed Lily toward Gianna who wrapped a protective arm around her, then I approached Luca. I was scared out of my mind, but I needed to get Fabiano away from him. Maybe New York and Chicago were trying to lay their feud to rest, but alliances could break in a blink. It wouldn't be the first time. Luca and his men were still the enemy.

"What a warm welcome we get. That's the infamous hospitality of the Outfit," said the other man with Luca; he had the same black hair but his eyes were darker. He was a couple of inches smaller than Luca and not as broad, but it was unmistakable that they were brothers.

"Matteo," Luca said in a low voice that made me shiver. Fabiano was still snarling and struggling like a wild animal, but Luca held him at arm-length.

"Fabiano," I said firmly, gripping his upper arm. "It's enough. That's not how we treat guests."

Fabiano froze, then gazed up at me over his shoulder. "He's not a guest. He wants to steal you away, Aria."

Matteo chuckled. "This is too good. I'm glad Father convinced me to come."

"Ordered you," Luca corrected, but he didn't take his eyes off of me. I couldn't return his gaze. My cheeks blazed with heat at his scrutiny. My father and his bodyguards made sure that Gianna, Lily and I weren't around men very often, and the ones he let near us were either family or ancient. Luca was neither family, nor old. He was only five years older than me, but he looked like a man and made me feel like a small girl in comparison.

Luca let go of Fabiano and I pulled him toward me, his back against my legs. I folded my hands over his small heaving chest. He didn't stop glaring at Luca. I wished I had his courage, but he was a boy, an heir to my father's title. He wouldn't be forced to obey anyone, except for the Boss. He could *afford* courage.

"I'm sorry," I said, even if the words tasted foul. "My brother didn't mean to be disrespectful."

"I did!" Fabiano shouted. I covered his mouth with my palm and he squirmed in my hold but I didn't let him go.

"Don't apologize," Gianna said sharply, ignoring the warning look I shot her. "It's not our fault that he and his bodyguards take up so much room in the corridor. At least, Fabiano speaks the truth. Everyone else thinks they need to blow sugar up his ass because he's going to be Capo—"

"Gianna!" My voice was like a whip. She snapped her lips shut, staring at me with wide eyes. "Take Lily and Fabiano to their rooms. Now."

"But—" She glanced behind me. I was glad I couldn't see Luca's expression.

"Now!"

She grabbed Fabiano's hand and dragged him and Lily away. I didn't think my first encounter with my future husband could possibly have gone any worse. Bracing myself, I faced him and his men. I expected to be greeted by fury, but I found a smirk on Luca's face instead. My cheeks were burning with embarrassment, and now that I was alone with the three men, nerves twisted my stomach. Mother would freak out if she found out I wasn't dressed up for my first meeting with Luca. I was wearing one of my favorite maxi dresses with sleeves that reached my elbows, and I was silently glad for the protection all the fabric offered me. I folded my arms in front of my body, unsure of what to do. "I apologize for my sister and brother. They are—" I struggled for a word other than rude.

"Protective of you," Luca said simply. His voice was even, deep, emotionless. "This is my brother Matteo."

Matteo's lips were pulled into a wide grin. I was glad he didn't try to take my hand. I didn't think I could have kept my composure if either of them had moved any closer. "And this is my right hand, Cesare." Cesare gave me the briefest nod before he returned to his task of scanning the corridor. What was he waiting for? We didn't have assassins stashed in secret trap doors.

I focused on Luca's chin and hoped it appeared as if I was actually looking at his eyes. I took a step back. "I should go to my siblings."

Luca had a knowing expression on his face, but I didn't care if he saw how uncomfortable, how *scared* he made me. Not waiting for him to excuse me – he wasn't my husband nor my fiancé yet – I turned and quickly walked off, proud that I hadn't given in to the urge to run.

*** 

Mother tugged at the dress Father had chosen for the occasion. For the meat show, as Gianna called it. No matter how much Mother tugged though, the dress didn't get any longer. I stared at myself in the mirror uncertainly. I'd never worn anything that revealing. The black dress was clinging to my butt and waist, and ended at my upper thighs; the top was a glittery golden bustier with black tulle straps. "I can't wear that, Mother."

Mother met my gaze in the mirror. Her hair was pinned up; it was a few shades darker than mine. She was wearing a floor-length elegant dress. I wished I was allowed something that modest. "You look like a woman," she whispered.

I cringed. "I look like a hooker."

"Hookers can't afford a dress like that."

Father's mistress had clothes that cost more than some people spent on a car. Mother put her hands on my waist. "You have a wasp waist, and the dress makes your legs look very long. I'm sure Luca will appreciate it."

I stared down at my cleavage. I had small breasts, even the push-up effect of the bustier couldn't change that. I was a fifteen-year-old dressed up to look like a woman.

"Here." Mother handed me five-inch black heels. Maybe I'd reach Luca's chin when I wore them. I slipped into them. Mother forced her fake smile onto her face and smoothed down my long hair. "Hold your head high. Fiore Cavallaro called you the most beautiful woman of Chicago. Show Luca and his entourage that you are more beautiful than any women in New York too. After all, Luca's *knows* almost all of them." The way she said it I was sure she'd read the articles about Luca's conquests as well, or maybe Father had told her something.

"Mother," I said hesitantly, but she stepped back. "Now go. I'll come after you, but this is your day. You should enter the room alone. The men will be waiting. Your father will present you to Luca and then we'll all come together in the dining room for dinner." She'd told me this dozens of times already.

For a moment, I wanted to take her hand and beg her to accompany me; instead I turned and walked out of my room. I was glad that my mother had forced me to wear heels in the last few weeks. When I arrived in front of the door to the fireplace lounge on the first floor in the west wing, my heart was beating in my throat. I wished Gianna was at my side, but Mother was probably warning her to behave right now. I had to go through this alone. Nobody was supposed to steal the show from the bride-to-be.

I stared at the dark wood of the door and considered running away. Male laughter rang out behind it, my father and the Boss. A room filled with the most powerful and dangerous men in the country and I was supposed to go in. A lamb alone with wolves. I shook my head. I needed to stop thinking like that. I'd made them wait too long already.

I gripped the handle and pressed down. I slipped in, not yet looking at anyone as I closed the door. Gathering my courage, I faced the room. Conversation died. Was I supposed to say something? I shivered and hoped they couldn't see it. My father looked like the cat that got the cream. My eyes sought Luca and his piercing stare rendered me motionless. I held my breath. He put down a glass with a dark liquid with an audible clank. If nobody said something soon, I'd flee the room. I quickly scanned the faces of the gathered men. From New York there were Matteo, Luca and Salvatore Vitiello, and two bodyguards: Cesare and a young man I didn't know. From the Chicago Outfit there were my Father, Fiore Cavallaro, and his son, the future head Dante Cavallaro, as well as Umberto and my cousin Raffaele whom I hated with the fiery passion of a thousand suns. And off to the side stood poor Fabiano who had to wear a black suit like everyone else. I could see that he wanted to run toward me to seek solace, but he knew what Father would say to that.

Father finally moved toward me, put a hand on my back and led me toward the gathered men like a lamb toward slaughter. The only man who looked positively bored out of his mind was Dante Cavallaro; he had only eyes for his Scotch. Our family had attended the funeral of his wife two months ago. A widower in his thirties. I would have felt pity for him if he didn't scare me senseless, almost as much as Luca scared me.

Of course Father steered me straight toward my future husband with a challenging expression as if he expected Luca to fall on his knees from awe. Going from his expression, Luca might as well have been staring at a rock. His gray eyes were hard and cold as they focused on my father.

"This is my daughter, Aria."

Apparently, Luca hadn't mentioned our embarrassing encounter. Fiore Cavallaro spoke up. "I didn't promise too much, did I?"

I wished the ground would open and swallow me whole. I had never been submitted to so much...attention. The way Raffaele looked at me made my skin crawl. He'd been initiated only recently and had turned eighteen two weeks ago. Since then he'd been even more obnoxious than before.

"You didn't," Luca said simply.

Father looked obviously put off. Without anyone noticing Fabiano had snuck up behind me and slipped his hand into mine. Well, Luca had noticed and was staring at my brother, which brought his gaze entirely too close to my naked thighs. I shifted nervously and Luca looked away.

"Maybe the future bride and husband want to be alone for a few minutes?" Salvatore Vitiello suggested. My eyes jerked in his direction and I didn't manage to hide my shock fast enough. Luca had noticed but he didn't seem to care.

My father smiled and turned to leave. I couldn't believe it.

"Should I stay?" Umberto asked. I gave him a quick smile, which disappeared when my father shook his head. "Give them a few minutes alone," he said. Salvatore Vitiello actually *winked* at Luca. They all filed out until only Luca, Fabiano and I were left.

"Fabiano," came my father's sharp voice. "Get out of there *now*."

Fabiano reluctantly let go of my hand and left, but not before sending Luca the deadliest look a five-year old could manage. Luca's lips quirked. Then the door closed and we were alone. What had Luca's father's wink meant?

I peeked up at Luca. I had been right: with my high heels, the top of my head graced his chin. He looked out of the window. He didn't spare me a single glance. Dressing me up like a hooker didn't make Luca any more interested in me. Why would he be? I'd seen the women he dated in New York. They would have filled out the bustier better.

"Did you choose the dress?"

I jumped, startled that he'd spoken. His voice was deep and calm. Was he ever anything but? "No," I admitted. "My father did."

Luca's jaw twitched. I couldn't read him and it was making me increasingly nervous. He reached into the inside of his jacket and for a ridiculous second I actually thought he was pulling a gun on me. Instead he held a black box in his hand. He turned toward me and I stared intently at his black shirt. Black shirt, black tie, black jacket. Black like his soul.

This was a moment millions of women dreamed off, but I felt cold when Luca opened the box. Inside sat a white gold ring with a big diamond in the center sandwiched between two marginally smaller diamonds. I didn't move.

Luca held out his hand when the awkwardness between us reached its peak. I flushed and extended my hand. I flinched when his skin brushed mine. He slipped the engagement ring on my finger, then released me.

"Thank you," I felt obligated to say the words and even look up into his face, which was impassive, though the same couldn't be said for his eyes. They looked angry. Had I done something wrong? He held out his arm and I linked mine through it, letting him lead me out of the lounge and toward the dining room. We didn't speak. Maybe Luca was disappointed enough with me that he'd cancel the arrangement? But he wouldn't have put the ring on my finger if that were the case.

When we stepped into the dining room, the women of my family had joined the men. The Vitiellos hadn't brought female company. Maybe because they didn't trust my Father and the Cavallaros enough to risk bringing women into our house.

I couldn't blame them. I wouldn't trust my father or the Boss either. Luca dropped his arm and I quickly joined my mother and sisters, who pretended to admire my ring. Gianna gave me a look. I didn't know what my mother had threatened her with to keep her silent. I could tell that Gianna had a scathing comment on the tip of her tongue. I shook my head at her and she rolled her eyes. Dinner was a blur. The men discussed business while we women remained quiet. My eyes kept drifting toward the ring on my finger. It felt too heavy, too tight, *entirely too much*. Luca had marked me as his possession.

\*\*\*

After dinner the men moved on to the lounge to drink and smoke and discuss whatever else needed to be discussed. I returned to my room, but couldn't fall asleep. Eventually, I put a bathrobe over my pajamas, slipped out of my room and crept downstairs. In a fit of craziness, I took the passage that led to the secret door behind the wall in the lounge. My Grandfather thought it was necessary to have secret escapes in the office and the fireplace lounge because that's where the men of the family usually held their meetings. I wondered what he thought would happen to the women after the men had all fled through the secret passage?

I found Gianna with her eyes pressed against the peephole of the disguised door. Of course, she was already there. She whirled around, eyes wide but relaxed when she spotted me.

"What's going on in there?" I said in a bare whisper, worried the men in the lounge would overhear us.

Gianna moved to the side, so I could peer through the second peephole. "Almost everyone's already gone. Father and Cavallaro have details to discuss with Salvatore Vitiello. It's only Luca and his entourage now."

I squinted through the hole, which gave me a perfect view of the chairs crowded around the fireplace. Luca leaned against the marble ledge of the fireplace, legs casually crossed, a glass of Scotch in his hand. His brother Matteo lounged in an armchair beside him, legs wide apart and that wolfish grin on his face. Cesare and the second bodyguard they'd called Romero during dinner sat in the other armchairs. Romero looked to be the same age of Matteo, so around eighteen. Barely men by society's standard, but not in our world.

"It could have been worse," Matteo said, grinning. He might not have looked quite as deadly as Luca, but something in his eyes told me he was only able to hide it better. "She could have been ugly. But, holy fuck, your little fiancée is an apparition. That dress. That body. That hair and face." Matteo whistled. It seemed as if he was provoking his brother on purpose.

"She's a child," Luca said dismissively. Indignation rose in me, but I knew I should be glad that he didn't look at me like a man looked at a woman.

"She didn't look like a child to me," Matteo said, then clucked his tongue. He nudged the older man, Cesare. "What do you say? Is Luca blind?"

Cesare shrugged with a careful glance at Luca. "I didn't look at her closely."

"What about you, Romero? You got functioning eyes in your head?"

Romero looked up, then quickly looked back down to his drink.

Matteo threw his head back and laughed. "Fuck, Luca, did you tell your men you'd cut their dicks off if they looked at that girl? You aren't even married to her."

"She's mine," Luca said quietly, sending a chill down my back with his voice, not to mention his eyes. He looked at Matteo, who shook his head. "For the next three years, you'll be in New York and she will be here. You can't always keep an eye on her, or do you intend to threaten every man in the Outfit. You can't cut off all of their dicks. Maybe Scuderi knows of a few Eunuchs who can keep watch over her."

"I'll do what I have to," Luca said, swirling the drink in his glass. "Cesare, find the two idiots who are supposed to guard Aria." The way my name rolled off his tongue made me shiver. I didn't even know I had two guards now. Umberto had always protected me and my sisters.

Cesare left immediately and returned ten minutes later with Umberto and Raffaele, both looked butt-hurt that they'd been summoned like dogs by someone from New York. Father was a step behind them.

"What's the meaning of this?" Father asked.

"I want to have a word with the men you chose to protect what's *mine*."

Gianna huffed beside me, but I pinched her. Nobody could know we were listening in on this conversation. Father would throw a fit if we revealed the position of his secret door.

"They are good soldiers, both of them. Raffaele is Aria's cousin, and Umberto has worked for me for almost two decades."

"I'd like to decide for myself if I trust them," Luca said. I held my breath. That was as close to an insult as he could get without actually insulting my father openly. Father's lips thinned, but he gave a curt nod. He remained in the room. Luca stepped up to Umberto. "I hear you are good with the knife."

"The best," Father interjected. A muscle in Luca's jaw twitched.

"Not as good as your brother, as rumor has it," Umberto said with a nod toward Matteo who flashed him a shark grin. "But better than any other man in our territory," Umberto admitted eventually.

"Are you married?"

Umberto nodded. "For twenty-one years."

"That's a long time," Matteo said. "Aria must look awfully delicious in comparison to your *old* wife." I stifled a gasp.

Umberto's hand twitched an inch toward the holster around his waist. Everyone saw it. Father watched like a hawk but didn't interfere. Umberto cleared his throat. "I've known Aria since her birth. She is a *child*."

"She won't be a child for much longer," Luca said.

"She will always be a child in my eyes. And I'm faithful to my wife." Umberto glared at Matteo. "If you insult my wife again, I'll ask your father for permission to challenge you in a knife fight to defend her honor and I'll kill you."

This would end badly.

Matteo inclined his head. "You could try." He bared his white teeth. "But you would not succeed."

Luca crossed his arms, then gave a nod. "I think you are a good choice, Umberto." Umberto stepped back, but kept his gaze fixed on Matteo who ignored him.

Luca's eyes settled on Raffaele and he dropped whatever civility had cloaked the monster within until that point. He moved so close to Raffaele that my cousin had to tilt his head back to return the stare. Raffaele tried to keep his expression arrogant and self-confident, but he looked like a Chihuahua pup trying to impress a Bengal tiger. Luca and he might as well have been two different species.

"He's family. Are you honestly going to accuse him of having an interest in my daughter?"

"I saw how you looked at Aria," Luca said, never taking his eyes off of Raffaele.

"Like a juicy peach you wanted to pluck," Matteo threw in, enjoying this entirely too much.

Raffaele's eyes darted toward my father, looking for help.

"Don't deny it. I know want when I see it. And you want Aria," Luca growled. Raffaele didn't deny it. "If I find out you are looking at her like that again. If I find out you are in a room alone with her. If I find out you touch as much as her hand, I will kill you."

Raffaele flushed red. "You aren't a member of the Outfit. Nobody would tell you anything even if I *raped* her. I could break her in for you." *God, Raffaele shut your mouth.* Couldn't he see murder in Luca's eyes? "Maybe I'll even film it for you."

Before I could even blink, Luca had thrown Raffaele to the ground and dug a knee into his spine, one of my cousin's arms twisted back. Raffaele struggled and cursed, but Luca held him fast. One of his hands gripped Raffaele's wrist while he reached under his vest with the other, pulling out a knife.

My legs turned weak. "Leave now," I told Gianna in a whisper. She didn't listen.

*Look away, Aria.*

But I couldn't. Father would surely stop Luca. But Father's expression was disgusted as he stared down at Raffaele. Luca's eyes sought Father's gaze – Raffaele wasn't his soldier. This wasn't even his territory. Honor demanded he got permission from the Consigliere – and when my father gave a nod, he brought the knife down and cut Raffaele's pinky off. The screams rang in my ears when my vision turned black. I bit down on my fist to stifle a sound. Gianna didn't. She let out a screech that could have woken the dead before she threw up. At least, she'd turned and aimed away from me. Her vomit spilled down the steps.

Behind the doors, silence reigned. They had heard us. I gripped Gianna's upper arms when the secret door was ripped open, revealing Father's furious face. Behind him stood Cesare and Romero, both with their weapons drawn. When they saw Gianna and me, they returned them to the holsters under their jackets.

Gianna didn't cry. She seldom did, but her face was pale and she leaned heavily against me. If I didn't have to hold her up, my own legs would have crumpled. But I had to be strong for her.

"Of course," Father hissed, scowling at Gianna. "I should have known it was you causing trouble again." He wrenched her away from me and into the lounge, raised his hand and slapped her hard across the face.

I took a step in his direction to protect her and Father lifted his arm again. I braced myself for the slap, but Luca caught my father's wrist with his left hand. His right hand was still grasping the knife he'd used to cut off Raffaele's finger. The knife and Luca's hand were coated with blood. My eyes widened. Father was the master of the house, the master over us. Luca's intervention was an insult against my father's honor.

Umberto drew his knife and Father had his hand on his gun. Matteo, Romero and Cesare had drawn their own guns. Raffaele was huddled on the floor, bent over his hand, his whimpers the only sound in the room. Had there ever been a red engagement?

"I didn't mean disrespect," Luca said calmly, as if war between New York and Chicago wasn't on the verge of breaking out. "But Aria is no longer your responsibility. You lost your right to punish her when you made her my fiancée. She's mine to deal with now."

Father glanced down at the ring on my finger, then inclined his head. Luca let go of his wrist, and the other men in the room relaxed slightly, but didn't put their weapons back. "That's true." He stepped back and gestured at me. "Then would you like the honor of beating some sense into her?"

Luca's hard gaze settled on me and I stopped breathing. "She didn't disobey me."

Father's lips thinned. "You are right. But as I see it Aria will be living under my roof until the wedding and since honor forbids me to raise my hand against her, I'll have to find another way to make her obey *me*." He glowered at Gianna and hit her a second time. "For every of your wrongdoings, Aria, your sister will accept the punishment in your stead."

I pressed my lips together, tears prickling in my eyes. I didn't look at Luca or Father, not until I could find a way to hide my hatred from them.

"Umberto, take Gianna and Aria to their rooms and make sure they stay there." Umberto sheathed his knife and gestured at us to follow him. I stepped past my father, dragging Gianna with me who had her head bowed. She stiffened as we stepped over the blood on the hardwood floor and the cut-off finger laying abandoned in it. My eyes darted to Raffaele who was clutching his wound to still the bleeding. His hands, his shirt and pants were covered with blood. Gianna retched as if she was going to throw up again.

"No," I said firmly. "Look at me."

She drew her eyes away from the blood and met my gaze. There were tears in her eyes and her lower lip had a cut that was dripping blood on her chin and her nightgown. My hand on hers tightened. *I'm here for you.* Our locked eyes seemed her only anchor as Umberto led us out of the room.

"Women," my father said in a scoffing tone. "They can't even bear the sight of a bit of blood." I could practically feel Luca's eyes boring into my back before the door closed. Gianna wiped her bleeding lip as we hurried after Umberto through the corridor and up the stairs. "I hate him," she muttered. "I hate them all."

"Shh." I didn't want her to talk like that in front of Umberto. He cared for us, but he was my father's soldier through and through.

He stopped me when I wanted to follow Gianna into her room. I didn't want her to be alone tonight. And I didn't want to be alone either. "You heard what your father said."

I glared at Umberto. "I need to help Gianna with her lip."

Umberto shook his head. "It's nothing. You two in a room together always bodes trouble. Do you think it's wise to irk your father any more tonight?" Umberto closed Gianna's door and gently pushed me in the direction of my room next to hers.

I stepped in, then turned to him. "A room full of grown men watches a man beat a helpless girl, that's the famous courage of *made men*."

"Your future husband stopped your father."

"From hitting *me*, not Gianna."

Umberto smiled like I was a stupid child. "Luca might rule over New York, but this is Chicago and your father is Consigliere."

"You admire Luca," I said incredulously. "You watched him cut off Raffaele's finger and you admire him."

"Your cousin is lucky The Vice didn't cut off something else. Luca did what every man would have done."

Maybe every man in our world.

Umberto patted my head like I was an adorable kitten. "Go to sleep."

"Will you be guarding my door all night to make sure I don't sneak out again?" I said challengingly.

"Better get used to it. Now that Luca's put a ring on your finger, he'll make sure you're always guarded."

I slammed the door shut. Guarded. Even from afar Luca would be controlling my life. I'd thought my life would go on as it used to until the wedding, but how could it when everyone knew what the ring on my finger meant? Raffaele's pinky was a signal, a warning. Luca had made his claim on me and would enforce it cold-bloodedly.

I didn't extinguish the lights that night, worried the darkness would bring back images of blood and cut-off limbs. They came anyway.

# CHAPTER THREE

My breath clouded as it left my lips. Even my thick coat couldn't protect me from Chicago's winter. Snow crunched under my boots as I followed mother along the pavement toward the brick building, which harbored the most luxurious wedding store in the Midwest. Umberto trailed closely behind, my constant shadow. Another of my father's soldiers made up the rear, behind my sisters.

Revolving brass doors let us into the brightly lit inside of the store and the owner and her two assistants immediately greeted us. "Happy birthday, Ms. Scuderi," she said in her lilting voice.

I forced a smile. My eighteenth birthday was supposed to be a day for celebration. Instead it only meant I was another step closer to marrying Luca. I hadn't seen him since that night he'd cut off Raffaele's finger. He'd sent me expensive jewelry for my birthdays, Christmas holidays, Valentine's days and the anniversary of our engagement but that was the extent of our contact in the last thirty months. I'd seen photos of him with other women on the internet, but even that would stop today when our engagement would be leaked to the press. At least in public he wouldn't flaunt his whores anymore.

I didn't kid myself into thinking he wasn't still sleeping with them. And I didn't care. As long as he had other women to screw, he'd hopefully not think about me in that way.

"Only six months until your wedding if I'm correctly informed?" the shop owner piped. She was the only person who looked excited.

No surprise really, she would make a lot of money today. The wedding that marked the final union of the Chicago and the New York mafia was supposed to be a splendid affair. Money was irrelevant.

I inclined my head. 166 days until I had to exchange one golden cage with another. Gianna gave me a look that made it clear what she thought of the matter, but she kept her mouth shut. At sixteen and a half, Gianna had finally learned to reign in her outbursts, *mostly*.

The shop owner led us into the fitting room. Umberto and the other man stayed outside the drawn curtains. Lily and Gianna plopped down on the plush white couch while Mother began browsing the wedding gowns on display. I stood in the middle of the room. The sight of all the white tulle, silk, gossamer, brocade and what it stood for, corded up my throat. I'd be a married woman soon. Quotes about love decorated the walls of the fitting room; they felt like a taunt considering the harsh reality that was my life. What was love but a silly dream?

I could feel the eyes of the shop owner and her assistants on me, and squared my shoulders before I joined my mother. Nobody could know that I wasn't the happy bride-to-be but a pawn in a game of power. Eventually, the shop owner approached us and showed us her most expensive gowns.

"What kind of gown would your future husband prefer?" she asked pleasantly.

"The naked kind," Gianna said, and my mother shot her a glare. I flushed, but the shop owner laughed as if it was all too delightful.

"There's time for that on the wedding night, don't you think?" She winked.

I reached for the most expensive dress in the collection, a dream of brocade; the bustier was embroidered with pearls and silvery threads forming a delicate flower pattern. "Those are platinum threads," the shop owner said. That explained the price. "I think your groom will be pleased with your choice."

Then she knew him better than I did. Luca was as much as stranger to me today as he had been almost three years ago.

*** 

The wedding would be held in the vast gardens of the Vitiello mansion in the Hamptons. Everyone was already abuzz with the preparations. I hadn't set foot into the house or even the premises yet, but my mother kept me up-to-date, not that I'd asked her to.

The moment my family had arrived in New York a few hours ago, my sisters and I had huddled together in our suite in the Mandarin Oriental Hotel in Manhattan. Salvatore Vitiello had suggested we live in one of the many rooms in the mansion until the wedding in five days, but my father had declined. Three years of tentative cooperation and they still didn't trust each other. I was glad. I didn't want to set foot into the mansion until I had to.

Father had agreed to let me share a suite with Lily and Gianna, so he and mother had a suite for themselves. Of course, a bodyguard was stationed in front of every of the three doors to our suite.

"Do we really have to attend the bridal shower tomorrow?" Lily asked, her bare legs swung over the backrest of the sofa. Mother always said Nabokov must have had Liliana in mind when he wrote Lolita. While Gianna provoked with her words, Lily used her body for that. She'd turned fourteen in April, a child that used her tentative curves to get a rise out of everyone around us. She looked like the teen model Thylane Blondeau, only her hair was a bit lighter and she didn't have a gap between her front teeth.

It worried me. I knew it was her way of rebelling against the gilded cage that was our life, but while Father's soldiers regarded her flirting with amusement, there were others out there that would love to misunderstand it.

"Of course, we have to," Gianna muttered. "Aria is the happy bride, remember?"

Lily snorted. "Sure." She sat up abruptly. "I'm bored. Let's go shopping."

Umberto wasn't enthused about the suggestion, even with another of my father's bodyguards at his side, he claimed it was almost impossible to keep us under control. Eventually he relented as he always did.

*** 

We were shopping in a store that sold sexy rocker-chick-like outfits that Lily desperately wanted to try on when I got a message from Luca. It was the first time he'd contacted me directly and for a long time I could only stare at my screen. Gianna peered over my shoulder in the dressing room. "'Meet me at your hotel at six. Luca.' How nice of him to *ask*."

"What does he want?" I whispered. I'd hoped I wouldn't have to see him until August 10th, the day of our wedding.

"Only one way to find out," Gianna said, checking her reflection.

***

I was nervous. I hadn't seen Luca in a long time. I smoothed my hair down, then straightened my shirt. Gianna had convinced me to wear the tight black skinny jeans I'd bought today. Now I wondered if something that drew less attention to my body might have been better. I still had fifteen minutes before Luca wanted to meet me. I didn't even know where yet. I assumed he'd call me once he arrived and ask me to come down into the lobby.

"Stop fiddling," Gianna said from her spot on the sofa, reading a magazine.

"I really don't think this outfit is a good idea."

"It is. It's easy to manipulate men. Lily is fourteen and has already figured it out. Father always says we're the weak sex because we don't carry around guns. We have our own weapons, Aria, and you'll have to start using them. If you want to survive a marriage with that man, you'll have to use your body to manipulate him. Men, even cold-hearted bastards like them, have a weakness and it hangs between their legs."

I didn't think Luca could be manipulated that easily. He didn't seem like someone who ever lost control, unless he wanted to and I really wasn't sure I wanted him to notice my body like that.

A knock made me jump and my eyes flew to the clock. It was still too early for Luca and he wouldn't really come up to our suite, would he?

Lily dashed out of her bedroom before Gianna or I could even move. She was wearing her rocker-chic outfit, tight leather pants and a tight black tee. She thought she looked so adult with it. Gianna and I thought she looked like a fourteen-year-old trying too hard.

She opened the door, jutting her hip out, trying to look sexy. Gianna groaned but I wasn't paying attention to her.

"Hi Luca," Lily piped. I walked closer so I could see Luca. He was staring down at Lily, obviously trying to figure out who she was. Matteo, Romero and Cesare stood behind him. Wow, he'd brought his entourage. Where was Umberto?

"You are Liliana, the youngest sister," Luca said, ignoring Lily's flirty expression.

Lily frowned. "I'm not that young."

"Yes, you are," I said firmly, walking up to her and putting my hands on her shoulders. She was only a couple of inches smaller than me. "Go to Gianna."

Lily gave me an incredulous look but then she slinked away.

My pulse was racing as I turned to Luca. His gaze lingered on my legs, then slowly moved up until it arrived at my face. That look hadn't been in his eyes the last time I'd seen him. And I realized with a start it was want. "I didn't know we'd meet in my suite," I said, then realized I should have greeted him, or at least tried to sound less rude.

"Are you going to let me in?"

I hesitated, then I stepped back and let the men walk past me. Only Cesare stayed outside. He closed the door even though I would have preferred to keep it ajar.

Matteo sauntered over to Gianna who quickly sat up and gave him her nastiest look. Lily of course smiled at him. "Can I see your gun?"

Matteo grinned at her but before he could reply, I said. "No, you can't."

I could feel Luca's eyes on me, lingering on my legs and butt again. Gianna gave me an I-told-you-so-look. She wanted me to use my body; the problem was I preferred Luca ignoring my body because everything else terrified me.

"You shouldn't be here alone with us," Gianna muttered. "It's not appropriate." I almost snorted. As if Gianna gave a damn about appropriateness.

Luca narrowed his eyes. "Where is Umberto? Shouldn't he be guarding this door?"

"He's probably on a toilet or cigarette break," I said, shrugging.

"Does it happen often that he leaves you without protection?"

"Oh all the time," Gianna said mockingly. "You see, Lily, Aria and I sneak out every weekend because we have a bet going who can pick up more guys." Lily let out her bell-like laugh.

"I want to have a word with you, Aria," Luca said fixing me with his cold stare.

Gianna rose from the sofa and came toward us. "I was joking, for god's sake!" she said, trying to step between Luca and me, but Matteo gripped her wrist and pulled her back. Lily watched everything with wide eyes and Romero stood against the door, pretending this didn't concern him.

"Let go of me, or I'll break your fingers," Gianna growled. Matteo raised his hands with a wide grin.

"Come on," Luca said, his hand touching my lower back. I swallowed a gasp. If he noticed, he didn't comment. "Where's your bedroom?"

My heartbeat stuttered as I nodded toward the door to the left. Luca led me in that direction, ignoring Gianna's protests. "I'll call our father! You can't do that."

We stepped into my bedroom and Luca closed the door. I couldn't help but be afraid. Gianna shouldn't have said those things. The moment Luca faced me, I said, "Gianna was joking. I haven't even kissed anyone yet, I swear." Heat crept into my face at the admission, but I didn't want Luca to get angry for something I hadn't even done.

Luca's gray eyes held me with their intensity. "I know."

My lips parted. "Oh. Then why are you angry?"

"Do I look angry to you?"

I decided not to reply.

He smirked. "You don't know me very well."

"That's not my fault," I muttered.

He touched my chin and I turned into a pillar of salt. "You are like a skittish doe in the clutches of a wolf." He didn't know how close that came to what I thought of him. "I'm not going to maul you."

I must have looked doubtful because he released a small laugh, lowering his head toward mine.

"What are you doing?" I whispered nervously.

"I'm not going to take you if that's what you're worried about. I can wait a few more days. I've waited three years after all."

I couldn't believe he'd said that. Of course, I knew what was expected on a wedding night, but I'd almost convinced myself that Luca wasn't interested in me that way. "You called me a child last time."

"But you aren't a child anymore," Luca said with a predatory smirk. His lips were less than an inch from mine. "You're making this really hard. I can't kiss you if you look at me like that."

"Then maybe I should give you that look on our wedding night," I challenged.

"Then maybe I'll have to take you from behind so I don't have to see it."

My face fell and I stumbled away, my back colliding with the wall.

Luca shook his head. "Relax. I was joking," he said quietly. "I'm not a monster."

"Aren't you?"

His expression hardened and he straightened, drawing up to his full height again. I regretted my words, even though they were the truth. "I wanted to discuss the matter of your protection with you," he said in an emotionless, formal voice. "Once you move into my penthouse after the wedding, Cesare and Romero will be responsible for your safety. But I want Romero at your side until then."

"I have Umberto," I protested, but he shook his head. "Apparently, he's taking too many toilet breaks. Romero won't leave your side from now on."

"Will he watch me when I shower too?"

"If I want him to."

I raised my chin, trying to quench my anger. "You would let another man see me naked? You must really trust Romero not to take advantage of the situation."

Luca's eyes blazed. "Romero is loyal." He leaned close. "Don't worry I'll be the only man to ever see you naked. I can't wait." His eyes traveled over my body.

I crossed my arms over my chest and averted my eyes. "What about Lily? She and Gianna share this suite with me. You saw how Lily can be. She will flirt with Romero. She will do anything to get a rise out of him. She doesn't realize what she could get herself into. I need to know that she's save."

"Romero won't touch your sister. Liliana is playing around. She's a little girl. Romero likes his women of age and willing."

'And you don't?' I almost asked but swallowed the words and nodded instead.

My eyes darted toward my bed. This was a horrible reminder of what would happen soon.

"There's something else. Are you taking the pill?"

Color drained from my face as I stared at him. "Of course not."

Luca scrutinized me with unsettling calm. "Your mother could have made you start it in preparation for the wedding."

I was pretty sure I was going to have a nervous breakdown any moment. "My mother would never do that. She won't even talk to me about these things."

Luca raised one eyebrow. "But you do know what happens between a man and a woman in a wedding night?"

He was mocking me, the bastard. "I do know what happens between normal couples. In our case, I think the word you're looking for is rape."

Luca's eyes flashed with emotion. "I want you to start taking the pill." He handed me a small packet. It was birth control.

"Don't I need to see a doctor before I start taking birth control?"

"We have a doctor who's been working for the Familia for decades. This is from him. You need to start taking the pill immediately. It takes 48 hours for them to start working."

I couldn't believe him. He seemed really eager to sleep with me. My stomach tightened. "And what if I don't?"

Luca shrugged. "Then I'll use a condom. Either way, on our wedding night you are mine."

He opened the door and gestured for me to move. As if in trance, I walked into the living area of the suite. I hadn't meant to make him angry, but now it was too late. It probably wasn't the last time anyway.

Umberto stood beside Gianna and Lily, looking annoyed. He frowned at Luca. "What are you doing here?"

"You should pay better attention in the future and keep your breaks to a minimum," Luca told him.

"I was gone for only a few minutes and there were guards in front of the other doors."

Gianna smirked. Matteo's eyes were locked on her. "What are you looking at?" she snapped.

Matteo leaned forward. "At your hot body."

"Then keep looking." She gave an one shoulder shrug. "Because that's all you ever get to do with my *hot body*."

"Stop it," Umberto warned.

I wasn't looking at him, but at Matteo who had a calculating expression on his face.

"Romero will take over the watch duty until the wedding," Luca said. Umberto opened his mouth, but Luca raised a hand. "It's done." He turned to Romero who straightened at once. They walked a few steps away from us. Gianna pressed up to me. "What does he mean?"

"Romero is my new bodyguard."

"He just wants to control you."

"Shh." I was watching Luca and Romero. After a moment, Romero glanced at Lily, then nodded and said something. They finally returned to us. "Romero will stay with you," Luca said simply. He was so cold since I'd as good as called him a monster.

"And what am I supposed to do?" Umberto asked.

"You can guard their door."

"Or you can join our stag party," Matteo suggested.

"I'm not interested," Umberto said.

Luca shrugged. "Suit yourself. Scuderi is coming with us."

My father would go with them? I didn't even want to know what they were up to.

Luca turned to me. "Remember what I told you."

I didn't say anything, only clutched the pill packet in my hand. Without another word, Luca and Matteo left. Romero held the door open. "You can leave too," he told Umberto who glared but walked out after a moment. Romero shut the door and locked it.

Gianna gaped. "You can't be *serious*."

Romero leaned against the door, arms clasped in front of him. He didn't react.

"Come, Gianna." I pulled her with me toward the couch and plopped down. Lily was already kneeling on the armchair, watching Romero in rapt attention. Gianna's eyes flitted down to my hand. "What's this?"

"Birth control."

"Don't tell me that asshole gave it to you just now so he can screw you on your wedding night."

I pressed my lips together.

"You aren't going to take them, right?"

"I have to. It won't stop Luca if I don't. He'll only be angry."

Gianna shook her head, but I gave her a pleading look. "I don't want to argue with you. Let's watch a movie, okay? I really need the distraction." After a moment, Gianna nodded. We picked out a random movie, but it was difficult to focus with Romero guarding us.

"Are you going to stand there all night?" I asked eventually. "You're making me nervous. Can't you sit down at least?"

He moved toward the vacant armchair and sank down. He shrugged off his jacket, revealing a white shirt and a holster holding two guns and a long knife.

"Wow," Lily breathed. She stood and walked over to him. He kept his attention on the door. She stepped in his way and he had no choice but to look up at her. She smiled. She quickly slipped into his lap and he tensed. I leaped off the sofa and wrenched her off him. "Lily, what's matter with you? You can't act like that. One day a man is going to take advantage of you." Many men had trouble understanding that provocative clothes and actions didn't mean a woman was *asking for it*.

Romero straightened in the chair.

"He won't hurt me. Luca forbid him, right?"

"He could steal your virtue you and cut your throat afterward, so you can't tell anyone," Gianna said off-handedly. I shot her a glare.

Lily's eyes grew wide.

"I wouldn't," Romero said, startling us with his voice.

"You shouldn't have said that," Gianna muttered. "Now she's going to fawn over you."

"Lily, go to bed," I ordered and she did under loud protest.

"I'm sorry," I said. "She doesn't know what she's doing."

Romero nodded. "Don't worry. I have a sister her age."

"How old are you?"

"Twenty."

"And how long have you been working for Luca?" Gianna turned off the TV to focus on her interrogation. I settled against the backrest.

"Four years, but I've been a made man for six years."

"You must be good if Luca chose you to protect Aria."

Romero shrugged. "Knowing how to handle myself in a fight isn't the main reason. Luca knows I'm loyal."

"Meaning you won't paw at Aria."

I rolled my eyes at Gianna. Romero probably regretted ever leaving his spot at the door. "Luca knows he can trust me with what's his."

Gianna's lips thinned. Wrong thing to say. "So if Aria came out of her room naked tonight and you got a hard-on because you can't really help it, Luca wouldn't cut off your dick?"

Romero was obviously taken aback. He stared at me, as if he actually worried I would do that. "Ignore her. I won't."

"Where are Luca and the other men going for stag night?"

Romero didn't reply.

"Probably a strip club and afterward one of the whorehouses the Familia has going," Gianna muttered. "Why is it that men can whore around while we have to save our virginity for the wedding night? And why can Luca fuck whoever he wants while Aria can't even kiss a guy?"

"I didn't make the rules," Romero said simply.

"But you make sure that we don't break them. You aren't our protector, you are our warden."

"Have you ever considered that I'm protecting guys who don't know who Aria is?" he asked.

I frowned.

"Luca would kill anyone who dared to touch you. Of course, you could go out, flirt with a guy and move on, because you wouldn't be the one Luca would gut."

"Luca isn't my fiancé," Gianna said.

"Your father would kill any man that got near you, because he wouldn't want anyone to spoil his most prized possessions."

For the first time, I realized that only because I'd been given to Luca that didn't mean Gianna wouldn't be forced to marry someone else. I felt suddenly very tired. "I'm going to bed."

I lay awake most of the night, thinking of ways to get out of the wedding, but the only option would be to run, and while Gianna would definitely come with me, what about Liliana? I couldn't keep them both save. And what about Fabiano? What about my mother? I couldn't leave everything behind. This was my life. I didn't know anything else. Maybe I was a coward, though marrying a man like Luca probably required more courage than running away.

# CHAPTER FOUR

The living room of the suite was decorated for the bridal shower. I'd hoped to be spared that tradition but my mother had insisted it would be an affront to the women of Luca's family if they couldn't meet me before the wedding.

I smoothed out the green cocktail dress. It was a color that was supposed to bring good luck. I knew my interpretation of what would be good luck at this point differed widely from Luca's and my father's interpretation.

Lily wasn't allowed to attend the bridal shower since she was deemed to young, but Gianna had argued her way into staying. Though I worried that there might be another reason behind mother's agreement. Gianna had turned seventeen a few days ago. That meant she was almost old enough to be married off as well. I pushed the thought aside. I could hear mother and Gianna arguing in the bedroom about what Gianna was supposed to wear when a knock sounded at the suite door. It was a bit early; the guests weren't supposed to arrive for another ten minutes.

I opened the door. Valentina stood in front of me, Umberto behind her. She was my cousin but five years older than me. Her mother and my mother were sisters. She smiled apologetically. "I know I'm early."

"It's okay," I said, stepping back so she could walk in. Umberto sat back on the chair outside my door. I really liked Valentina, so I didn't mind spending some time alone with her. She was tall and graceful, with dark-brown, almost black hair and eyes that were the darkest green imaginable. She wore a black dress with a pencil skirt that reached her knees. Her husband Antonio had died six months ago, and my wedding would be the first time that she'd wear something other than black. Sometimes widows, especially older women, were expected to wear mourning for a year after their husband's death, but Valentina was only twenty-three. Luca's age. I caught myself wishing her husband had died sooner so she could have married Luca and then I felt horrible. I shouldn't be thinking like that. Romero hovered beside the window.

"Could you please wait outside? A bridal shower is no place for a man."

He tilted his head, then walked out without another word.

"Your husband sent you his own bodyguard?" Valentina asked.

"He isn't my husband yet."

"No, you're right. You look sad," she said with a knowing expression as she sank down on the sofa. Champagne, soft drinks and an array of fingerfood were set up on a table behind it.

I swallowed. "So do you." And I felt immediately stupid for saying something like that.

"My father wants me to remarry," she said, twisting her wedding band.

My eyes widened. "So soon?"

"Not right away. Apparently he's already talking to someone."

I couldn't believe it. "Can't you say no? You were already married."

"But it was a childless marriage, and I'm too young to stay alone. I had to move back in with my family. My father insisted on it to protect me."

We both knew that code. Women always needed protection from the outside world, especially if they were in a marriageable age. "I'm sorry," I said.

"It is what it is. You know that as well as I do."

I laughed bitterly. "Yeah."

"I saw your husband when I visited the Vitiello mansion with my parents yesterday. He's...imposing."

"Terrifying," I added quietly. Valentina's expression softened, but our conversation was cut short when Mother and Gianna came out of the bedroom. And soon after that more guests arrived.

The gifts were everything from lingerie over jewelry to certificates for a day in a luxury spa in New York. The lingerie was the worst though, and when I opened the gift from Luca's stepmother Nina I had trouble keeping a straight face. I lifted the barely-there white nightgown and smiled tightly. The entire middle was see-through and it was so short it wouldn't even cover much of my legs. Beneath it in the gift box was an even smaller piece of clothing; white lace panties that revealed most of my butt and were held together by a bow in the back. A chorus of appreciative murmurs came from the women around me.

I gaped at the lingerie. Gianna tipped her finger inconspicuously against her temple.

"This is for your wedding night," Nina said with a calculating glint in her eyes. "I bet Luca will love unwrapping you. We need to please our husbands. Luca will certainly expect something this daring."

I nodded. "Thank you."

Had Luca maybe set his stepmother up to give this to me? I wouldn't put it past him. Not after he'd gotten birth control for me. My stomach twisted with worry, and it got only worse when the woman started talking about their wedding nights.

"I was so embarrassed when it was time for the presentation of the sheets!" Luca's cousin Cosima stage-whispered.

"The presentation of the sheets?" I asked.

Nina's smile was patronizing when she said, "Didn't your mother explain it to you?"

I glanced at my mother who pressed her lips together, two red blotches appearing on her cheeks.

"It's a Sicilian tradition that the Familia has proudly upheld for generations," Nina explained, eyes fixed on my face. "After the wedding night, the women of the groom's family come to the bridal pair to collect the sheets they spent the night on. Then those sheets are presented to the fathers of the bride and the groom and whoever else wants to see proof that the marriage has been consummated and that the bride was pure."

Cosima giggled. "It's also called tradition of the bloody sheets for that reason."

My face was frozen.

"That's a barbaric tradition!" Gianna hissed. "Mother, you can't allow it."

"It's not up to me," Mother said.

"That's right. We won't abandon our traditions." Nina turned to me. "And from what I know you've been well protected from male attention so there's nothing for you to fear. The sheets will prove your honor."

Gianna's lips curled, but all I could think about was that this tradition meant I definitely had to sleep with Luca.

## CHAPTER FIVE

The afternoon before the wedding day, my family moved out of the Mandarin Oriental and headed for the Vitiello mansion in the Hamptons. It was a huge building inspired by Italian palazzos surrounded by almost three acres of park-like grounds. The driveway was long and winding, and led past four double garages and two guesthouses until it ended in front of the mansion with its white front and red shingled roof. White marble statues stood at the base of the double staircase leading up to the front door.

Inside, coffered ceilings, white marble columns and floors, and a view of the bay and the long pool through the panorama windows took my breath away. Luca's father and stepmother led us toward the second floor of the left wing where our bedrooms were situated.

Gianna and I insisted on sharing a room. I didn't care if it made us look immature. I needed her at my side. From the window we could watch how the workers began setting up the huge pavilion that would serve as church tomorrow. Beyond it the ocean churned. Luca wouldn't arrive until the next day so we couldn't cross paths by accident before the wedding, which would mean bad luck. I honestly didn't know how I could have any more bad luck than I already had.

*** 

"Today's the day!" Mother said with fake cheer.

I dragged myself out of bed. Gianna pulled the blankets over her head, grumbling something about it being too early.

Mother sighed. "I can't believe you shared a room like five year olds."

"Someone had to make sure Luca didn't sneak in," Gianna said from beneath the blanket.

"Umberto patrolled the corridor."

"As if he would protect Aria from Luca," Gianna muttered, finally sitting up. Her red hair was a mess.

Mother pursed her lips. "Your sister doesn't need protection from her husband."

Gianna snorted, but Mother ignored her and ushered me into the bathroom. "We have to get you ready. The Beautician will be here any second. Grab a quick shower."

As the hot water poured down on me, realization set in. This was it, the day I'd been dreading for so long. Tonight I'd be Aria Vitiello, wife to the future Capo dei Capi, and former virgin. I leaned against the shower cabin. I wished I were like other brides. I wished I could enjoy this day. I wished I didn't have to look forward to my wedding night with trepidation, but I'd learned a long time ago that wishing didn't change a thing.

When I stepped out of the shower, I felt cold. Even my fluffy bathrobe couldn't stop my shivering. Someone knocked and Gianna entered with a cup and a bowl in her hand. "Coffee and fruit salad. Apparently you aren't allowed to have pancakes because it could cause bloating. What bullshit."

I took the coffee but shook my head at the food. "I'm not hungry."

"You can't go all day without eating or you'll faint when you walk down the aisle." She paused. "Though, on second thought, I'd love to see Luca's face when you do."

I sipped at the coffee, then took the bowl from Gianna and ate a few pieces of banana. I really didn't want to faint. Father would be furious, and Luca probably wouldn't be too happy about it either.

"The beautician has arrived with her entourage. You could think they need to prettify an army of fishwives."

I smiled weakly. "Let's not make them wait."

Gianna's worried gaze followed me as I walked into the bedroom, where Lily and my mother were already waiting with the three beauticians. They began their work at once, waxing our legs and armpits. When I thought the torture was over, the Beautician asked. "Bikini zone? Do you know what your husband prefers?"

My cheeks exploded with heat. Mother actually looked at me for an answer. As if I knew the first thing about Luca and his preferences, especially concerning body hair.

"Maybe we could call one of his whores," Gianna suggested.

Mother gasped. "Gianna!"

Lily looked clueless about the whole situation. She might have been the queen of flirting but that was all.

"I'll remove everything except for a small triangle, okay?" The beautician said in a gentle voice and I nodded, giving her a grateful smile. It took hours to get us ready. When our make-up was in place and my hair was pinned up in an elaborate updo that would later hold the veil and the diamond headpiece, my aunts Livia and Ornatella came in carrying my wedding dress as well as the bridesmaid dresses for Lily and Gianna. There was only one hour left until the wedding ceremony.

***

I stared at my reflection. The dress was gorgeous; the chapel train fanned out behind me, the platinum embroidery glittering wherever the sunlight hit it, and the empire waist was accentuated by a white satin ribbon.

"I love the sweetheart neckline. It gives you a breathtaking cleavage," Aunt Livia gushed. She was Valentina's mother.

"Luca will surely appreciate it," Aunt Ornatella said.

Something on my face must have made my mother realize I was close to having a nervous breakdown, so she ushered my aunts out. "Let the three girls have a moment."

Gianna stepped into view beside me. Her red hair contrasted beautifully with the mint dress. She opened the box with the necklace. Diamonds and pearls surrounded by intricate white gold threads. "Luca doesn't spare any costs, does he? That necklace and your headpiece probably cost more than most people pay for their house."

The conversation and laughter of the gathered guests carried up from the gardens through the open window into the room. Every now and then a clunk could be heard.

"What's that noise?" I asked, trying to distract myself. Gianna walked over to the window and peered out. "The men are taking off their guns and putting them into plastic boxes."

"How many?"

Gianna cocked an eyebrow.

"How many guns does each man put away?"

"One." She frowned, then it dawned on her, and I nodded grimly. "Only a fool would leave the house with less than two guns."

"Then why the show?"

"It's symbolic," I said. *Like this horrid wedding.*

"But if they all want peace, why not attend unarmed? It's a wedding, after all."

"There have been red weddings before. I saw pictures from a wedding where you couldn't tell the color of the bride's dress anymore. It was soaked in blood."

Lily shuddered. "That won't happen today, right?"

Anything was possible. "No, Chicago and New York need each other too much. They can't risk spilling blood among each other as long as the Bratva and the Taiwanese pose a threat."

Gianna snorted. "Oh great, that's comforting."

"It is," I said firmly. "At least we know nobody will come to harm today." My stomach twisted into a knot. Except for me, maybe. Probably.

Gianna wrapped her arms around me from behind and rested her chin on my bare shoulder. "We could still run. We could get you out of your dress and sneak out. They're all busy. Nobody would notice."

Lily nodded her head vigorously and got up from where she'd perched on the bed.

Luca would notice. I forced a brave smile. "No. It's too late."

"It's not," Gianna hissed. "Don't give up."

"There would be blood on my hands if I broke the agreement. They would kill each other in retribution."

"They all have blood on their hands. Every single fucking person in the garden."

"Don't curse."

"Really? A lady doesn't curse," Gianna mimicked our Father's voice. "Where did it get you to behave like an obedient little lady?"

I looked away. She was right. It had brought me straight into the arms of one of the deadliest men in the country.

"I'm sorry," Gianna whispered. "I didn't mean it."

I linked our fingers. "I know. And you are right. Most of the people in the garden have blood on their hands and would deserve to die, but they are our family, the only one we got. And there are innocents like Fabiano."

"Fabiano will have blood on his hands soon enough," Gianna said bitterly. "He'll become a killer."

I didn't deny it. Fabiano would start his initiation process at twelve. If what Umberto had said was true, Luca had killed his first man at eleven. "But he's innocent now, and there are other children out there as well, and women."

Gianna fixed me with a hard look in the mirror. "Do you really believe that one of us is innocent?"

Being born into our world meant being born with blood on your hands. With every breath we took, sin was engraved deeper into our skin. Born in blood. Sworn in blood like the motto of the New York Cosa Nostra. "No."

Gianna smiled grimly. Lily walked over to the bed and picked up my veil attached to the headpiece. I bent my knees so she could fix it atop my head. She gently smoothed it out.

"I wish you were marrying for love. I wish we could giggle about your wedding night. I wish you didn't look so fucking sad," Gianna said fiercely.

The silence between us stretched. Lily eventually nodded toward the bed. "Is this where you'll sleep tonight?"

My throat tightened. "No, Luca and I will spend the night in the master bedroom." I didn't think I'd get much, if any, sleep.

A knock sounded and I squared my shoulders, putting on my outside face. Bibiana and Valentina stepped in, followed by mother.

"Wow, Aria, you are gorgeous. Your hair looks like spun gold," Valentina said. She was already wearing her bridesmaid dress and the mint color looked gorgeous with her dark hair. Technically, only unmarried women were allowed to be bridesmaids but my Uncle had insisted we make an exemption for Valentina. He was really keen to find a new husband for her. Bibiana wore a floor-length maroon dress with long sleeves, despite the summer heat. It was probably meant to hide how thin she'd gotten.

I forced a smile. Mother took Lily's arm. "Come on, Liliana, your cousins need to talk to your sister." She led Lily out of the room, then looked back at Gianna who sat cross-legged on the sofa. "Gianna?"

Gianna ignored her. "I'm staying. I won't leave Aria alone."

Mother knew better than to argue with my sister when she was in a mood and so she closed the door.

"What are you supposed to talk to me about?"

"Your wedding night," Valentina said with an apologetic smile. Bibiana made a face, which reminded me how young she was. Only twenty-two. She'd gotten thin. I couldn't believe they'd chosen to send those two to talk to me about my wedding night. Bibiana's face spoke of her unhappiness. Since her wedding to a man almost thirty years her senior, she'd been fading away. Was that meant to soothe my fears? And Valentina had lost her husband six months ago in an altercation with the Russians. How could they expect her to talk about wedded bliss?

I smoothed my dress nervously.

Gianna shook her head. "Who sent you anyway? Luca?"

"Your mother," Bibiana said. "She wants to make sure you know what's expected of you."

"Expected of her?" Gianna hissed. "What about what Aria wants?"

"It's what it is," Bibiana said bitterly. "Tonight Luca will expect to claim his rights. At least, he's good looking and young."

Pity for her kindled in me, but at the same time my own anxiety made it hard to console her. She was right. Luca was good looking. I

66

couldn't deny it, but that didn't change the fact that I was terrified of being intimate with him. He didn't strike me as a man who was gentle in bed. My stomach lurched again.

Valentina cleared her throat. "Luca will know what to do."

"You just lie on your back and give him what he wants," Bibiana added. "Don't try to fight him; that will only make it worse."

We all stared at her and she looked away.

Valentina touched my shoulder. "We're not doing a good job at consoling you. Sorry. I'm sure it'll be alright."

Gianna snorted. "Maybe mother should have invited one of the women Luca's fucked to the wedding. They could have told you what to expect."

"Grace is here," Bibiana said, then she turned red, and stammered. "I mean, that's only a rumor. I—" She looked toward Valentina for help.

"One of Luca's old girlfriends is here?" I whispered.

Bibiana cringed. "I thought you knew. And she wasn't really his girlfriend, more like a plaything. Luca's been with many women." She snapped her mouth shut. I was fighting for control. I couldn't let people see how weak I was. Why did I even care if Luca's whore was at the wedding?

"Okay," Gianna said getting up. "Who the fuck is Grace and why the fuck is she invited to this wedding?"

"Grace Parker. She's the daughter of a New York senator who's on the payroll of the Mafia," Valentina explained. "They had to invite his family."

Tears blurred my vision and Gianna rushed toward me. "Oh don't cry, Aria. It's not worth it. Luca's an asshole. You knew that. You can't let his actions get to you."

Valentina handed me a Kleenex. "You'll ruin your make-up."

I blinked a few times until I had a grip on my emotions. "I'm sorry. I'm just being emotional."

"I think it's best if you leave now," Gianna said sharply, not even looking at Bibiana and Valentina. There was rustling and then the door opened and closed. Gianna wrapped her arms around me. "If he hurts you, I'll kill him. I swear it. I'll take one of those fucking guns and put a hole into his head."

I leaned against her. "He survived the Bratva and the Triad, and he's the most feared fighter in the New York familia, Gianna. He'd kill you first."

Gianna shrugged. "I'd do it for you."

I pulled back. "You're still my little sister. I should protect you."

"We will protect each other," she whispered. "Our bond is stronger than their stupid oaths and the Omerta and their blood vows."

"I don't want to leave you. I hate that I have to move to New York."

Gianna swallowed. "I'll visit often. Father will be glad to be rid of me."

There was a knock and Mother walked in. "It's time." She scanned our faces but didn't comment. Gianna took a step back, eyes burning into me. Then she turned and walked out. Mother's eyes zoomed in on the white lace garter on my vanity. "Do you need help putting it on?"

I shook my head and slid it up until it came to rest on my upper thigh. Later tonight Luca would remove it with his mouth and throw it into the group of gathered bachelors. I smoothed down my wedding dress.

"Come," Mother said. "Everyone's waiting." She handed me my flower bouquet, a beautiful arrangement of white roses, mother of pearl roses, and pink ranunculas.

We walked in silence through the empty house, my heels clacking on the marble floors. My heart was pounding in my chest as we stepped through the glass sliding door onto the veranda overlooking the backyard and the beach. The front of the garden was occupied by the huge white pavilion where the wedding ceremony would be held. But behind the pavilion dozens of tables had been set up for the following feast. Voices carried over to me from inside the pavilion where the guests were waiting for my arrival. A path of red rose petals led from the veranda toward the entrance of the pavilion. I followed mother into the small room between the outside and the main part of the pavilion. Father was waiting and straightened when we entered. Mother gave him the briefest nod before slipping into the makeshift chapel. His smile was earnest when he offered me his arm. "You look beautiful," he said quietly. "Luca won't know what hit him."

I ducked my head. "Thanks, Father."

"Be a good wife, Aria. Luca is powerful and once he takes his father's place, his word will be law. Make me proud, make the Outfit proud."

I nodded, my throat too tight for words. The music started to play: a string quartet and a piano. Father lowered my veil. I was glad for the extra layer of protection, no matter how thin. Maybe it would hide my expression from afar.

Father led me toward the entrance and gave a low command. The fabric was pulled apart, revealing the long aisle and the many hundred guests to either side of it. My eyes were drawn to the end of the aisle where Luca stood. Tall and imposing in his charcoal suit and vest with the silver tie and the white shirt. His groomsmen were dressed in a vest and dress pants of a lighter grey, and wore no jacket and a bowtie instead of a tie. Fabiano was one of them, with only eight much shorter than the men.

My father tugged me along and my legs seemed to carry me on their own accord as my body shook with nerves. I tried not to look at Luca and instead watched Gianna and Liliana from the corner of my eye. They were the first two bridesmaids and seeing them gave me the strength to hold my head high and not bolt for the outside.

White rose petals covered my path and were squashed under my shoes. Kind of symbolic in itself, though I was sure it wasn't meant to be.

The walk took forever and yet it was over too soon. Luca extended his hand, palm upwards. My father gripped the corners of my veil and lifted it, then he handed my hand over to Luca, whose gray eyes seemed to burn up with an emotion I couldn't place. Could he feel me shaking? I didn't meet his gaze.

The priest in his white frock greeted us, then the guests, before he began his opening prayer. I tried not to pass out. Luca's grip was the one thing keeping me focused. I had to be strong. When the priest finally came to the closing lines of the Gospel, my legs could barely hold me up. He announced the rite of marriage and the guests all rose from their chairs.

"Luca and Aria," the priest addressed us. "Have you come here freely and without reservation to give yourselves to each other in marriage? Will you love and honor each other as man and wife for the rest of your lives?"

Lying was a sin, but so was killing. This room *breathed* sin. "Yes," Luca said in his deep voice, and a moment later my own 'yes' followed. It came out firm.

"Since it is your intention to enter into marriage, join your right hands, and declare your consent before God and his Church." Luca clasped my hands. His were hot against my cold skin. We faced each other and I had no choice but to look up into his eyes. Luca spoke first, "I, Luca Vitiello, take you, Aria Scuderi, to be my wife. I promise to be true to you in good times and in bad, in sickness and in health. I will love you and honor you all the days of my life." How sweet the lies sounded from his mouth.

I recited the words expected of me and the priest blessed our rings.

Luca picked up my ring off the red cushion. My fingers shook like leaves in the breeze as I raised them, my heartbeat hummingbird quick. Luca's strong hand was firm and steady as he took mine. "Aria, take this ring as a sign of my love and fidelity. In the name of the Father, and of the Son, and of the Holy Spirit."

He slipped the ring onto my finger. White gold with twenty small diamonds. What was meant as a sign of love and devotion for other couples was nothing but a testament of his ownership of me. A daily reminder of the golden cage I'd be trapped in for the rest of my life. Until death do us part wasn't an empty promise as with so many other couples that entered the holy bond of marriage. There was no way out of this union for me. I was Luca's until the bitter end. The last few words of the oath men swore when they were inducted into the mafia, could just as well have been the closing of my wedding vow:

'I enter alive and I will leave dead.'

It was my turn to say the words and slip the ring onto Luca's finger. For a moment, I wasn't sure if I could manage. The tremor rocking my body was so strong that Luca had to steady my hand and help me. I hoped nobody had noticed, but as usual Matteo's keen eyes rested on my fingers. He and Luca were close; they'd probably laugh about my fear for a long time.

I should have run when I still had the chance. Now as hundreds of faces from the Chicago and New York Familias stared back at us, flight was no longer an option. Nor was divorce. Death was the only acceptable end to a marriage in our world. Even if I still managed to escape Luca's watchful eyes and that of his henchmen, my breach of our agreement would mean war. Nothing my father could say would prevent Luca's Familia from exercising vengeance for making them lose face.

My feelings didn't matter, never had. I'd been growing up in a world where no choices were given, especially to women.

This wedding wasn't about love or trust or choice. It was about duty and honor, about doing what was expected. A bond to ensure peace.

I wasn't an idiot. I knew what else this was about: money and power. Both were dwindling since the Bratva, the Triad and other smaller crime organizations had been trying to expand their influence into our territories. The Italian Familias across the US needed to lay their feuds to rest and work together to beat down their enemies. I should be honored to marry the oldest son of the New York Familia. That's what my father and every other male relative had tried to tell me since my betrothal to Luca. I knew that, and it wasn't as if I hadn't had time to prepare for this exact moment, and yet fear corseted my body in a relentless grip.

"You may kiss the bride," the priest said.

I raised my head. Every pair of eyes in the pavilion scrutinized me, waiting for a flicker of weakness. Father would be furious if I let my terror show, and Luca's Familia would use it against us. But I had grown up in a world where a perfect mask was the only protection afforded to women and had no trouble forcing my face into a placid expression. Nobody would know how much I wanted to escape. Nobody but Luca. I couldn't hide from him, no matter how much I tried. My body wouldn't stop shaking and his grip on my hands tightened. As my gaze met Luca's cold gray eyes, I could tell that he knew. How often had he instilled fear in others? Recognizing it was probably second nature to him.

He bent down to bridge the ten inches he towered over me. There was no sign of hesitation, fear or doubt on his face. My lips trembled against his mouth. My first kiss, if it could even be called that. His eyes bored into me, even as he pulled back. Their message was clear: *You are mine.*

Not quite. But I would be tonight. A shudder passed through me, and Luca's eyes narrowed briefly before his face broke into a tight smile as we faced the applauding guests. He could change his expression in a heartbeat. I had to learn it too if I wanted to stand any chance in this marriage.

Luca and I walked down the aisle past the standing and clapping guests, and left the pavilion. Outside, dozens of waiters were waiting with glasses of Champagne and small plates with Canapées. It was now our turn to accept the blessings and congratulations of every guest before we could move on to the tables and sit down for dinner. Luca took two glasses of Champagne and handed one to me. Then he grabbed my hand again and it didn't appear as if he had any attention to let go any time soon. He bent down, lips brushing my ear and whispered. "Smile. You are the happy bride, remember?"

I stiffened, but I forced my brightest smile onto my face as the first guests piled out of the pavilion and lined up to talk to us.

My legs began to hurt as we'd made it through half of our guests. The words directed at us were always the same. Praise for me on my beauty and congrats to Luca for having such a beautiful wife – as if that was an achievement – always followed by not so hidden hints about the wedding night. I wasn't sure if my face remained as bright through all of them. Luca kept glancing at me as if to make sure I kept up the charade.

Bibiana and her husband were next. He was small, fat and bald. When he kissed my hand I had to stop myself from shuddering. After a few mandatory words of congrats, Bibiana gripped my arms and pulled me toward her body to whisper into my ear. "Make him be good to you. Make him love you if you can. It's the only way to get through this."

She let go of me and her husband wrapped his arm around her waist, meaty hand on her hip, then they were gone.

"What did she say?" Luca asked.

"Nothing," I said quickly, glad for the next well-wishers that prevented Luca from asking more questions. I nodded and smiled, but my mind whirred around what Bibiana had said. I wasn't sure if anyone could make Luca do anything he didn't want to do. Could I make him *want* to be good to me? Could I make him *want* to love me? Was he even capable of such an emotion?

I risked a glance up at him as he talked to a soldier of the New York mob. He was smiling. Feeling my eyes on him, he turned and for a moment our gazes locked. There was darkness and a burning possessiveness in his eyes that sent a shiver of fear down my back. I doubted there was a flicker of gentleness or love in his black heart.

"Congrats, Luca," a high female voice said. Luca and I turned toward it and something in his demeanor shifted ever so slightly.

"Grace," Luca said with a nod.

My eyes froze on the woman, even though her father Senator Parker had started talking to me. She was beautiful in an artificial way with a too narrow nose, full lips and a cleavage that made my moderate chest look like child's play. I didn't think any of it was natural. Or maybe my jealousy was talking. I dismissed the thought as quickly as it had come.

With a look in my direction, she leaned up and said something to Luca. His face remained a passive mask. Finally, she turned to me and actually pulled me into a hug. I had to force myself not to stiffen. "I should warn you. Luca's a beast in the bedroom and hung like one too. It'll hurt when he takes you and he won't care. He doesn't care about you or your silly emotions. He will fuck you like an animal. He will fuck you bloody," she murmured, then she stepped back and followed after her parents.

I could feel the color drain from my face. Luca reached for my hand and I flinched, but he clasped it anyway. I steeled myself and ignored him. I couldn't face him now, not after what that woman had just said. I didn't care that it was required to invite her and her parents. Luca should have kept them away.

I could tell Luca got frustrated with my continued refusal to meet his gaze as we spoke to the last few guests. When we walked toward the tables that had been set up under a roof of garlands attached to wooden beams, he said, "You can't ignore me forever, Aria. We are married now."

I ignored that as well. I was hanging onto my composure with desperate abandon and still I could feel it slipping through my fingers like sand. I could not, I *would not* break into tears at my own wedding, especially since nobody would mistake them for tears of happiness.

Before we could take our seats, a chorus of 'Bacio, Bacio' broke out among our guests. I'd forgotten about that tradition. Whenever the guests shouted the words we'd have to kiss until they were satisfied. Luca pulled me against his rock-hard chest and pressed another kiss against my lips. I tried in vain not to be as stiff as a porcelain doll, to no avail. Luca released me and finally we were allowed to sit down.

Gianna took a seat beside me, then leaned over to whisper in my ear. "I'm glad he didn't shove his tongue down your throat. I don't think I could get any food down if I had to witness that." I was glad too. I was already tense enough. If Luca actually tried to deepen a kiss in front of hundreds of guests, I might lose it altogether.

Matteo sat beside Luca and said something to him that made both of them laugh. I didn't even want to know what kind of lewd joke that might have been. The rest of the seats at our table belonged to my parents, Fabiano and Lily, Luca's father and step-mother, as well as Fiore Cavallaro and his wife and their son Dante. I knew I should be starving. The only thing I'd eaten all day were the few pieces of banana in the morning, but my stomach seemed content to live on fear alone.

Matteo rose from his chair after everyone had settled down and clinked his knife against the Champagne glass to silence the crowd. With a nod toward Luca and me, he began his toast. "Ladies and gentlemen, old and new friends, we've come here today to celebrate the wedding of my brother Luca and his stunningly beautiful wife Aria..."

Gianna reached for my hand under the table. I hated having the attention of everyone on me, but I mustered up a bright smile. Matteo soon made several inappropriate jokes that had almost everyone roaring and even Luca leaned back in his chair with a smirk, which seemed to be the only form of smile he allowed himself most of the time. After Matteo, it was my father's turn; he praised the great collaboration of the New York mob and the Chicago Outfit, making it sound as if this was a business merger and not a wedding feast. Of course he also dropped a few hints that it was a wife's duty to obey and please her husband.

Gianna clutched my hand so tightly by then that I was worried it would fall off. At last, it was Luca's father's turn to toast us. Salvatore Vitiello wasn't quite as impressive but whenever his eyes settled on me, I had to stifle a shiver. The only good thing about listening to the toast was that nobody could call 'Bacio, Bacio' and that Luca's attention was focused elsewhere. That reprieve was short-lived however.

The servers began piling the tables with antipasti; everything from veal Carpaccio, Vitello Tonnato, Mozzarella di Bufala, an entire leg of parma ham, over a selection of Italian cheeses, octopus salad, marinated calamari as well as green salads and ciabiatta. Gianna grabbed a piece of bread and tore into it, then said, "I wanted to make a toast as your bridesmaid but Father forbade it. He seemed worried I would say something to embarrass our family."

Luca and Matteo glanced our way. Gianna hadn't bothered lowering her voice and pointedly ignored Father's death glare. I tugged at her arm. I didn't want her to get in trouble. With a huff, she filled her plate with antipasti and dug in. My plate was still empty. A server filled my glass with white wine and I took a sip. I'd already drunk a glass of Champagne; that combined with the fact that I hadn't eaten much all day made me feel slightly foggy.

Luca put a hand on mine, preventing me from taking another gulp. "You should eat." If I hadn't felt the eyes of everyone at the table on me, I'd have ignored his warning and downed the wine. I grabbed a slice of bread, took a bite, then put the rest onto my plate. Luca's lips tightened but he didn't try to coax me into eating more, not even when soup was served and I let it go back untouched. They served lamb roast for the main course. The sight of the whole lambs made my stomach turn but it was traditional. The cook rolled a rotisserie table toward us, since we had to be served first. Luca as the husband got the first slice and before I could decline he told the cook to give me a slice as well. The center of the table was loaded with roasted rosemary potatoes, truffled mashed potatoes, grilled asparagus and much more.

I forced a bite of lamb and potato into my mouth before I set down my cutlery. My throat was too tight for food. I washed it down with another gulp of wine. Luckily Luca was busy talking to the men at the table about a club the Russians had attacked in New York. Even Dante Cavallaro, the future Boss of the Outfit looked almost animated when he talked about business.

A band started playing when dinner was over, the signal that it was time for the obligatory dance. Luca stood, holding out his hand. I let him pull me to my feet, and at once 'Bacio, Bacio' rang out. Gianna narrowed her eyes and searched the guests, as if she was thinking of attacking the culprit who'd started the chanting.

When Luca tugged me toward him, I stumbled against his chest as dizziness caught up with me. Luckily, nobody noticed because Luca's arms around me held me firm. His eyes pierced mine as he lowered his lips and brushed them against mine. The band played faster and faster, urging us to finally enter the dance floor; the tables had been set up in circles around it. Luca kept his arm around my waist as he led me toward the center. To everyone around us it looked like a loving embrace but it was the only thing keeping me upright.

Luca pulled me against his chest for the waltz and I had no choice but to rest my cheek against it. I could feel a gun under his vest. Even the groom couldn't come to his wedding unarmed. For the first time I was glad for Luca's strength. He had no trouble keeping me on my feet during the dance. When it ended, he leaned down. "Once we're back at the table, you'll eat. I don't want you to pass out during our celebration and much less during our wedding night."

I did as he asked and forced down a few more bites of now cold potato and meat. Luca's alert gaze kept checking on me while he talked to Matteo. The dance floor was filled with other people now. Lily rose from her chair and asked Romero to dance. No surprise there. He couldn't refuse her of course. Neither could I refuse when Luca's father asked me for a dance. After that I was handed from one man to the next until I lost count of their names and faces. All through it Luca's eyes followed my every move, even when he danced with the women of our families. Gianna, too, couldn't escape the dance floor. I caught her dancing with Matteo at least three times and her face got more sullen by the minute.

"May I?"

I startled at the distantly familiar voice that sent a thrill of fear through my body. Dante Cavallaro took the place of whomever I'd danced with before. He was tall, albeit not as tall as Luca, and not as muscled. "You don't look impressed with the festivities."

"Everything's perfect," I said mechanically.

"But you didn't choose this marriage."

I gaped at him. His dark blonde hair and blue eyes gave him a look of cold efficiency while Luca radiated fierce brutality. Different sides of the same coin. In a few years the East Coast and Midwest would tremble under their judgement. I snapped my mouth shut. "It's an honor."

"And your duty. We all have to do things we don't want to. Sometimes it might seem as if we don't have any choice at all."

"You are a man. What do you know about not having a choice?" I said harshly, then stiffened and ducked my head. "I'm sorry. That was out of turn." I couldn't talk to someone who was practically my Boss like that. Then I remembered he no longer was. I didn't fall under the rule of the Chicago Outfit anymore. With my marriage, I'd become part of the New York mob and thus Luca's and his father's rule.

"I think your husband is eager to have you back in his arms," Dante said with a tilt of his head, then handed me over to Luca who gave him a hard look. Two predators facing off.

Once we were out of earshot of Dante Cavallaro, Luca looked down at me. "What did Cavallaro want?"

"Congratulate me on the festivities."

Luca gave me a look that made it clear he didn't believe me. There was a hint of mistrust in his expression.

The music stopped and Matteo clapped his hands, silencing the guests. "Time to throw the garter!"

Luca and I stopped as the guests gathered around the dance floor to watch the show. A few even stood on chairs or held up their kids so everyone could get a good look. Luca knelt before me under the cheers of our guests and raised his eyebrows. I gripped my gown and lifted it up to my knees. Luca slid his hands up my calves, over my knees and up my thighs. I stilled completely at the feel of his fingers on my naked skin. Goose-bumps erupted all over my body. The touch was light and not uncomfortable, and yet it terrified me.

Luca's eyes were intent as they watched my face. His fingers brushed the garter on my right thigh and he pushed my gown up for everyone to see, revealing the entire length of my leg. I gripped the hem and he put his arms behind his back, then he bent over my thigh, his lips brushing the skin under the garter. I sucked in a deep breath but tried to keep my face in happy-bride mode. Luca closed his teeth around the edge of the garter and pulled it down my leg until it landed in a heap at my white high heels. I raised my foot so Luca could pick the piece of lace up. He straightened and presented the garter to the applauding crowd. I forced a smile and clapped as well. The only person who wasn't smiling was Gianna.

"Bachelors," Luca called in his deep voice. "Gather around. Maybe you'll be the lucky one to marry next!"

Even the youngest boys stepped forward, Fabiano among them. He was scowling. Mother had probably forced him to participate. I winked at him and he poked out his tongue. I couldn't help but laugh, the first genuine gesture I'd managed during the wedding feast.

Luca's eyes darted toward me, a strange expression on his face. I quickly looked away. Luca raised his arm, the garter in his fist before he thrust it into the cluster of waiting men.

Matteo snatched it out of the air with an impressive lunge. "Any willing Outfit ladies out there that want to further the bond between our families?" he boomed, wiggling his eyebrows.

Cheering and laughter sounded from many married and unmarried women. Of course, Lily was among them, jumping up and down with a bright smile. Everything was a game for her. I didn't want Matteo's eyes on her, I didn't even want her name in his mind when he thought of marriage. As was tradition he had to pick an unmarried woman to dance with.

Luca stepped close to me, his arm sneaking around my waist in casual possessiveness. I flinched at the unexpected contact and Luca's body became rigid.

Matteo extended his hand toward Lily who looked close to exploding from excitement over being chosen. My chest tightened. I knew it was a joke right now. Nobody took a fourteen-year-old girl seriously.

As Luca and I waltzed over the dance floor, I kept an eye on Lily and Matteo. His hand was high on her back, his expression teasing. He didn't look like a man who'd set his eyes on his future wife.

"If my brother married your sister, you'd have family in New York," Luca said.

"I won't let him have Lily." The words were fierce. How could I be tough when it came to protecting my sister but not when it was about me?

"It's not Lily he wants."

My eyes flew to Gianna who stood with her arms wrapped around her chest, eyes like a hawk as they followed us. Father wouldn't give away another of his daughters to New York. If he wanted to strengthen the position of our family in the Chicago Outfit, he needed to make sure he had enough family around him. After the waltz was over, a faster beat began and the dance floor was once again flooded with guests.

Luca started dancing with my mother and I used the moment to slip away. I needed a few moments to myself or I'd lose it. I lifted my gown off the ground and hurried to the edge of the garden where grass met the bay before I walked down the few steps that led to the dock where a yacht was lying in wait. To my right a long beach stretched out. The ocean was black under the night sky and the breeze tugged at my dress and ripped strands from my updo. I stepped out of my high heels and jumped off the dock, my feet landing in the cool sand. Closing my eyes, I listened to the sound of the waves. The wooden boards creaked and I tensed before glancing over my shoulder and spotting Gianna. She shook off her own shoes and joined me on the beach, wrapping an arm around me.

"Tomorrow you'll leave for New York and I'll head back to Chicago," she whispered.

I swallowed hard. "I'm scared."

"Of tonight?"

"Yes," I admitted. "Of tonight and every night that follows. Of being alone with Luca in a city I don't know, surrounded by people I know even less, people who might still be the enemy. Of getting to know Luca and finding out he's the monster I think he is. Of being without you and Lily and Fabiano."

"We will come to visit as often as Father allows it. And about tonight." Gianna's voice turned hard. "He can't force you."

I let out a choked laugh. Sometimes I forgot that Gianna was younger than me. These were the moments that reminded me. "He can. He *will*."

"Then you'll fight him with all you've got."

"Gianna," I said in a whisper. "Luca is going to be Capo dei Capi. He's a born fighter. He'll laugh at me if I try to resist. Or my refusal will make him angry and then he'll really want to hurt me." I paused. "Bibiana told me I should give him what he wants, that I should try to make him be good to me, try to make him love me."

"Stupid Bibiana, what does she know?" Gianna glared at me. "Look at her, the way she cowers in front of that fat fool. How she lets him touch her with his sausage fingers. I'd rather die than lie under a man like that."

"Do you think I can make Luca love me?"

Gianna shook her head. "Maybe you can make him respect you. I don't think men like him have a heart to be capable of love."

"Even the most cold hearted bastards have a heart."

"Well, then it's as black as tar. Don't waste your time on love, Aria. You won't find it in our world."

She was right of course, but I couldn't help hoping.

"Promise me you'll be strong. Promise me you won't let him treat you like a whore. You are his wife."

"Is there a difference?"

"Yeah, whores at least get to sleep with other men and don't have to live in a golden cage. They are better off."

I snorted. "You are impossible."

Gianna shrugged. "It made you smile." She turned and her expression darkened. "Luca sent his lapdog. Maybe he was worried you'd run."

I followed her gaze to find Romero standing at the crest of the small hill overlooking the bay and the dock.

"We should have taken that yacht and run away."

"Where could I run? He'd follow me to the end of the world." I glanced at the elegant golden watch around my wrist. I didn't know Luca, but I knew men of his kind. They were possessive. Once you belonged to them, there was no escaping. "We should go back. The wedding cake will be presented soon."

We put our shoes back on and walked back toward the noise. I ignored Romero but Gianna scowled at him. "Does Luca need you for everything? Or can he at least take a piss on his own?"

"Luca is the groom and needs to attend to the guests," Romero said simply, but of course it was a reprimand in my direction.

Luca's eyes settled on me the moment I returned to the festivities. Many guests were already drunk, and some had moved up to where the pool was and were taking a swim fully clothed. Luca held his hand out and I bridged the distance between us and took it. "Where were you?"

"I just needed a moment to myself."

There was no time for further discussions as the cook rolled a table with our wedding cake toward the center. It was white, had six tiers and was decorated with peach flowers. Luca and I cut it under another round of applause, followed by 'Bacio, Bacio' and put the first piece onto our plate. Luca picked up a fork and fed me a bit as a sign that he'd provide for me, and I then fed him a piece as a sign that I'd take care of him as a good wife was supposed to.

It was close to midnight when the first shouts rang out that suggested Luca and I retire to the bedroom. "You wed her, now bed her!" Matteo shouted, throwing his arms up and bumping into a chair. He'd drunk his fair share of wine, whiskey, Grappa and whatever else he could get his hands on. Luca, on the other hand, was sober. The small inkling of hope I'd harbored that he'd be too drunk to consummate our marriage evaporated. Luca's answering grin, all predator, all hunger, all want, made my heart pound in my chest. Soon most of the men and even many women joined in the chorus.

Luca rose from his chair and I did the same, even though I wanted to cling to it with desperate abandon, but I had no choice. A few looks of understanding and compassion from other women were directed my way, but they were almost as bad as the jeering.

Gianna rose from her chair but Mother gripped her upper arm, holding her back. Salvatore Vitiello shouted something about a bed sheet, but the sound and colors seemed dimmed to me, as if I was trapped in fog. Luca's grip around my hand as he led me toward the house was the only thing keeping me in motion. My body seemed on autopilot. A large crowd, mainly consisting of men, followed after us, their chant of "Bed her, Bed her!" growing louder as we entered the house and ascended the staircase toward the second floor where the master bedroom was. Fear was an insistent throbbing in my chest.

I tasted copper and realized I'd bitten the inside of my cheek hard. We finally arrived in front of the dark wooden double doors of the master bedroom. The men kept clapping Luca's back and shoulders. Nobody touched me. I would have wilted if they had. Luca opened the door and I walked in, glad to bring some distance between the leering crowd and myself. The shouting rang in my head and it was all I could do not to clamp my hands over my ears. "Bed her! Bed her!"

Luca slammed the door shut. Now we were alone for our wedding night.

# CHAPTER SIX

The commotion in front of the door stopped except for Matteo who was still shouting lewd suggestions of what Luca could do to me, or I to him.

"Shut up, Matteo, and go find a whore to fuck," Luca shouted.

Silence reigned outside. My eyes wandered toward the king-sized bed in the center of the room and terror gripped me. Luca had his own whore to fuck tonight and until the end of days. The price for my body hadn't been paid in money, but it might as well have been. I wrapped my arms around my middle, trying to quench my panic.

Luca turned around to me with a predatory look on his face. My legs turned weak. Maybe if I fainted, I'd be spared, and even if he didn't care if I was conscious and took me anyway, at least I wouldn't remember anything. He thrust his jacket over the armchair next to the window, the muscles in his forearms flexing. He was muscle and strength and power, and I might as well have been made from glass. One wrong touch and I would shatter.

Luca took his time admiring me. Wherever his eyes touched my body, they branded me as his possession, the word 'mine' edged into my skin over and over again.

"When my father told me I was to marry you, he said you were the most beautiful woman the Chicago Outfit had to offer, even more beautiful than the woman in New York."

To offer? As if I was a piece of meat. I dug my teeth into my tongue.

"I didn't believe him." He stalked up to me and grabbed my waist. I swallowed the gasp and forced myself to be still as I stared at his chest. Why did he have to be so tall? He leaned down until his mouth was less than an inch from my throat. "But he told the truth. You are the most beautiful woman I've ever seen, and tonight you are mine." His hot lips touched my skin. Could he feel the terror pounding in my veins? His hands on my waist tightened. Tears pressed against my eyeballs, but I forced them back. I wouldn't cry, but Grace's words slammed into my brain. *He'll fuck you bloody.*

*Be strong.* I was a Scuderi. Gianna's words flashed in my mind. *Don't let him treat you like a whore.*

"No!" The word ripped from my throat like a battle cry. I wrenched myself away from him, stumbling a few steps back. Everything seemed to still then. What had I just done?

Luca's expression was stunned, then it hardened. "No?"

"What?" I snapped. "Have you never heard the word 'no' before?" *Shut up, Aria. For God's sake shut up.*

"Oh, I hear it often. The guy whose throat I crushed he said it over and over and over again until he couldn't say it anymore."

I took a step back, bristling. "So you're going to crush my throat too?" I was like a cornered dog, biting and snapping, but my opponent was a wolf. A very big and dangerous wolf.

A cold smile twisted his lips. "No, that would defy the purpose of our marriage, don't you think?"

I shuddered. Of course, it would. He couldn't kill me. At least not if he wanted to maintain peace between Chicago and New York. That didn't mean he couldn't beat or force himself on me. "I don't think my father would be happy if you hurt me."

The look in his eyes made me take another step back. "Is that a threat?"

I averted my eyes from his. My father might risk war over my death – not because he loved me, but to keep face –, but definitely not over a few bruises or rape. For my father it wouldn't even be rape; Luca was my husband and my body was his to take whenever he wanted. "No," I said softly. I hated myself for being submissive like a bitch bowing to her alpha, almost as much as I hated him for making me do it.

"But you deny me what's mine?"

I glared. Damn being submissive. Damn my father for selling me off like cattle, and damn Luca for accepting the offer. "I can't deny you something that you don't have the right to take in the first place. My body doesn't belong to you. It's mine."

'He will kill me', the thought shot through my mind a second before Luca drew himself up before me. Six foot five was scarily tall. I saw his hand move in my peripheral vision and flinched in anticipation of the blow, my eyes slamming shut. Nothing happened. The only sound was Luca's harsh breathing and the pounding of my pulse in my ears. I risked a peek up at him. Luca was staring at me, his eyes like a stormy summer sky. "I could take what I want," he said, but the viciousness was gone from his voice.

There was no use denying it. He was much stronger than me. And even if I screamed nobody would come to my help. Many men in my and Luca's family would probably even hold me down to make it easer for him, not that Luca would have any trouble restraining me. "You could," I admitted. "And I would hate you for it until the end of my days."

He smirked. "Do you think I care about that? This isn't a marriage of love. And you do already hate me. I can see it in your eyes."

He was right on both accounts. This wasn't about love and I hated him already, but hearing him say it crushed the last bit of foolish hope I had. I didn't say anything.

He gestured at the squeaky clean sheets of the bed. "You heard what my father said about our tradition?"

My blood turned ice cold. I had, but until now I'd put it out off my mind. My courage had been for nothing. I stepped up to the bed and stared down at the sheets, my eyes boring into the spot where the proof of my lost virginity would have to be. Tomorrow morning the women of Luca's family would knock at our door and take with them the sheets to present them to Luca's and my father, so they could inspect the proof of our consummated marriage. It was a sick tradition, but not one I could evade. The fight drained out off me.

I could hear Luca coming up behind me. He grasped my shoulders and I closed my eyes. I wouldn't make a sound. But not crying was a losing battle. The first tears already clung to my lashes, then dripped onto my skin and burned a trail down my cheeks and chin. Luca slid his hands over my collarbones, then down to the edge of my dress. My lips quivered and I could feel a tear dropping from my chin. Luca's hands tensed against my body.

For a moment, neither of us moved. He turned me to face him and pushed my chin up. His cold gray eyes scanned my face. My cheeks were wet with silent tears but I made no sound, only returned his gaze. He dropped his hands, jerked back with a string of Italian curses, and then he drove his fist into the wall. I gasped and jumped back. I pressed my lips together as I watched Luca's back. He was facing the wall, shoulders heaving. I quickly wiped the tears off my face.

*You've done it. You've made him really angry.*

My eyes darted toward the door. Maybe I could reach it before Luca. Maybe I could even get outside before he caught up with me, but I'd never make it off the premises. He turned around and removed his vest, revealing a black knife and gun holster. His fingers closed around the handle of the knife, his knuckles already turning red from the impact with the wall, and he pulled it out. The blade was curved like a claw: short, sharp and deadly. It was black like the handle, so it couldn't easily be seen in the dark. A Karambit knife for close combat. Who knew Fabiano's obsession with knives would ever be of use for me? Now I could at least identify the knife that would cut me open. Hysteric laughter wanted to fight its way out of my throat but I swallowed it.

Luca stared intently at the blade. Was he trying to decide which part of me to slice open first?

*Beg him.* But I knew it wouldn't save me. People probably begged him all the time and from what I heard it never saved them. Luca didn't show mercy. He would become the next Capo dei Capi in New York and he would rule with cold brutality.

Luca came toward me and I flinched. A dark smile curled his lips. He pressed the sharp tip of the knife into the soft skin below the crook of his arm, drawing blood. My lips parted in surprise. He put the knife down on the small table between the two armchairs, grabbed a glass and held his wound over it, then watched his blood drip down without a flicker of emotion before finally disappearing in the adjoining bathroom.

I heard water running and then he returned into the bedroom. The mix of water and blood in the glass had a light red color. He approached the bed, dipped his fingers into the liquid and then smeared it onto the center of the sheet. My cheeks flushed with realization. I approached him slowly and stopped when I was still out of arm-reach, not that it would do me much good. I stared down at the stained sheets. "What are you doing?" I whispered.

"They want blood. They get blood."

"Why the water?"

"Blood doesn't always look the same." *He would know.*

"Is it enough blood?"

"Did you expect a blood bath?" He gave me a sardonic smile. "It's sex, not a knife fight."

'He will fuck you bloody'. The words were burnt into my brain but I didn't repeat them.

Just how many virgins have you taken to know about this? And how many of them came willingly into your bed? The words lay on the tip of my tongue, but I wasn't suicidal.

"Won't they know that it's your blood?"

"No." He walked back over to the table and poured Scotch into the glass with water and blood. His eyes held mine as he downed it in one gulp. I couldn't help but wrinkle my nose in disgust. Was he trying to intimidate me? Drinking blood really wasn't necessary for that. I'd been terrified of him before I'd ever met him. I'd probably still be terrified of him when I bowed my head over his open casket.

"What about a DNA test?"

He laughed. It wasn't exactly a joyful sound. "They will take me by my word. Nobody will doubt that I've taken your virginity the moment we were alone. They won't because I am who I am."

*Yes, you are.* Then why did you spare me? Another thought to never leave my lips. But Luca must have been thinking the same because his dark brows drew together as his eyes roamed the length of my body.

I stiffened and took a step back.

"No," he said in a low voice. I froze. "That is the fifth time you shied back from me tonight." He set down the glass and took the knife in his hand. Then he advanced on me. "Did your father never teach you to hide your fear from monsters? They give chase if you run."

Maybe he expected me to contradict his claim to be a monster, but I wasn't that good a liar. If there were monsters, the men in my world belonged to them. When he arrived in front of me, I had to tilt my head back to look him in the face.

"That blood on the sheets needs a story," he said simply as he brought the knife up. I flinched and he murmured. "That's six times."

He hooked the blade under the edge of the bodice of my wedding dress and slowly moved the knife down. The fabric gave way until it finally pooled at my feet. The blade never once touched my skin. "It's tradition in our family to undress the bride like this."

His family had many disgusting traditions.

Finally I stood before him in my tight white corset with its laces in the back and my panties with the bow over my butt. Goosebumps covered every inch of my body. Luca's gaze was like fire on my skin. I drew back.

"Seven," he said quietly.

Anger surged through me. If he was tired of me flinching away from him, then maybe he should stop being so intimidating.

"Turn around."

I did as he ordered, and the sharp intake of his breath made me regret it instantly. He moved closer and I felt a gentle tug on the bow that was holding my panties up. 'A present to unwrap. How could any man possibly resist?' The words of Luca's stepmother popped unwantedly into my head. I knew that below the bow the top of my butt would be in the open. *Say something to distract him from that stupid bow over your butt.*

"You already bled for me," I said in a shaky voice, and then almost inaudible. "Please don't." My father would be ashamed of my open display of weakness. But he was a man. The world was his for the taking. Women were his for the taking. And we women were always supposed to give without protest.

Luca didn't say anything but his knuckles brushed the skin between my shoulder blades as he raised the knife to my corset. With a hiss the fabric came apart under the blade. I brought my hands up before that barrier of protection could fall as well and pressed the corset against my chest.

Luca wrapped his arm across my chest possessively, trapping my arm under his and gripped my shoulder, pressing me against him. I gasped when something hard poked me in the lower back. That wasn't his gun. Heat flooded my cheeks and fear gripped my body.

His lips brushed my ear. "Tonight you beg me to spare you, but one day you're going to beg me to fuck you." No. Never, I swore to myself. His breath was hot against my skin and I closed my eyes. "Don't think because I don't claim my rights tonight that you aren't mine, Aria. No other man will ever have what belongs to me. You are mine." I nodded, but he wasn't done yet. "If I catch a man kissing you, I'll cut out his tongue. If I catch a man touching you, I'll cut off his fingers, one at a time. If I catch a guy fucking you, I'll cut off his dick and his balls, and I'll feed them to him. And I'll make you watch."

He dropped his arm and stepped back. From the corner of my eye, I watched him stride over to the armchair and sink down in it. He reached for the bottle of Scotch and poured himself a generous amount. Before he could change his mind, I quickly walked into the bathroom, closed the door and turned the lock, then cringed at how stupid that was. A lock wasn't any protection from him, neither was a door. Nothing in this world could protect me.

I scrutinized my face in the mirror. My eyes were red and my cheeks wet. I let the remains of my corset drop to the floor and picked up the nightgown that one of the servants had folded on the chair for me. A choked laugh escaped my mouth after I'd put it on over my bow panties. The part over my breasts was made from lace, but at least it wasn't see-through; unlike the entire middle of the nightgown. It was the finest gossamer I'd ever seen and it didn't leave anything to the imagination. My bare stomach and the panties were on display. It ended above my knees with a hem of more lace. I could just as well walk out of this room naked and be done with it, but I wasn't that brave.

I washed my makeup off, brushed my teeth, let down my hair, and when I couldn't prolong the inevitable any longer, I grabbed the door handle. Would it be so bad if I slept in the bathroom?

Taking a deep breath, I opened the door and stepped back into the bedroom. Luca was still sitting in the armchair. The scotch bottle was almost half empty. Drunk men were never a good thing. His eyes found me and he laughed without humor. "That's what you choose to wear when you don't want me to fuck you?"

I flushed at his crude language. It was the Scotch talking, but I couldn't tell him to stop drinking. I was toeing the line as it was. "I didn't choose it." I crossed my arms, torn between staying on my feet and slipping under the covers of the bed. But lying down felt like a bad idea. I didn't want to make myself any more vulnerable than I already was. But standing in front of Luca half-naked wasn't the best choice either.

"My stepmother?" he asked.

I nodded simply. He put down his glass and rose. Of course, I flinched. His expression darkened. He didn't say anything as he walked past me into the bathroom, not even when I gasped as his arm brushed mine. The moment the door closed, I released a harsh breath. Slowly I approached the bed, my eyes finding the light red stain. I perched on the edge of the mattress. Water was running in the bathroom, but eventually Luca would come back out.

I lay down on the edge of the mattress, turned on my side and pulled the covers up to my chin, then squeezed my eyes shut, willing myself to fall asleep. I wanted this day to end, even if it was only the beginning of many hellish days and nights to come.

The water stopped and a few minutes later Luca emerged from the bathroom. I tried to make my breathing even to appear as if I was already sleeping. I risked a quick peek through half-closed eyes, my face mostly covered by the blanket, and turned to stone. Luca was only wearing black briefs. And if Luca was impressive when dressed, he was a whole new level of intimidating when half-naked. He was pure muscle and his skin was littered with scars, some thin and long as if a knife had sliced cleanly through, and some round and rigged as if a bullet had torn into his flesh. Letters were inked into the skin over his heart. I couldn't read them from afar but I had a feeling it was their motto. 'Born in Blood. Sworn in Blood. I enter alive and I leave dead'.

He walked over to the main light switch and turned it off, bathing us in darkness. Suddenly I felt like I was alone in a forest at night, knowing that somewhere something was stalking me. The bed dipped under Luca's weight and I clutched the edge of the bed. I pressed my lips together, allowing myself only shallow breaths.

The mattress shifted when Luca lay down. I held my breath, waiting for him to reach out for me and take what was *his*. Would it always be like this? Would I be miserable for the rest of my life? My nights filled with fear?

The pressure of the last few weeks, or maybe even years crashed down on me. Helplessness, fear and anger washed over me. Hatred for my father filled me up, but even worse was the hot knife of disappointment and sadness. He'd given me to a man he didn't know anything about, except for his reputation as a skilled killer, had offered me to the enemy to do with as he pleased. The man who should have protected me from harm had shoved me into the arms of a monster for the sole purpose of securing power.

Hot tears spilled out of my eyes but the weight on my chest didn't lift. It grew heavier and heavier until I couldn't hold it in anymore and a gasped sob burst out of me. *Get yourself under control, Aria.* I tried to fight it, but another choked sob slipped past my lips.

"Will you cry all night?" came Luca's cold voice out of the blackness. Of course, he wasn't asleep yet. For a man in his position, it was best to always keep an eye open.

I buried my face into the pillow but now that the floodgates had opened, I couldn't close them again.

"I can't see how you could possibly have cried any worse, if I'd taken you. Maybe I should fuck you to give you a real reason to cry."

I pulled my legs up against my chest, making myself as small as possible. I knew I needed to stop. I hadn't been beaten or worse, but I couldn't get a grip on my emotions.

Luca moved and a soft light flooded the room. He'd turned on the lamp on his nightstand. I waited. I knew he was watching me but I kept my face pressed against the pillow. Maybe he'd leave the room if he got fed up with the noise. He touched my arm and I jerked so violently that I would have fallen off the bed if Luca hadn't pulled me toward him.

"That's enough," he said in a low voice.

That voice. I stilled immediately and let him roll me onto my back. Slowly I uncurled my legs and arms, and lay as unmoving as a corpse.

"Look at me," he ordered, and I did. Was that the voice that had made him notorious? "I want you to stop crying. I want you to stop flinching from my touch."

I nodded numbly.

He shook his head. "That nod means nothing. Don't you think I recognize fear when it stares back at me? The moment I turn out the light, you'll be back crying as if I'd fucking raped you."

I didn't know what he wanted me to do. It wasn't as if I enjoyed being scared out of my mind. Not that fear was the only reason for my break down, but he wouldn't understand. How could he possibly understand that I felt like my life was ripped away from me? My

102

sisters, Fabiano, my family, Chicago, were all I had ever known and now I had to give them up.

"So to give you peace of mind and shut you up, I'm going to swear an oath."

I licked my lips, tasting the saltiness of tears on them. Luca's fingers tensed on my arm. "An oath?" I whispered.

He took my hand and pressed my palm against the tattoo over his heart. I exhaled as his muscles flexed under my touch. He was warm, the skin much softer than I'd anticipated.

"Born in blood, sworn in blood, I swear that I won't try to steal your virginity or harm you in any way tonight." His lips quirked and he nodded toward the cut on his arm. "I already bled for you, so that seals it. Born in blood. Sworn in blood." He covered my hand with his over the tattoo, looking at me expectantly.

"Born in blood, sworn in blood," I said softly. He released my hand and I lowered it to my stomach, stunned and confused. An oath was a big deal. Without another word, he extinguished the light and returned to his side of the bed.

I listened to his rhythmic breathing, knowing that he wasn't asleep. I closed my eyes. He wouldn't break his oath.

# CHAPTER SEVEN

Sunlight hit my face. I tried to stretch but an arm was thrown over my waist and a firm chest pressed against my back. It took me a moment to remember where I was and what had happened yesterday and then I stiffened.

"Good, you're awake," Luca said in a voice that was gruff with sleep.

Realization hit me. Luca. My husband. I was a married woman, but Luca had kept his promise. He hadn't consummated the marriage. I opened my eyes. Luca's hand gripped my hip and he turned me on my back. He was propped up on one elbow as his eyes took in my face. I wished I knew what he was thinking. It was strange to be in bed with a man. I could feel Luca's heat, even though our bodies weren't touching. In the sunlight the scars on his skin were somehow less prominent than last night, but his muscles were just as impressive. I wondered how they'd feel to the touch.

He reached up and took a strand of my hair between two fingers. I held my breath, but he released it after a moment, his face becoming calculating. "It won't be long until my step-mother, my aunts and the other married women of my family knock at our door to gather up the sheets and carry them into the dining room where undoubtedly everyone else is already waiting for the fucking spectacle to begin."

A blush spread over my cheeks and something in Luca's eyes changed, some of the coldness replaced by another emotion. My eyes found the small cut on Luca's arm. It hadn't been deep and was already scabbing.

Luca nodded. "My blood will give them what they want. It'll be the foundation of our story, but we'll be expected to fill in the details. I know I'm a convincing liar. But will you be able to lie in everyone's face, even your mother's, when you tell them about our wedding night? Nobody can know what happened. It would make me look weak." His lips tightened with regret. Regret of having spared me and gotten himself in the position of depending on my lying skills.

"Weak because you didn't want to rape your wife?" I whispered.

Luca's fingers on my hip tightened. I hadn't even realized they were still there. *Make him want to be good to you*, Bibiana's words flitted through my mind. Luca was a monster, there was no doubt about it. He couldn't be anything else in order to survive as a leader in our world, but maybe I could make him keep the monster in chains when he was with me. It was more than I'd hoped for when he'd led me toward the bedroom last night.

Luca smiled coldly. "Weak for not taking what was mine for the taking. The tradition of bloody sheets in the Sicilian mafia is as much a proof of the bride's purity as of the husband's relentlessness. So what do you think will it say about me that I had you lying half naked in my bed, vulnerable and *mine*, and yet here you are untouched as you were before our wedding?"

"Nobody will know. I won't tell anyone."

"Why should I trust you? I don't make a habit of trusting people, especially people who hate me."

I rested my palm against the cut on his arm, feeling his muscles flex beneath my touch. *Make him be good to you, make him love you.* "I don't hate you." He narrowed his eyes, but it was mostly the truth. I would have hated him if he had forced himself on me. I certainly hated what the marriage to him meant for me, but I didn't know him well enough for real hate. Maybe it would come with time. "And you can trust me because I am your wife. I didn't choose this marriage but I can at least choose to make the best out of our bond. I have nothing to gain from betraying your trust, but everything to gain by showing you that I'm loyal."

There was a flicker of something, maybe respect in his expression. "The men waiting in that living room are predators. They prey on the weak and they've been waiting for more than a decade for a sign of weakness from me. The moment they see one, they'll pounce."

"But your father—"

"If my father thinks I'm too weak to control the Familia, he'll gladly let them tear me apart."

What kind of life was it to have to be strong all the time even around your closest family? At least, I had my sisters and my brother, and even to some extent my mother and people like Valentina. Women were forgiven weakness in our world.

Luca's eyes were hard. Maybe this would be the moment he decided it really wasn't worth the risk and take me, but when his gaze finally settled back on my face the darkness was at bay.

"What about Matteo?"

"I trust Matteo. But Matteo is hot-headed. He'd get himself killed trying to defend me."

It was strange talking to Luca, to my husband like this, almost like we knew each other. "Nobody will doubt me," I said. "I'll give them what they want to see."

Luca sat up and my eyes were drawn to the tattoo, then took in the muscles of his chest and stomach. My cheeks heated when I met Luca's gaze.

"You should be wearing more than this bad excuse for a nightgown when the harpies arrive. I don't want them to see your body, especially your hips and upper thighs. It's better when they wonder if I left marks on you," he said. Then he smirked. "But we can't hide your face from them."

He bent over me and his hand came toward my face. I squeezed my eyes shut, flinching.

"This is the second time you thought I was going to hit you," he said in a low voice.

My eyes flew open. "I thought you said..." I trailed off.

"What? That everyone expects you to have bruises on your face after a night with me? I don't hit women."

I remembered when he'd stopped my father from slapping me. He'd never raised his hand against me. I knew many men in the

107

Chicago Outfit had a strange code of rules they followed. You couldn't stab a man in the back, but you could cut his throat that way for example. I wasn't sure what made one better than the other. Luca seemed to have his own rules as well. Crushing someone's throat with your bare hands was acceptable, hitting your wife was not.

"How am I supposed to believe you can convince everyone we've consummated our marriage when you keep flinching away from my touch?"

"Believe me, the flinching will make everyone believe the lie even more because I definitely wouldn't have stopped flinching away from your touch if you'd *taken what's yours*. The more I flinch the more they will take you for the monster you want them to think you are."

Luca chuckled. "I think you might know more about playing the game of power than I expected."

I shrugged. "My father is Consigliere."

He tilted his head in acknowledgement, then he brought his hand up and cupped my face. "What I meant earlier was that your face doesn't look like you've been kissed."

My eyes widened. "I've never..." But of course he knew that already.

His lips collided with mine and my palms came up against his chest, but I didn't push him away. His tongue teased my lips, demanding entrance. I gave in and hesitantly touched my tongue to his. I wasn't sure what to do and looked at Luca wide eyed, but he took lead, as his tongue and lips ravished my mouth. It was strange allowing that sort of intimacy, but it wasn't unpleasant. I lost track of time as he kissed me, demanding and possessive, his hand warm against my cheek. His stubble rubbed against my lips and skin, but the friction made me tingle instead that it bothered me. I could feel the restrained strength as his body pressed against me. Eventually he pulled back, eyes dark with desire. I shivered, not only from fear.

Insistent knocking sounded and Luca swung his legs out of bed and stood. I sucked in a breath at the sight of the bulge in his briefs.

He smirked. "A man is supposed to have a boner when he wakes up beside his bride, don't you think? They want a show, they'll get a show." He nodded toward the bathroom. "Now go and grab a bathrobe."

I quickly leaped out of bed with its stained bedsheet and hurried into the bathroom where I grabbed the long white satin bathrobe and put it over my nightgown before I picked up the remnants of my corset that I'd dropped last night.

When I stepped back into the bedroom, I watched Luca putting his gun and knife holster on over his naked chest, another knife strap with a longer hunting knife onto his forearm covering the small cut, and reposition his stiffness so it was even more obvious.

My cheeks hot, I moved further into the room and threw the corset down beside my ruined wedding dress. Luca was a magnificent sight with his tall frame, muscles and holster, not to mention the bulge in his pants. A hint of curiosity filled me. How did he look without the pants?

I leaned against the wall beside the window and wrapped an arm around myself, suddenly worried that someone would realize Luca hadn't slept with me. These were all married women. Would they see something wasn't right?

I braced myself when he opened the door wide, standing before the gathered women in all his half-naked glory. There were gasps, giggles and even a few muttered Italian words, which might have been prayers or curses, they were spoken too fast and quiet for me to hear. I had to stifle a snort.

"We've come to collect the sheets," Luca's stepmother said in what was barely hidden glee.

Luca stepped back, opening the door wider. At once several women stepped in, their eyes darting to the bed and the stain, then to me. I knew my face was red, even though it wasn't my blood on the sheets. How could these women jump at the chance to see proof of my taken virginity? Didn't they have any compassion? Maybe they thought it was only fair I went through the same as they had. I looked away, unable to bear their scrutiny. Let them make from that what they wanted. Most guests had left, especially politicians and other non-mafia folk; only the closest family was supposed to bear witness to the presentation of the sheets, but from the number of women gathered in the corridor and in the bedroom, you wouldn't have known.

Only women of marriage age were allowed to be present when the sheets were taken down – as not to frighten the pure virgin eyes of younger girls. I could see my aunts among the spectators, as well as my mother, Valentina and Bibiana, but the women from Luca's family were in the front since it was their tradition, not ours. Now it is yours as well, I reminded myself with a twinge. Luca met my eyes briefly from across the room. We shared a secret now. I couldn't help but feel grateful toward my husband, even though I didn't want to be grateful for something like that. But in our world you had to be thankful for the smallest kindness, especially from a man like Luca, especially when he didn't have to be kind.

Luca's stepmother Nina and his cousin Cosima began stripping the bed. "Luca," Nina said with feigned indignation. "Did nobody tell you to be gentle to your virgin bride?"

That actually got her a few embarrassed giggles and I lowered my eyes, even though I wanted to scowl at her. Luca did a fine job of that, then he flashed her a wolfish smile that raised the hairs on my neck. "You are married to my father. Does he strike you as a man who teaches his sons to be gentle to *anyone*."

Her lips thinned but she didn't stop smiling. I could feel everyone's eyes on me and squirmed under the attention. When I risked a peek toward my family, I could see shock and pity on many of their faces.

"Let me through!" came Gianna's panicked voice. My head shot up. She was fighting her way through the gathered women and avoided Mother who tried to stop her. Gianna wasn't even supposed to be here. But when did Gianna ever do what she was supposed to do? She shoved a very thin woman out of her way and staggered into the bedroom. Her face flashed with disgust when she spotted the sheets Luca's stepmother was holding up and spreading over Cosima's outstretched arms.

Her eyes found my face, lingering on my swollen lips, disheveled hair and my arms, which were still wrapped around my middle. I wished there was a way to let her know I was fine, that it wasn't as it looked, but not with all those women around us. She turned to Luca, who at least didn't have a boner anymore. The look in her eyes would have sent most people running. Luca raised his eyebrows with a smirk.

She took a step in his direction. "Gianna," I said quietly. "Will you help me get dressed?" I let my arms fall to my sides and walked toward the bathroom, trying to wince now and then as if I was sore and hoping I wasn't overdoing it. I'd never seen a bride, or anyone else, after they'd supposedly lost their virginity. The moment the door closed behind Gianna and me, she threw her arms around me. "I hate him. I hate them all. I want to kill him."

"He didn't do anything," I murmured.

Gianna pulled back and I put my finger to my lips. Confusion filled her face. "What do you mean?"

"He didn't force me."

"Just because you didn't fight him doesn't mean it wasn't rape."

I covered her mouth with my hand. "I'm still a virgin."

Gianna stepped back so my hand dropped from her lips. "But the blood," she whispered.

"He cut himself."

She stared at me in disbelief. "Do you have Stockholm syndrome?"

I rolled my eyes. "Shh. I'm telling the truth."

"Then why the show?"

"Because nobody can know. Nobody. Not even Mother or Lily. You can't tell anyone, Gianna."

Gianna frowned. "Why would he do that?"

"I don't know. Maybe he doesn't like to hurt me."

"That man would kill a baby fawn if it looked at him the wrong way."

"You don't know him."

"Neither do you." She shook her head. "Don't tell me you trust him now. Just because he didn't fuck you last night doesn't mean he won't do it soon. Maybe he prefers to do it in his penthouse with a view over New York. You are his wife and any man with a working dick would want to get into your pants."

"Father really wasted all of his lady comments on you," I said with a smile. Gianna kept glaring. "Gianna, I knew when I married Luca that I would have to sleep with him eventually, and I accepted that. But I'm glad that I get the chance to at least get to know him a bit better first." Though I wasn't sure I'd like the parts of him I'd get to know. But his kisses hadn't been unpleasant at all. My skin still warmed when I thought of it. And Luca definitely was nice to look at. Not that good looks could cancel out cruelness, but so far he hadn't been cruel to me, and somehow I thought he wouldn't be, at least not intentionally.

Gianna sighed. "Yeah, you're probably right." She sank down on the toilet lid. "I didn't sleep all night from worry about you. Couldn't you have sent me a text saying Luca didn't pop your cherry?"

I began undressing. "Sure. And then Father or Umberto check your mobile and see it, and I'm doomed."

Gianna's eyes scanned me from head to toe as I stepped into the shower, probably still looking for a sign that Luca had manhandled me.

"You still have to act as if you hate Luca when you see him later, or people will get suspicious," I told her.

"Don't worry. That won't be a problem because I still hate him for taking you away from me, and for *being him.* I don't believe for one second that he's capable of kindness."

"Luca can't know I told you either." I turned the shower on and let the hot water wash away the last hints of tiredness. I needed to be fully alert for the show in the living room later. My tense muscles began relaxing as the stream of water massaged them.

"You can't come in," Gianna said angrily, startling me. "I don't care that you are her husband." I opened my eyes to see Luca pushing his way into the bathroom. Gianna stepped in his way. I quickly turned my back to them.

"I need to get ready," Luca growled. "And there's nothing here that I haven't already seen."

Liar. "Now leave, or you'll see your first cock, girl, because I'm going to undress now."

"You arrogant asshole, I—"

"Leave!" I shouted.

Gianna left, but not without calling Luca by a few choice words. The door banged shut and we were alone. I wasn't sure what Luca was doing and I wouldn't turn around to check. I couldn't hear him from the splashing of the water. I knew I couldn't stay in the shower forever, so I shut off the water and faced the room.

Luca was spreading shaving cream on his chin with a brush, but his eyes were watching me in the mirror. I resisted the urge to cover myself, even though I felt a blush spreading over my body. He set the brush down and reached for one of the plush bath towels hanging over the heated towel rack, then walked over to me, still in his briefs. I opened the shower and took the towel from him with a quick thanks. He didn't move, eyes unfathomable as they roamed my body. I wrapped the towel around myself, then stepped out. Without high heels, the top of my head only reached Luca's chest.

"I bet you're already regretting your decision," I said quietly. I didn't need to explain; he knew what I meant.

Without a word, he returned to the wash table, picked up the brush and resumed what he'd been doing before. I was on my way into the bedroom, when his voice startled me, "No." I glanced back and met his eyes. "When I claim your body I want you writhing beneath me in pleasure and not fear."

# CHAPTER EIGHT

I was already dressed in an orange summer maxi dress and a golden belt to accentuate my waist when Luca stepped out of the bathroom in nothing but a towel. I sat on the chair in front of my vanity, putting on make-up, but froze with the mascara brush inches from my eye when I saw Luca. He walked toward the wardrobe and picked out black pants and a white shirt before he dropped his towel without shame. I didn't look away fast enough and was rewarded with his firm backside. I lowered my eyes and busied myself with checking my nails until I dared to face the mirror again and put on mascara.

Luca buttoned his shirt, except for the upper two. He strapped a knife to his forearm and rolled the sleeve over it, then put a gun holster around his calf. I turned around. "Do you ever go anywhere without guns?" No chest holster today because it couldn't be hidden well with only a white shirt.

"Not if I can avoid it." He considered me. "Do you know how to shoot a gun or use a knife?"

"No. My father doesn't think women should get involved in fights."

"Sometimes fights come to you. The Bratva and the Triad don't make a difference between men and women."

"So you've never killed a woman?"

His expression tightened. "I didn't say that." I waited for him to elaborate but he didn't. Maybe it was for the best.

I stood, smoothing out my dress, nervous about meeting my father and Salvatore Vitiello after the wedding night. "Good choice," Luca said. "The dress covers your legs."

"Someone could lift the skirt and inspect my thighs."

It was meant as a joke but Luca's lips pulled into a snarl. "Someone tries to touch you, they lose their hand."

I didn't say anything. His protectiveness thrilled and scared me in equal parts. He waited for me at the door and I approached him uncertainly. His words from the bathroom still rang in my ears. *Writhe in pleasure.* I wasn't sure I was even close to being relaxed enough around him for anything coming close to pleasure. Gianna was right. I couldn't allow myself to trust him that easily. He could be manipulating me.

He rested his hand on my lower back as we walked out. When we reached the top of the stairs, I could already hear conversation and a few scattered guests were talking in small groups in the huge entrance hall.

I froze. "Are they all waiting to see a bloody sheet?" I whispered, appalled.

Luca peered down at me, smirking. "Many of them, especially the women. The men might hope for dirty details, others might hope to talk about business, ask a favor, get on my good side." He gently pressed me forward and we walked down the steps.

Romero was waiting at the foot of the stairs, his brown hair in disarray. He tilted his head toward Luca, then gave me a brief smile. "How are you?" he asked me, then grimaced, the tips of his ears actually turning red.

Luca chuckled. I didn't know any of the other men in the hall, but they all gave Luca winks or broad grins. Embarrassment crept up my neck. I knew what they were all thinking, could practically feel them undressing me with their eyes. I shifted closer to Luca and he curled his fingers around my waist.

"Matteo and the rest of your family are in the dining room."

"Poring over the sheets?"

"As if they could read them like tea leaves," Romero confirmed, then gave me an apologetic look. He didn't seem to suspect anything.

"Come," Luca said, nudging me toward the double doors. The moment we stepped into the dining room, every pair of eyes was on us. The women of the family were gathered on one side of the room, divided into small clusters, while the men were sitting around the long dining table, which was piled with Ciabatta, grapes, ham, mortadella, cheese, fruit platters, and biscotti. I realized I was actually quite hungry. It was already almost lunch time. Matteo snuck up beside Luca and me, an espresso in his hand.

"You look like shit," Luca said.

Matteo nodded. "My tenth espresso and I'm still not awake. Drank too much last night."

"You were trashed," Luca said. "I'd have had your tongue cut out for some of the things you said to Aria if you weren't my brother."

Matteo grinned at me. "I hope Luca didn't do half of the things I suggested."

I wasn't sure what to say to that. Matteo still made me nervous. He exchanged a look with Luca, who ran a thumb over my side, making me jump.

"Quite a work of art you presented us," Matteo said with a nod toward the back of the room where the sheets were draped over a kind of coat rack for better display.

I tensed. What did he mean?

But Luca didn't look worried, instead he shook his head. Salvatore Vitiello and my father were waving at us to join them and it would have been impolite to make them wait any longer. Father rose when we arrived at the table and wrapped me in his arms. I was surprised by this open display of affection. He touched the back of my head and whispered, "I'm proud of you."

I gave him a forced smile when we pulled apart. Proud for what? For losing my virginity? For spreading my legs?

Salvatore put a hand on my and Luca's shoulders, and gave us a smile. "I hope we can expect small Vitiello's soon."

I managed not to let my shock show. Hadn't Luca mentioned that I was on birth control?

"I want to enjoy Aria alone for a long while. And with the Bratva closing in, I wouldn't want to have children to worry over," Luca said tightly. There was no word to describe how relieved I was about Luca's words. I really wasn't ready for children. I had already enough changes thrown my way without the added bonus of a baby.

His father nodded. "Yes, yes, of course. Understandable."

After that they launched into a conversation about the Bratva and it became pretty clear I was dismissed. I slipped out of Luca's grasp and walked toward the women. Gianna met me halfway. "Disgusting," she muttered with a scowl toward the sheets.

"I know."

I looked around, but couldn't see Fabiano or Lily. "Where are—"

"Upstairs in their room with Umberto. Mother didn't want them to be there for the reveal of the sheets." She leaned in conspiratorially. "I'm so glad you're finally here. Those women have been sharing their bloody sheet stories for hours. What the fuck is wrong with the New York Familia? If I hear one more word about it, I'm going to give them a real bloodbath."

"Now that I'm here, I doubt they'll be talking about anything but the bloody sheets over there," I muttered. It turned out I was right. Almost every woman felt the need to hug me and offer me words of advice that only made me nervous. *It'll get better. Sometimes it takes a bit for a woman to be comfortable.* And the best: *Believe me it took me years to enjoy it.*

Mother kept her distance. I wasn't sure why. Valentina didn't say anything as she wrapped her arms around me, just touched her palm to my cheek and smiled, before stepping back to make room for another woman. Mother stood with her hands clasped in front of her, disapproval written across her face. I was glad she wasn't sharing stories of her wedding night with Father. I stepped toward her and she pulled me into a tight hug. Like my father she wasn't an overly affectionate person but I was glad for her closeness. ""I wish I could have protected you from all this," she whispered before pulling back. There was a flicker of guilt on her face. I nodded. I didn't blame her. What could she have done? Father wouldn't have let her talk him out of the agreement.

"Luca can't stop watching you. You must have left quite an impression on him," Luca's stepmother said teasingly.

I turned to her and smiled politely. Luca probably just wanted to make sure I didn't give away our secret by accident. From the corner of my eye, I saw the door at the back open and Lily slink in, followed by Fabiano. They'd probably used Umberto's toilet break to get away. Gianna made a face when our brother stopped in front of the sheets.

I excused myself and walked over to them with Gianna at my heels. Mother was wrapped up in overly polite conversation with Luca's stepmother.

"What are you doing here, you little Monster?" Gianna asked, grasping Fabiano's shoulders.

"Why's there blood on the sheets?" he half shouted. "Has someone been killed?"

Gianna burst into laughter while Lily looked honestly distressed by the sight of the sheets. I supposed it burst her bubble of fairy tale princes and lovemaking under the stars. The men at the table behind us also started laughing, and Fabiano's face scrunched up in anger. Although he was only eight, he had a temper. I hoped he'd calm down soon, or he'd get in trouble once he was initiated. Gianna ruffled his hair.

"Are you going to New York with Luca?" Fabiano asked suddenly.

I bit my lip. "Yeah."

"But I want you to come home with us."

I blinked, trying to hide my anguish over hearing him say that. "I know."

Lily tore her eyes away from the sheets for a moment. "Won't you go on a honeymoon?"

"Not right now. The Russians and the Taiwanese are giving Luca trouble."

Fabiano nodded as if he understood, and maybe he did. With every year that passed he'd learn more of the dark world he lived in.

"Stop staring at the sheets," Gianna said in a low voice, but Lily seemed too caught up in the sight.

Her face scrunched up. "I think I'm going to be sick." I wrapped an arm around her shoulder and steered her outside. She shook in my grip.

"Hold it back," I ordered as we half ran out of the room, everyone's eyes following us. We stumbled into the hall. "Where's the bathroom?" This mansion had too many rooms.

Romero motioned us to the end of the hall and opened a door, then closed it when we were inside. I held Lily's hair as she threw up in the toilet bowl, then made her sit down on the ground. I wiped her face with a wet towel and a bit of soap. "I still feel strange."

"Put your head between your knees." I crouched before her. "What's the matter?"

She gave a small shrug.

"I'll get you some tea." I straightened.

"Don't let Romero see me like this."

"Romero isn't…" I trailed off. Lily obviously had a crush on him. It was futile, but I could at least allow her that small fantasy, when the sight of the sheets had already distressed her so much. "I'll keep him out," I promised instead and slipped out of the bathroom.

Romero and Luca waited in front of it.

"Is your sister okay?" Luca asked. Was he actually concerned or only polite?

"The sheets made her queasy."

Romero's expression darkened. "They shouldn't allow young girls to witness something like that. It'll only scare them." He glanced at Luca as if catching himself. But Luca waved dismissively. "You are right."

"Lily needs some tea."

"I can get it for her, and stay with her so you can return to your guests," Romero suggested.

I smiled. "That's nice, but Lily doesn't want you to see her."

Romero frowned. "Is she scared of me?"

"You sound like that isn't a possibility," I said with a laugh. "You are a soldier of the mafia. What's not to be scared of?" I decided not to play with him anymore and lowered my voice. "But that's not it. Lily has a major crush on you and doesn't want you to see her like that." That, and I didn't want any of Luca's men alone with Lily until I knew them better.

Luca grinned. "Romero, you still got it. Capturing the hearts of fourteen-year-old girls left and right." Then he turned his attention to me. "But we have to return. The women will be mortally offended if you don't give them all your attention."

"I'll take care of Lily," Gianna said, appearing in the hall with Fabiano.

I smiled. "Thanks," I said as I brushed her hand in passing. The moment I was back in the dining room, the women flocked around me again, trying to extract more details from me. I pretended to be too embarrassed to speak about it – which I would have been – and only gave them vague answers. Guests eventually started to leave, and I knew it would soon be time to say goodbye to my family and leave for my new life.

***

Fabiano pressed his face against my ribs almost painfully and I stroked his hair, feeling him tremble. Father was watching with a disapproving frown. He thought Fabiano was too old to show emotions like that, as if a boy couldn't be sad. They would have to leave for the airport soon. Father needed to return to Chicago to conduct business as usual. I wished they could have stayed longer, but Luca and I would leave for New York today as well.

Fabiano sniffed, then pulled back, looking up at me. Tears pressed against my eyes but I held them back. If I started crying now, things would only get harder for everyone, especially Gianna and Lily. They both hovered a couple of steps behind Fabiano, waiting for their turn to say good-bye. Father stood already beside the black rental Mercedes, impatient to leave.

"I will see you again soon," I promised, but I wasn't sure when soon would be. Christmas? That was still four months away. The thought settled like a heavy stone in the pit of my stomach.

"When?" Fabiano jutted out his lower lip.

"Soon."

"We don't have forever. The plane will leave without us," Father said sharply. "Come here, Fabiano."

With a last longing look at me, Fabiano shuffled over to Father who immediately began scolding him. My heart felt so heavy, I wasn't sure how it could stay in my chest without crushing my ribs. Luca pulled up behind the Mercedes in his steel-gray Aston Martin Vanquish and got out, but my attention shifted to Lily who threw her arms around me, and after a moment Gianna joined in the hug. My sisters, my best friends, my confidantes, my *world*.

I couldn't hold back the tears anymore. I never wanted to let them go. I wanted to take them with me to New York. They could live in our apartment, or even get their own. At least, then I'd have someone whom I loved and who loved me back.

"I'm going to miss you so much," Lily whispered between hiccupped sobs. Gianna didn't say anything. She only pressed her face into the crook of my neck and cried. Gianna, who almost never cried. My strong, impulsive Gianna. I wasn't sure how long we held onto each other, and I didn't care who saw this open display of weakness.

Let them all see what true love meant. Most of them would never experience it.

"We have to leave," Father called. Gravel crunched.

I lifted my face. Mother walked up to us, briefly touched my cheek, then took Lily's arm and led her away from me. Another piece of myself gone. Gianna didn't loosen her iron grip on me.

"Gianna!" Father's voice was like a whip.

She raised her head, eyes red, her freckles standing out even more. We locked gazes and for a moment neither of us said anything. "Call me every day. Every single day," Gianna said fiercely. "Swear it."

"I swear," I choked out.

"Gianna, for Christ's sake! Do I have to come get you?"

She backed away from me slowly, then she whirled around and practically fled into the car. I walked a few steps after them as their car drove down the long driveway. Neither of my sisters turned around. I was relieved when they finally turned a corner and were gone. I cried for myself for a while and nobody interrupted me. I knew I wasn't alone. At least, not in the physical sense.

When I finally turned around, Luca and Matteo stood on the steps behind me. Luca stared at me with a look I didn't have the energy to read. He probably thought me pathetic and weak. That was the second time I'd cried in front of him. But today hurt worse. He came down the steps while Matteo stayed behind.

"Chicago isn't the end of the world," Luca said calmly.

He couldn't understand. "It might as well be. I've never been separated from my sisters and brother. They were my whole world."

Luca didn't say anything. He gestured at his car. "We should leave. I have a meeting tonight."

I nodded. Nothing kept me here. Everyone I cared about was gone.

"I'll be behind you," Matteo said, then headed for a motorcycle.

I sank into the taupe colored leather seats of the Aston Martin. Luca closed the door, walked around the hood and settled behind the steering wheel.

"No bodyguard?" I asked tonelessly.

"I don't need bodyguards. Romero is for you. And this car doesn't exactly have room for additional passengers." He started the engine, the deep rumbling filling the inside. I faced the window as we drew away from the Vitiello mansion. It felt surreal that my life could change so drastically because of a wedding. But it had, and would only change further.

# CHAPTER NINE

The drive to New York passed in silence. I was glad Luca hadn't tried to make conversation. I wanted to be alone with my thoughts and sadness. Soon skyscrapers rose up around the car as we crept through New York at a glacial pace. I didn't care. The longer the drive took the longer I could pretend I didn't have a new home, but eventually we pulled into an underground garage. We got out of the car without a word and Luca took our bags from the trunk. Most of my belongings had already been brought to Luca's apartment a few days ago but this would be the first time I saw where he lived.

I lingered next to the car as Luca headed for the elevator doors. He glanced over his shoulder and stopped as well. "Thinking about running?"

*Every single day.*

I walked up to him. "You would find me," I said simply.

"I would." There was steel in his voice. He jabbed a card into a slot and the elevator doors glided open, revealing marble, mirrors and a small chandelier. The elevator made it clear that this wasn't a normal apartment building. We stepped inside, and nerves twisted my stomach.

I'd been alone with Luca last night and during the ride here but the thought of being alone in his penthouse was somehow worse. This was his kingdom. Who was I kidding? Pretty much all of New York was his empire. He leaned against the mirrored wall and watched me as the elevator began its ascend. I wished he'd say something, *anything really*. It would distract me from the panic rising up my throat. My eyes flitted to the screen showing which floor we were on. We were already on floor twenty and hadn't stopped yet.

"The elevator is private. It leads only to the last two floors of the building. My penthouse is at the top and Matteo has his apartment on the floor below."

"Can he come into our penthouse whenever he wants?"

Luca scanned my face. "Are you scared of Matteo?"

"I'm scared of the both of you. But Matteo seems more volatile while I doubt you'd ever do anything you don't want to do. You seem like someone who's always firmly in control."

"Sometimes I lose control."

I twisted my wedding ring around my finger, avoiding his eyes. That was information I didn't need to know.

"You have nothing to worry about when it comes to Matteo. He's used to coming over to my place whenever he wants, but things will change now that I'm married. Most of our business takes place somewhere else anyway."

The elevator beeped and came to a stop, then the doors slid apart. Luca gestured for me to step out first. I did and immediately found myself in a huge living space with sleek white sofas, dark hardwood floors, a modern glass and metal fireplace, black sideboards and tables, as well as avant-garde chandeliers. There was hardly any color at all, except for a few pieces of modern art on the walls and art pieces made from glass. But the entire wall facing the elevator was glass. The windows opened the view toward a terrace and roof garden, and beyond that skyscrapers and Central Park. The ceiling opened up above the main part of the living area and a staircase led up to the second floor of the penthouse.

I walked farther into the apartment and tilted my head up. Glass banisters allowed a clear view of the upper floor: a bright gallery with several doors branching off of it.

An open kitchen took up the left side of the living area and a massive black dining table marked the border between dining and living area. I could feel Luca's eyes on me as I took everything in. I approached the windows and peered out. I'd never lived in an apartment; even a roof garden didn't change the fact that it was a high prison.

"Your things are in the bedroom upstairs. Marianna wasn't sure if you wanted to put them away yourself, so she left them in your suitcases."

"Who's Marianna?"

Luca came up behind me. Our gazes met in the reflection in the window. "She's my housekeeper. She's here a couple of days per week."

I wondered if she was also his mistress. Some men in our world actually dared to insult their wives by bringing their whores into their own home. "How old is she?"

Luca's lips twitched. "Are you jealous?" He rested his hands on my hips and I tensed. He didn't pull away, but I could see anger crossing his face. But I also noted that he didn't answer my question.

I stepped out of his hold and headed for a glass door leading out onto the roof garden. I turned to Luca. "Can I go outside?"

His jaw was tight. He wasn't stupid. He had noticed how quickly I'd shaken off his touch. "This is your home now too."

It didn't feel that way. I'm not sure it ever would. I opened the door and stepped outside. It was windy and distant honking carried up from the streets below. White lounge furniture took up the terrace but beyond it a small well-kept garden stretched out toward a glass barrier. There was even a square in-ground Jacuzzi big enough for six people. Two sunchairs were set up beside it. I strode toward the edge of the garden and let my gaze wander over Central Park. It was a beautiful view.

"You're not thinking about jumping, are you?" Luca asked, gripping the banister beside me.

I tilted my face up to him, trying to gauge if this was his attempt at humor. He looked serious. "Why would I kill myself?"

"Some women in our world see it as their only way to gain freedom. This marriage is your prison."

I appraised the distance between the roof and the ground. Death was certain. But I'd never considered killing myself. Before doing that, I'd run. "I wouldn't do that to my family. Lily, Fabi and Gianna would be heartbroken."

Luca nodded. I couldn't read his expression and it was driving me crazy. "Let's go back inside," he said, putting a hand on my lower back and steering me into the apartment. He closed the door, then turned back to me. "I have a meeting in thirty minutes, but I'll be back in a few hours. I want to take you to my favorite restaurant for dinner."

"Oh," I said, surprised. "Like a date?"

The corners of Luca's mouth twitched, but he didn't smile. "You could call it that. We haven't been on a real date yet." He wrapped an arm around my middle and pulled me against him. I froze, and the lightness disappeared from his eyes.

"When will you stop being afraid of me?"

"You don't want me to be afraid of you?" I'd always thought it would make his life easier if I was terrified of him. Would make it easier to keep me in check.

Luca's dark brows drew together. "You are my wife. We'll spend our lives together. I don't want a cowering woman at my side."

That really surprised me. Mother loved Father but she also feared him. "Are there people out there who don't fear you?"

"A few," he said before lowering his head and pressing his lips against mine. He kissed me without hurry until I relaxed under his touch and parted my lips for him. I raised my arm and hesitantly touched the back of his neck, my fingers brushing his hair. My other hand pressed against his chest, enjoying the feel of his muscles. He pulled away.

"I have half a mind to cancel this fucking meeting." He rubbed his thumb over my lips. "But there's still more than enough time for this later." He glanced at his watch. "I really need to go now. Romero will be here when I'm gone. Take your time and look around." With that he headed for the door and left.

For a moment, I stared at the door, wondering if anyone would stop me if I walked out of this building. Instead I moved toward the staircase and walked up to the second floor. Only one of the white doors was ajar and I pushed it open. The master bedroom opened up before me. As with the living area, an entire wall was made up of windows overlooking New York. The king-sized bed was facing them. I wondered how it would be to watch the sunrise from bed. The wall behind the bed was upholstered with black fabric. At the end of the room a doorway led into a walk-in closet and to its right I could see a freestanding bathtub through the glass wall separating the bedroom from the bathroom.

I walked toward it. Even from the bathtub you could watch the city. Despite the glass wall, the washbasins and the shower weren't visible from the bedroom, and the toilet was in its own small room.

"Aria?"

I gasped. My heart pounded in my chest as I slowly followed the voice and found Romero on the gallery, carrying my bags. "I didn't mean to startle you," he said when he saw my face. I nodded. "Where do you want me to put your bags?"

I'd forgotten Luca had dropped them on the sofa. "I don't know. Maybe the walk-in closet?"

He strode past me and set the bags down on a bench in the closet. My three suitcases as well as two moving boxes were beside it. "Do you know if I need to dress up for tonight? Luca said he wants to take me to his favorite restaurant, but he didn't tell me if it has a dress code."

Romero smiled. "No. Definitely no dress code."

"Why? Is it a KFC?" I'd actually never eaten at a KFC. Father and Mother would have never taken us to a place like that. Gianna, Lily and I had once convinced Umberto to take us to a McDonalds but that was really the whole extent of my experience with fast-food joints.

"Not really. I think Luca wants to surprise you."

I doubted that. "Maybe I should unpack then." I gestured at my suitcases.

Romero kept a careful distance to me. He was nice but professional. "Do you need help?"

I really didn't want Romero to touch my underwear. "No. I'd prefer to be alone."

Compassion filled Romero's face before he turned and left. I waited until I was certain that he was back downstairs before I opened the first box. On top was a photo of me with Gianna, Lily and Fabi. I cried for the third time in less than twenty-four hours. I'd seen them only this morning, so how could I already feel so alone?

*** 

When Luca came home almost five hours later, I'd changed into a skirt and a flimsy, sleeveless blouse. Despite my best efforts, my eyes were still slightly red from crying. There was a limit to what make-up could do. Luca noticed immediately, his gaze lingering on my eyes, then darting to the photo of my family on the nightstand.

"I wasn't sure which was your side. I can move it to the other nightstand if you want," I said.

"No, it's okay." Exhaustion was written plainly on his face.

"Was the meeting okay?"

Luca looked away. "Let's not talk about it. I'm starving." He held out his hand and I took it and followed him to the elevator. He was tense and barely said a word as we rode in his car. I wasn't really sure if he expected me to make conversation, and I was too emotionally drained to put up an effort.

When we stopped at a red light, he glanced over. "You look great."

"Thanks."

He parked the car in a gated parking area where they stashed the cars on top of each other, then we headed down a street with small restaurants offering everything from Indian cuisine, over Libanese to Sushi. He stopped at a Korean restaurant and held the door open for me. Stunned I walked in into the crowded, narrow inside.

Small tables were set closely together and a bar at the front offered alcoholic beverages with labels I couldn't even read. A waiter came up to us and upon spotting Luca, he led us toward the back of the restaurant and gave us the last available table. The people at the table beside ours stared at Luca with wide eyes, probably wondering how he'd fit. I took the seat on the bench running the entire length of the room and Luca folded himself into the chair across from me. The man beside him shifted his chair to the side, so Luca would have more room. Did they know who he was or were they being polite?

"You look surprised," Luca said after the waiter had taken our drink orders and left us with the menu.

"I didn't think you'd go for Asian food, considering *everything*." That was all I could say in a crowded restaurant, but Luca knew I was talking about the Taiwanese Triad.

"This restaurant is the best Asian restaurant in town, and it doesn't belong to an Asian *chain*."

I frowned. Was it under the protection of the Familia?

"It's independent."

"There are independent restaurants in New York?"

The couple at the table beside us gave me a strange look. For them our conversation was probably more than a little weird.

"A few, but we're in negotiations right now."

I snorted.

Luca pointed at my menu. "Do you need help?"

"Yeah, I've never tried Korean."

"The marinated silk tofu and the bulgogi beef are delicious."

"You eat *tofu*?"

Luca shrugged. "If it's prepared like this, then yes."

I shook my head. This was surreal. "Just order what you think is best. I eat everything except for liver."

"I like women that eat more than salad."

The waiter returned and took our orders. I fumbled with the chopsticks, trying to figure out the best way to use them.

"Have you never used sticks before?" Luca asked with a smirk. Was he mocking me?

"My parents only took us to their favorite Italian restaurant and I wasn't really allowed to go anywhere alone." Bitterness rang in my voice.

"You can go anywhere you want now."

"Really? Alone?"

Luca lowered his voice. "With Romero or me, or Cesare when Romero isn't available."

Of course.

"Here, let me show you." He took his own chopsticks and held them up. I tried to imitate his grip and after a few tries, I managed to move the sticks without dropping them. When our food arrived, I realized that it was much harder to grab onto something with sticks.

Luca watched with obvious amusement as I took three tries to bring a piece of tofu to my lips.

"No wonder New York girls are so thin if they eat like this all the time."

"You are more beautiful than all of them," he said. I scanned his face, trying to figure out if he was being truthful, but as usual his face was unreadable. I allowed myself to admire his eyes. They were unusual with their darker ring around the gray. They weren't exactly cold right now, but I remembered them being that way.

Luca snatched a piece of marinated beef and held it out in front of me. My eyebrows shot up in surprise. Luca mirrored my expression but his was more challenging. I leaned forward and closed my lips around the sticks, then pulled back, savoring the taste of the bulgogi beef. Luca's eyes seemed to darken as he watched me.

"Delicious," I said. Luca picked up a piece of Tofu next and I took it eagerly. This was better than trying to wrangle the chopsticks into submission.

I was grateful that Luca showed me this normal side of him. It gave me hope. Maybe that was his intention, but I didn't care.

***

The relaxation I'd felt during dinner evaporated when Luca and I returned to our penthouse and stepped into the bedroom. I went into the bathroom and took my time getting ready before I returned.

Luca's eyes took in my long dark satin nightgown. It reached my calves but had a slit that went up to my thighs. It was still much more modest than the horrible thing I'd worn on our wedding night. And yet I was sure there was desire in his eyes.

Once he'd disappeared into the bathroom, I walked toward the window and busied myself watching the nightly skyline. I was almost as nervous as last night. I knew I wasn't ready for more than kissing. I didn't turn when I heard Luca come up beside me. His impressive stature was reflected in the windows. Like yesterday he was only wearing briefs. I watched him reach out for me, and every muscle in my body tensed. If he noticed my reaction, he didn't let it show. He trailed a knuckle down the length of my spine, sending a tingling sensation through my body. When I didn't react he extended his hand, palm upward, an invitation not a command, and yet I knew there was only one right answer.

I faced him, but my eyes were drawn to the long scar on his palm. I ran my fingertips over it. "Is that from the blood oath?" I peered up into his unreadable face. I knew during the initiation ceremony, men had to let blood while reciting the words of the oath.

"No. This is." He turned his other hand where a small scar marred his palm. "That," he said with a nod toward the scar I was still touching. "...happened in a fight. I had to stave off a knife attack with my hand."

I wanted to ask him about the first time he killed a man, but he curled his fingers around my wrist and led me toward the bed. My throat became too tight for words when he sat on the mattress and pulled me between his legs. I tried to relax into his kiss and when he made no move to take things further I actually felt the tension slip away and began to enjoy his experienced mouth, but then he lay back and pulled me onto the bed with him.

His kisses became more forceful and I could feel his erection pressed up against my thigh. Still I didn't pull back. I could do this. I knew it was coming. His hand cupped my breast and I stiffened despite my best intentions not to. He didn't remove it, but didn't move it either. His kisses made thinking difficult. Would it really be so bad to sleep with Luca? He drew back a couple of inches and trailed kisses toward my ear. "I've never wanted to fuck a woman as much as I want to fuck you right now."

I froze. His words made me feel cheap. He was my husband and he had a right to my body, if you asked anyone in our family anyway, but I deserved better than that. I didn't want to be fucked like he was used to doing with other women. I was his wife. I wanted more. I turned my head and pushed my palms against his chest. After a moment, he relented.

"I don't want this," I said, not bothering to hide my disgust from him.

I didn't look at him but I could practically feel his frustration. What did he think? That I would suddenly feel comfortable enough to sleep with him because he'd taken me out for dinner once? Was that how it worked with his other girls? For a long time he did nothing but stare at me, then he untangled himself from me.

He shut off the light without a word and lied on his side of the bed. I wished he'd at least hold me. This was my first night so far away from my family. It would have been nice if he'd at least comforted me, but I didn't ask him to. Instead I pulled the covers up and closed my eyes.

***

When I woke the next morning, Luca was gone. There was no note, not even a text on my phone. He was really pissed. I shoved my blankets off. *Bastard.* He knew I didn't know anyone in New York and yet he didn't care. I grabbed my laptop and opened my email account. Gianna had already sent me three new emails. The last one was almost threatening. I picked up the phone. Only hearing her voice was enough to make me feel better. I didn't need Luca or anyone else, as long as I had Gianna.

The scent of coffee and something sweeter eventually drew me out of the bedroom and downstairs. Pans were clanking in the kitchen and as I turned the corner, I found a small, plump woman who looked old enough to be my Grandma at the stove, making pancakes. Her dark grey hair was secured with a hairnet. Romero was perched on a stool at the bar attached to the kitchen island, a cup of coffee in front of him. He turned when I approached, his eyes taking in my nightgown before jerking his head away. Really?

The woman turned and smiled kindly. "You must be Aria. I'm Marianna."

I walked up to her to shake her hand but she pulled me into a hug, pressing me against her ample chest. "You are a beauty, *bambina*. No wonder Luca is smitten with you."

I swallowed a snide comment. "That smells delicious."

"Sit. Breakfast is ready in a couple of minutes. It's enough for Romero and you."

I sat beside Romero on a stool. He was still pointedly looking the other direction. "What's your problem? I'm not naked," I said when I couldn't take it anymore.

Marianna laughed. "The boy is worried Luca finds out he ogled his girl."

I shook my head, annoyed. If Romero insisted on being a coward, he'd have to eat with closed eyes. I wasn't putting a bathrobe on because I needed a bodyguard in my own home.

*** 

I was already dozing off when Luca came home that night. While he'd spent his day outside doing God knows what I was a prisoner in this stupid penthouse. The only people who kept me company were Marianna and Romero, but she'd left after preparing dinner and Romero wasn't exactly the most communicative company. I watched as Luca emerged from the bathroom, freshly showered. He barely acknowledged me. Did he think I cared? When he lied down beside me and extinguished the lights, I said into the darkness. "Can I walk through the city tomorrow?"

"As long as you take Romero with you," was his short reply.

I swallowed my hurt and frustration. When he'd taken me to his favorite restaurant I'd thought he'd try to make this marriage work but it had only been a ploy to get me into bed. And now he punished me with the silent treatment.

But I didn't need him, never would. I drifted off to the sound of his rhythmic breathing.

I awoke in the middle of the night from a nightmare. Luca's arm was wrapped around me, my body spooned by his. I could have pulled away, but his closeness felt too good. A part of me still wanted this marriage to work.

***

I missed Gianna and Lily so much, it was almost a physical thing.

Romero tried to be invisible but he was always there. "Do you want to go shopping?"

I almost laughed. Did he think shopping made everything better? Maybe that worked for some people, but definitely not for me. "No, but I'd like to grab something to eat. Gianna sent me an email with a few restaurants she wants to try when she visits. I'd like to go to one of them today."

Romero looked uncertain for an instant, and I exploded. "I asked Luca for permission a couple of nights ago, so you don't have to worry. I'm allowed to leave this prison."

He frowned. "I know. He told me."

This was ridiculous. I left him standing in the middle of the living area and hurried up the stairs to the bedroom. I quickly changed into a nice summer dress and sandals, grabbed my bag and sunglasses before heading back down. Romero hadn't moved from his spot. Why couldn't he pretend he was something other than my bodyguard?

"Let's go," I ordered. If he wanted to act like my bodyguard, I'd treat him that way. Romero pulled a jacket over his shirt to hide his holster, then pushed the elevator button. We didn't talk during the ride down. This was actually the first time I saw the lobby of the apartment building. It was sleek, black marble, modern art, white high gloss counter behind which a middle-aged receptionist in a black suit sat. He inclined his head toward Romero before his eyes zoomed in on me with obvious curiosity. "Good day, Mrs. Vitiello," he said in an overly polite voice. I almost stumbled at hearing him call me that. It was easy to forget I wasn't a Scuderi anymore. After all, my husband was never present.

I nodded in acknowledgement, then quickly rushed outside. Heat blasted against my body as I left the air-conditioned building. Summer in the city, nothing to be excited about. The smell of exhaust and garbage seemed to carry through the streets like fog. Romero was a step behind me and I wondered how he could bear the heat in his dress-up.

"I think we need to take a taxi," I said, as I stepped toward the curb. Romero shook his head but I'd already raised my arm and a taxi swerved to the side and stopped beside me.

***

Romero hung a few steps back, his alert gaze on my back. It was driving me crazy. People were giving us strange looks. "Can you please walk beside me?" I asked as we walked down Greenwich Street where the restaurant was. "I don't want people to think you're guarding me." He was probably still pissed that I'd made him take a taxi, instead of the black BMW that screamed mafia from afar.

"I'm guarding you."

I stopped until he fell into step beside me. The outside of the restaurant was surrounded by wild flowers growing in terracotta pots and the inside reminded me of British pubs I'd read about. It seemed as if every single of the waiters was tattooed, and the tables were set so closely together you could have eaten from your neighbor's plate. I could see why Gianna would love it.

Romero's lips twisted in obvious disapproval. It was probably a bodyguard's nightmare. "Do you have a reservation?" A tall woman with a septum piercing asked.

"No." Romero narrowed his eyes as if he couldn't believe someone was actually asking something like that. I loved it. Here I wasn't Aria, wife of Luca Vitiello. "But it's just the two of us. And we won't take long," I said politely.

The woman looked between Romero and me, then smiled. "You have 1 hour. You are a cute couple."

She turned to lead us toward our table, which was why she didn't see Romero's expression. "Why didn't you correct her?" he asked quietly.

"Why should I?"

"Because we aren't a couple. You are Luca's."

"I am. And I'm not."

Romero didn't argue again, but I could tell it made him uncomfortable to act like we were anything but bodyguard and his boss's wife. I ate a salad with the most delicious dressing and enjoyed watching the people around us, while Romero ate a burger and monitored our surroundings. I couldn't wait to take Gianna here. Sadness filled me at the thought. I had never been so lonely in my life. Only two days into my new life and I really didn't know how to survive the many thousand days that would follow. "So Luca will be home late again tonight?"

"I suppose," Romero said evasively.

After we'd eaten, I forced Romero to stroll through the neighborhood of the restaurant for a bit longer, but eventually I got frustrated with his stiff posture and obvious discomfort, and agreed to return to the apartment.

***

When the taxi pulled up in front of the apartment building, Romero paid the driver and I slipped out of the car. As I approached the glass front, I noticed one of Luca's cousins sitting inside the lobby. What was she doing here? We hadn't talked more than a few sentences at the wedding and I hadn't gotten the impression that she was interested in friendship. Confused, I stepped into the lobby. Cosima's eyes snapped to me and she walked up to me without hesitation and hugged me to my surprise, then she pressed something into my hand. "Here. Don't let Romero or anyone else see it. Now smile."

I did, stunned. I could feel a folded piece of paper and what felt like a key in my palm. I quickly stashed them in my purse when Romero appeared beside me. "What are you doing here, Cosima?" There was a hint of suspicion in his voice.

She flashed her teeth at him. "I wanted to see how Aria was doing and asked her if we could meet for lunch soon. But now I need to go. I have a hair appointment." She gave me a warning look, then she walked out, high heels clacking on the marble floor.

Romero was watching me. "What did she say?"

"What she told you," I said, raising my chin. "I want to go up now." He wanted me to act like his boss, so he couldn't expect me to open up to him. He nodded and led me toward the elevator with a curt nod toward the two receptionists.

The moment we entered the penthouse, I excused myself and headed into the guest bathroom. I pulled out what Cosima had given me and unfolded the piece of paper.

Aria,

The key is for one of the apartments the Vitiello's own. Come over tonight at ten pm to see what your husband is really up to while you warm his bed. Be careful and quiet, and don't tell anyone. Romero will try to stop you. Shake him off.


The address was at the bottom of the page. The note wasn't signed and it was written with a computer. Was it from Cosima? It would make sense. I read it over and over again. It could be a trick, or worse: a trap, but curiosity burned through me. Luca hadn't exactly been the most present husband. The only problem was how to get to the apartment and how to get rid of Romero. He never left my side.

\*\*\*

I convinced Romero to go out to dinner to a restaurant that according to google maps was only a five-minute walk from the address Cosima had given me. When Romero used the guest bathroom in our apartment, I used the moment to take a small gun Luca kept in one of the top drawers in the walk-in closet. I'd noticed it when I'd unpacked my suitcases and folded my clothes into drawers. I hid it in the side pocket of my bag. Even though I didn't have much experience with guns, I knew how to handle them in theory. Better safe than sorry.

\*\*\*

It was quarter past nine. Romero and I had just finished our starter, when I stood to head for the bathroom. Romero pushed back his chair and was about to stand as well.

I glared. "You won't follow me to the bathroom. Do you think I will get lost on the way? People will be staring. Nobody knows who I am here. I'm safe."

Romero sank back down. The bathroom was past a corner, closer to the door than our table. I slipped out of the restaurant, took flats from my purse and put them on. Then I hurried toward the address. It would take at least five minutes before Romero would venture toward the bathroom and hopefully even longer before he'd barge in to check on me.

When I arrived in front of the brownstone building, I hesitated. It didn't have a reception, only a narrow corridor and a steep staircase. Then I took a deep breath and entered. The key said the apartment was on the third floor. I took the elevator hidden in a dark corner behind the stairs. During the ride up, doubt overcame me. Maybe I shouldn't have listened to the letter. The elevator came to a halt and the door rattled open. My eyes darted to the button that would take me back to the ground floor but instead I stepped out and found the apartment door. It wasn't completely shut.

My heart fluttered with fear. This seemed like a really bad idea, but curiosity was stronger than worry. I pushed the door open and peered in. The living room was dark and empty, but light was coming from somewhere else. I rested my hand on the gun in my purse, then crept further in, but froze when I heard a woman cry out. "Yes! Harder!"

Dread settled in me as I followed the voice. I had heard it before. The light was spilling out of an open door. I stopped in front of it, hesitating. I could still turn around and pretend I'd never received the letter. Another moan drifted out of the room and I peaked inside. Heat rushed up my face, then seemed to drain out of my body completely. Grace Parker was on her knees and forearms on the bed while Luca fucked her from behind. The slaps of his body hitting her ass filled the silence, only occasionally disrupted by her encouraging cries and moans. Luca's eyes were closed as his fingers dug into her hips and he rammed into her over and over again. Grace turned her head to meet my eyes, and smiled triumphantly. Bile traveled up my throat. So this was what Luca had been up to the last two nights.

For a crazy moment, I considered taking the gun out and throwing it at her head. I wouldn't shoot her, even if I wanted to. I wasn't a mobster. I wasn't Luca. My shoulders slumped and I took a step back. I needed to get away. Luca's eyes shot open, hand reaching for a gun on the bed beside him but then he found me. He jerked, then froze.

"What's the matter, Luca?" Grace asked, wiggling her ass against him. He was still buried inside her. Luca and I stared at each other and I could feel tears gathering in my eyes.

I whirled around and ran. I needed to get away. Just away. The moment I stepped out of the elevator on the first floor, I began shaking but I didn't stop. I rushed outside almost bumping into

Romero who must have followed my phone's GPS. He stumbled back, looked at my face, then at the building and his eyes widened. He knew. Everyone seemed to know, except for stupid me.

I stormed away, running faster than I'd ever run in my life. When I crossed the street toward the underground station, I caught a glimpse of Luca in an unbuttoned shirt and pants staggering out of the door. Romero was already chasing me.

But I was fast. Years of working out on the treadmill finally paid off. I practically flew down the steps, fumbled for the Metro card my sisters and I had purchased before the wedding after we'd forced Umberto to show us the subway. I managed to squeeze into the already closing doors of a subway wagon. I wasn't even sure where it was going. But as I saw Luca and Romero heading for the tracks, all that mattered was that it was taking me away. Away from the triumphant smile Grace had given me, from the sound of Luca's body pounding her ass, from his betrayal.

On our wedding night I'd told Luca I didn't hate him. I wished he'd ask me again today. I sank down on a free seat, but I was still shaking. Where was I going?

I couldn't run away. Luca was probably already sending every soldier after me. I let out a choked laugh and got a few strange looks from other passengers. What did they know? They were free.

I grabbed my mobile and called Gianna. She answered at the second ring. "Aria?"

"I caught Luca in bed with Grace." More people looked my way. What did it even matter? They didn't know who I was. The wedding announcements in the newspaper had never included a photo of me. I really didn't need any more attention.

"Holy fuck."

"Yeah." I got out at the next station as I began telling the whole story to Gianna. I quickly moved away from the underground because that would be the place they'd look first. Eventually I landed in a loud and dark place where burgers and beer were sold. I ordered a coke and a burger, though I had no intention of drinking or eating.

"Where are you now?" Gianna asked.

"Somewhere. I don't even know. In a restaurant, sort of."

"Be careful." I didn't say anything. "Are you crying?"

I was. Again I stayed silent.

"Don't. Not when I'm not around to console you and kick Luca's fucking ass. I knew he was an asshole. Fucking bastard. You haven't slept with him yet, right?"

"No, I haven't. That's probably why he's off cheating on me."

"Don't you dare blaming yourself, Aria. Any decent man would have kept his dick in his pants or used his hand."

The burger and a coke arrived, and I thanked the waitress who lingered beside my table for a couple of seconds, her gaze lingering on my tears. I gave her a smile and she finally took the hint and left.

"What will you do now? Are you thinking of coming back home?"

"Do you really think Father will let me leave Luca because he cheated on me? Father has had a mistress for *years*." Nor would Luca allow it. I was his, as Romero never ceased to remind me.

"Men are all pigs."

"I can't forget the look Grace gave me. She looked like she'd won."

"She wanted you to see it, she wanted to humiliate you." Gianna fell silent. "You are the wife of the future Capo dei Capi. If someone humiliates you, they are practically insulting Luca."

"Well, he was busy helping her insult me."

Gianna snorted. "I hope his dick falls off."

"I'm not holding my breath."

"I bet Romero's getting his ass kicked for letting you slip away. Serves him right."

I almost felt sorry for Romero, but then I reminded myself that he'd known about Grace all along. It had been written all over his face. God, how many people knew? Were they all laughing about me behind my back?

"Are you talking to Aria?" I could hear Lily's excited voice in the background. "That's none of your business. Get out of my room, you little snoop."

"I want to talk to her! She's my sister too!"

"Not now. This is private." There was shouting, then the bang of a door, followed by fists hammering against wood. My heart swelled with warmth and I smiled. This had been my life not too long ago. Now I only had a cheating husband to return to.

"So what now?" Gianna asked eventually.

"I honestly don't know." I paid and left the restaurant, returning to roaming the streets. It was dark but they were still crowded with people on their way home from dinner or on their way to a club or bar.

"You can't let him treat you like that. You must fight back."

"I don't know if fighting Luca is something I want to do."

"What can he do to you? You aren't his enemy or his soldier, and he said he didn't beat women, nor would he force himself on you. What's left? Lock you in your room without dinner?"

I sighed.

"Maybe you should cheat on him. Go to a club, find a hot guy and sleep with him."

That would go over well with Luca. "He'd kill him. I don't want blood on my hands."

"Then do something else. I don't care as long as you pay Luca back for what he's doing to you. He'll probably just keep cheating on you. Fight back."

But Gianna was the fighter. I preferred subtle tactics. "I should get rid of this phone now. I need more time to think and don't want Luca to track me down."

"Call me as soon as you can. No matter the time. If I don't hear from you tomorrow morning, I don't care who I have to take down to fly to New York."

"Okay. Love you." Before Gianna could say any more, I turned my phone off, disabled it and threw it into a dustbin before walking the streets aimlessly. It was past midnight and I was getting tired. The only thing that kept me going was the image of Luca going crazy because he couldn't find me. He hated not being in control. And now I'd slipped away from him. I wished I could see it.

I bought a coffee and wrapped my fingers around the warm paper cup as I leaned against the facade of the coffee shop and let my eyes wander over the thinning number of passerby. Every time a couple walked past me, holding hands, kissing and laughing and being in love, my chest tightened. My eyes burnt from exhaustion and my earlier crying. I was so tired.

I hailed a taxi and let it take me to our apartment building. As I stepped into the lobby, the receptionist immediately picked up the phone. Good dog, I wanted to say. Instead I twisted my mouth into a smile and stepped into the elevator, then slipped in the card so it would take me to the right floor. I was almost calm now, at least on the outside. Was Luca in the penthouse? Or was he out hunting me? Or maybe he'd returned to his whore and let his men do the work for him. When I'd woken with Luca's arms around me, or when he'd kissed me, I'd let myself believe that maybe I could make him love me. When we'd had dinner together I'd thought I could fall for him.

I entered the penthouse. Romero was there and practically sagged with relief. "She's here," he said into his phone, then nodded before ending the call.

"Where's Luca? Back with his whore?"

Romero frowned. "Searching for you."

"I'm surprised he bothers. He could have sent you or one of his other lapdogs. After all you do everything he says. Even cover for him while he's out cheating on me." Romero didn't say anything. I wasn't sure why I was lashing out at him.

I walked away.

"Where are you going?"

"I'm going to undress and shower. If you want to watch, be my guest." Romero stopped but his eyes followed me up the stairs. I slammed the bedroom door shut after me, then locked it before walking into the bathroom to take a shower. I turned the temperature as high as I could bear but the water couldn't wash away the images that had taken refuge in my brain. Luca buried in Grace. Her smile. The sound of his hips slamming against her ass. I wasn't exactly sure what I was feeling. Disappointment. Jealousy? I hadn't chosen Luca, but he was my husband. I wanted him to be faithful to me. I wanted him to want only me. I wanted to be enough.

There was banging at the bedroom door when I got out of the shower. I wrapped a towel around myself and slowly walked out of the bathroom into the bedroom.

"Aria, let me in!" There was anger in his voice. He was *angry*?

I dropped the towel and slipped a silk nightgown over my body.

"I'm going to kick in the door, if you don't let me in."

I'd like to see you do it. Maybe you'll dislocate a shoulder.

"Aria, open the fucking door!"

I was too tired to keep playing with him. I wanted this day to be over. I wanted sleep to magically take away my memory. I unlocked the door, then turned and walked back to the bed. The door flew open, banging against the wall and Luca stormed in. He grasped my arm and fury burned through me. How dare he lay hands on me after gripping that whore's ass with them?

"Don't touch me!" I shrieked, wrenching out of his grip. He was panting, eyes wild with emotion. His hair was a mess and his shirt wasn't buttoned properly. Matteo stood in the doorway, Romero and Cesare a few steps behind.

"Where have you been?" he said in a low voice, he reached for me again and I stumbled back. "No! Don't ever touch me again. Not when you use those same hands to touch your *whore.*"

His face became very still. "Out, everyone. Now."

Matteo turned and he and the other two men disappeared from view.

"Where have you been?"

"I wasn't cheating on you if that's what you're worried about. I would never do that. I think faithfulness is the most important thing in a marriage. So you can calm yourself now, my body is still only yours." I practically spat the last few words. "I only walked around the city."

"You walked around New York at night *alone*?"

I stared into his eyes, hoping he could see how much I hated him for what I'd seen, how much it hurt to know he respected me so little. "You have no right to be angry with me, Luca. Not after what I saw today. You cheated on me."

Luca snarled. "How can I be cheating when we don't even have a real marriage? I can't even fuck my own wife. Do you think I'll live like a monk until you decide you can stand my closeness?"

That arrogant pig. He and my father had made sure I didn't even talk to other men until my wedding to Luca. "God forbid. How dare I expect my husband to be faithful to me? How dare I hope for this small decency in a monster?"

"I'm not a monster. I've treated you with respect."

"Respect?" My voice rose higher. "I caught you with another woman! Maybe I should go out, bring a random guy back with me and let him fuck me in front of your eyes. How would that make you feel?"

Suddenly he flung me on the bed and was on top of me, my arms pinned above my head. Pushing through the choking fear, I said. "Do it. Take me, so I can really hate you." His eyes were the most terrifying thing I'd ever seen.

His nostrils flared. I turned my face away and closed my eyes. He was breathing harshly, his grip on my wrists too tight. My heart pounded against my ribcage as I lay unmoving beneath him. He shifted and pressed his face into my shoulder, releasing a harsh breath. "God, Aria."

I opened my eyes. He released my wrists but I kept my arms above my head. Slowly he raised his eyes. The anger was gone from his face. He reached for my cheek but I turned away. "Don't touch me with *her* on you."

He sat up. "I'm going to take a shower now, and we will both calm down and then I want us to talk."

"What's there left to talk about?"

"Us. This marriage."

I lowered my arms. "You fucked a woman in front of my eyes today. Do you think there's still a chance for this marriage?"

"I didn't want you to see that."

"Why? So you could cheat in peace and quiet behind my back?"

He sighed, and began unbuttoning his shirt. "Let me take a shower. You were right. I shouldn't disrespect you further by touching you like this."

I shrugged. Right now I didn't think I'd ever want him to touch me again, no matter how many showers he took. He disappeared in the bathroom. The shower ran for a long time. I sat against the headboard, sheets pulled up to my hip when Luca finally emerged. I averted my eyes when he dropped his towel and put on boxer shorts, then he slipped into bed beside me with his back against the headboard. He didn't try to touch me. "Did you cry?" he asked in a puzzled voice.

"Did you think I wouldn't care?"

"Many women in our world are glad when their husbands use whores or take on a mistress. As you said, there are few love marriages. If a woman can't stand her husband's touch, she won't mind him having affairs to satisfy his needs."

I scoffed. "His needs."

"I'm not a good man, Aria. I never pretended otherwise. There are no good men in the mafia."

My eyes rested on the tattoo over his heart. "I know." I swallowed. "But you made me think that I could trust you and that you wouldn't hurt me."

"I never hurt you."

Did he really not get it? "It hurt seeing you with *her*."

His expression softened. "Aria, I didn't get the feeling that you wanted to sleep with me. I thought you'd be glad if I didn't touch you."

"When did I say that?"

"When I told you I wanted you, you pulled back. You looked disgusted."

"We were kissing and you said you wanted to fuck me more than any other women. Of course, I pulled back. I'm not some whore you can use when you feel like it. You are never home. How am I supposed to get to know you?" He looked frustrated. Mafia men seemed even more clueless than normal men. "What did you think? I've never done anything. You are the only man I kissed. You knew that when we married. You and my father even made sure it was the case, and despite that you expect me to go from never even having kissed a guy to spreading my legs for you. I wanted to take it slow. I wanted to get to know you so I could relax, I wanted to kiss you and *do other things* first before we slept together."

Realization finally settled on his features, then he smirked. "Other things? What kind of other things?"

I glared. I wasn't in the mood for jokes. "This is useless."

"No, don't." He turned my face back to him, then dropped his hand. He'd learned his lesson. "I get it. For men the first time isn't a big deal, or at least it wasn't for the men I know."

"When was your first time?"

"I was thirteen and my father thought it was time for me to become a real man since I'd already been initiated. 'You can't be a virgin and a killer'. That's what he said." Luca smiled coldly. "He paid two noble prostitutes to spend a weekend with me and teach me everything they knew."

"That's horrible."

"Yeah, I suppose it is," Luca said quietly. "But I was a thirteen year old teenage boy who wanted to prove himself. I was the youngest member in the New York Familia. I didn't want the older men to think of me as a boy. And I felt like a big deal when the weekend was over. I doubt the prostitutes were overly impressed with my performance but they pretended that I was the best lover they'd ever had. My father probably paid them extra for it. It took me a bit to figure out that not all women like it if you come all over their face when they give you a blowjob."

I wrinkled my nose and Luca let out a laugh. "Yeah," he murmured, then reached for a strand of my hair, and let it glide over his finger. I wasn't sure why he always did that. "I was really worried tonight."

"Worried that I'd let someone have what's yours."

"No," he said firmly. "I knew, I *know* you are loyal. Things with the Bratva are escalating. If they got their hands on you..." He shook his head.

"They didn't."

"They *won't*."

I shifted away from his hand that had moved on from my hair to my throat. I didn't want his touch. He sighed. "You're going to make this really difficult, aren't you?"

I stared.

"I'm sorry for what you saw today."

"But not sorry for what you did."

He looked exasperated. "I rarely say I'm sorry. When I say it, I mean it."

"Maybe you should say it more often."

He took a deep breath. "There's no way out of this marriage for you, neither for me. Do you really want to be miserable?"

He was right. There was no way out. And even if there was, what for? My father would marry me off to the next man. Maybe a man like Bibiana's husband. And no matter how much I wanted to deny it, I could imagine developing feelings for the Luca I saw in the restaurant. It wouldn't have hurt so much seeing him with that woman, if I didn't. When he'd touched my hair or kissed me or wrapped his arms around me during the night, I'd felt myself wanting to fall in love with him. I wished I could hate him with all my heart. If Gianna had been in my stead, she would rather have gone through life hating her husband and being miserable than ever giving him and our father the satisfaction of coming to care for him. "No," I said. "But I can't pretend I never saw you with her."

"I don't expect you to, but let's just pretend our marriage begins today. A clean start."

"It's not that easy. What about her? Tonight wasn't the first time you were with her. Do you love her?" My voice trembled as I said it.

Luca noticed of course. He looked at me as if I was a puzzle he couldn't figure out. "Love? No. I don't have feelings for Grace."

"Then why do you keep seeing her? The truth."

"Because she knows how to suck a cock and because she's a good fuck. Truthful enough?"

I flushed. Luca brushed a finger over my cheek. "I love it when you blush whenever I say something dirty. I can't wait to see your blush when I do something dirty to you."

Why couldn't he stop to touch me? "If you really want to make this marriage work, if you *ever want the chance* to do something dirty to me, then you'll have to stop seeing other women. Maybe other wives don't care, but I won't have you touch me as long as there is anyone else."

Luca nodded. "I promise. I'll touch only you from now on."

I considered him. "Grace won't like it."

"Who gives a fuck what she thinks?"

"Won't her father give you trouble?"

"We pay for his campaigns and he has a son following in his footsteps who needs our money soon as well. What does he care about a daughter who isn't good for anything but shopping and eventually marrying a rich man?" The same could be said for me and every other woman in our world. Sons could follow in their father's footsteps, they could become members of the mafia. I still

163

remembered how much Father had celebrated when he'd found out his fourth child was finally a son.

"She probably hoped you'd be that man."

"We don't marry outsiders. Never. She knew that, and it wasn't like she was the only woman I fucked."

I gave him a look. "You said it yourself. You have your needs. So how can you tell me you won't cheat on me again soon if you get tired of waiting for me to sleep with you?"

Luca tilted his head, eyes narrowed in thought. "Do you intend to make me wait long?"

"I think we both have very different concepts of the word 'long wait'."

"I'm not a patient man. If long means a year…" He trailed off. I couldn't believe him.

"What do you want me to say, Aria? I kill and blackmail and torture people. I'm the Boss of men who do the same when I order them to, and soon I'll be the Capo dei Capi, the leader of the most powerful crime organization on the East coast, and probably the US. You thought I'd take you against your will on our wedding night and now you are angry because I don't want to wait months to sleep with you?"

I closed my eyes. "I'm tired. It's late." It was so late it was actually early.

"No," Luca said, touching my waist. "I want to understand. I'm your husband. It's not like you are like other girls who can choose the man they're going to lose it to. Are you scared I'm going to be rough with you because of what you saw today? I won't be. I told you I want you to writhe beneath me in pleasure, and while that probably won't happen the first time I take you, I'll make you come as often as you want with my tongue and my fingers until you can come when I'm in you. I don't mind going slow, but what do you want to wait for?"

I watched him through half-lidded eyes. For something that will never happen: that you'll want to *make love* to me and not *take* me like I'm your possession. Part of me didn't want to settle for less, the other part knew I had to. 'Love is something girls hope for when they don't know better, something women long for when they lie awake at night, and something they'll only ever get from their children. Men don't have time for such notions.' That's what my father always said. "I won't make you wait for months," I said instead of what I really wanted to say, then I fell asleep.

# CHAPTER TEN

Luca cancelled his plans for the next day and sent Matteo out to do whatever needed to be done. As a woman in our world, you quickly learned not to ask too many questions because the answers were rarely good.

Luca got ready first and when I walked into the kitchen dressed and showered, he was staring into the fridge with a frown on his face. "Can you cook?"

I snorted. "Don't tell me you've never made breakfast for yourself?"

"I usually grab something on my way to work, except on the days when Marianna is here and prepares something for me." His eyes scanned my body. I'd chosen shorts, a tanktop and sandals since it was supposed to get really hot today. "I love your legs."

I shook my head, then walked toward him to peek into the fridge. He didn't step back and our arms brushed. This time I managed not to flinch. His touch wasn't uncomfortable and when he didn't startle me, I could actually imagine enjoying it. The fridge was well stocked. The problem was I'd never cooked either, but I wouldn't mention that to Luca. I grabbed the egg carton and red peppers, and set them down on the kitchen counter. It couldn't be that hard to prepare an omelet. I'd watched our cook a few times in the past.

Luca leaned against the kitchen island and crossed his arms as I grabbed a pan from the cupboard and turned on the stove. I glanced over my shoulder at him. "Won't you help me? You can chop the peppers. You know how to handle a knife from what I hear."

That made the corners of his lips twitch but he pulled a knife out of the block and stepped up to my side. The top of my head came only up to his chest with my flat sandals. I had to admit I kind of liked it. I handed him the pepper and pointed toward a wooden cutting board because I got the feeling Luca would have started chopping right on the expensive black granite countertops. We worked in silence but Luca kept sneaking glances at me. I put a bit of butter into the pan, then seasoned the beaten eggs. I wasn't sure if I needed to add milk or cream, but decided against it. I poured the eggs into the sizzling pan.

Luca pointed his knife at the chopped peppers. "What happens to these?"

"Shit," I whispered. The peppers should have gone in first.

"Have you ever cooked?"

I ignored him and chucked the peppers into the pan with the eggs. I'd turned the stove to maximum heat and soon the hint of a burning smell reached my nose. I quickly grabbed a spatula and tried to flip the omelet over, but it stuck to the pan. Luca was watching me with a smirk.

"Why don't you make coffee for us?" I snapped as I scraped the half burnt eggs from the bottom of the pan.

When I thought the eggs were safe to eat, I spooned them onto two plates. They didn't really look all that tasty. Luca's brows rose when I put a plate down in front of him. He sank down on the barstool and I hopped onto the one beside him. I watched him as he picked up the fork and speared a piece of egg, then brought it to his lips. He swallowed, but it was obvious he wasn't too impressed. I took a bite as well and almost spat it back out. The eggs were too dry and too salty. I dropped my fork and gulped down half of my coffee, not even caring that it was hot and black. "Oh my God, that's disgusting."

There was a hint of amusement in Luca's face. The more relaxed expression made him look so much more approachable. "Maybe we should go out for breakfast."

I glowered at my coffee. "How hard can it be to make an omelet?"

Luca let out what might have been a laugh. Then his eyes flitted back down to my bare legs, which were almost touching his. He put his hand down on my knee and I froze with my cup against my lips. He didn't do anything, just lightly traced his thumb back and forth over my skin. "What would you like to do today?"

I pondered that, even if his hand was very distracting. I was alternating between wanting to shove it off my knee and ask him to keep caressing me. "The morning after our wedding night, you asked me if I knew how to fight, so maybe you can teach me how to use a knife or a gun, and maybe some self-defense."

Surprise crossed Luca's face. "Thinking about using them against me?"

I huffed. "As if I could ever beat you in a fair fight."

"I don't fight fair."

Of course he didn't. "So will you teach me?"

"I want to teach you a lot of things." His fingers tightened on my knee.

"Luca," I said quietly. "I'm serious. I know I have Romero and you but I want to be able to defend myself if something happens. You said it yourself, the Bratva won't care that I'm a woman."

That got him. He nodded. "Okay. We have a gym where we work out and do fight training. We could go there."

I smiled, excited about getting out of the penthouse and doing something useful. "I'll grab my workout clothes." I hopped off the stool and ran upstairs.

***

Thirty minutes later we parked in front of a shabby building. I was bursting with excitement, and I was glad to have something to distract myself from what had happened yesterday. Luca and I got out of the car and he carried our bags as we headed through a rusty steel door. Security cameras were everywhere and a middle-aged man sat in a nook that held a table and chair as well as a TV. Two guns were in his holster. He straightened when he saw Luca, then he spotted me and his eyes grew wide.

"My wife," Luca said with a hint of warning and the man's gaze jerked away from me. Luca put a hand on the small of my back and guided me through another door that led into a huge hall. There were a boxing ring, all kinds of exercise machines, dummies for fight and knife training, and a corner with mats where a few man were sparring. I was the only woman.

Luca grimaced. "Our changing rooms are men only. We don't usually have female visitors."

"I know you'll make sure nobody sees me naked."

"You bet I will."

I laughed, and a few faces turned our way, then more until everyone was staring. They quickly returned to what they'd been doing before when Luca led me toward a door on the side, but they kept throwing badly disguised glances my way. A few of the older men called out a greeting to Luca. He opened the door, then stopped. "Let me check if someone's in there." I nodded, then leaned against the wall as Luca disappeared inside the changing room. The moment he was gone, I could feel the full force of the men's attention shifting my way. I tried not to let them see how nervous their scrutiny made me and almost breathed a sigh of relief when Luca came back out, followed by a few men who pretended they didn't notice me. I wondered what Luca had told them.

"Come." He held the door open for me and we walked into a low ceilinged room filled with humidity and the smell of too many hard-working male bodies. I scrunched my nose up. Luca laughed. "We're not catering to sensitive female noses."

I grabbed by bag from him and walked toward a locker. Luca followed and set his own bag down on the scratched wooden bench.

"Aren't you going to give me some privacy?" I asked, hands on the hem of my shirt.

Luca raised one eyebrow at me before removing his holster and then pulling his own shirt over his head, revealing his muscled tanned

170

torso. He dropped his shirt on the bench, then reached for his belt, still that challenging look in his eyes.

Gritting my teeth, I turned my back to him and slid my tanktop over my head. I reached behind me to open the clasp of my bra, but Luca's hand was there and did it for me expertly. Bastard. Of course, he could open a bra with one finger. I grabbed my jogging bra and put it on, trying not to think about Luca who was undoubtedly watching every move. I stripped off my shorts and could have kicked myself for choosing a thong this morning. I pulled it down as well, and heard Luca sucking in his breath when I bent forward slightly. My cheeks blasted with heat, realizing what kind of view I'd just given him. I snatched one of the plain black panties I always wore when I worked out on the treadmill, then I put my jogging shorts on over them and turned back around to Luca. He'd put on black sweatpants and an ultra tight white shirt that showed his spectacular body. There was a bulge in his pants. All because of my butt?

"That's what you're wearing for self-defense lessons?"

I looked down at myself. "I don't have anything else. This is what I'm wearing when I go jogging." The shorts were tight and ended high up on my thighs, but I didn't like too much fabric when I ran.

"You realize I'll have to kick every guy's ass who looks at you the wrong way, right? And looking like that my men will have a hard time not looking at you the wrong way."

I shrugged. "It's not my job to make them control themselves. Just because I'm wearing revealing clothes doesn't mean I'm inviting them to look. If they can't behave themselves, that's their problem."

Luca led me out of the changing room and toward the sparring mats. The men there immediately backed away and they were pointedly not looking at me. I followed Luca toward a display of knives. His eyes scanned them, then he chose one with a long smooth blade and handed it to me. He didn't take one for himself.

He positioned himself across from me, looking utterly relaxed. He must have known everyone was watching us, but he acted as if he couldn't care less. This wasn't private. He had to put up a show for his men. "Attack me, but try not to cut yourself."

"Won't you get a knife too?"

Luca shook his head. "I don't need one. I'll have yours in a minute."

I narrowed my eyes at his self-assured tone. He was probably right, but I didn't like him saying it. "So what am I supposed to do?"

"Try to land a hit. If you manage to cut me, you win. I want to see how you move."

I took a breath and tried to forget the men watching me. I tightened my grip on the knife, then I dashed forward. Luca moved fast. He dodged my jab, grabbed my wrist and whirled me around until my back collided with his chest.

"You don't have my knife yet," I gasped out. His fingers around my wrist tightened a fraction, uncomfortably but not painfully. His lips brushed my ear. "I would have to hurt you to get it. I could break your wrist for example or just bruise it." He released me and I stumbled forward.

"Again," Luca said. I tried a few times, but didn't even get anywhere close to cutting him. For my next try, I decided to stop playing fair. I advanced on him, then as he made a grab for me, I aimed a kick between his legs. The men cheered, but Luca's hand caught my foot before it could make impact and before I knew what was happening I landed on my back with a heavy thud. My breath rushed out of me and the knife slipped out of my hand. I squeezed my eyes shut. Luca touched my stomach and my muscles constricted under his warm palm. "Are you okay?" he asked quietly.

I opened my eyes. "Yeah. Just trying to catch my breath." Then I scanned the crowd. "Don't you have a soldier who's only five foot something and terrified of his own shadow who would be willing to fight me?"

"My men aren't terrified of anything," Luca said loudly. He held out his hand and pulled me to my feet. He addressed his soldiers. "Anyone willing to fight my wife?"

Of course nobody stepped forward. They were probably worried Luca would skin them alive. Some of them shook their heads, chuckling.

The shadow of a grin crossed Luca's face. "You'll have to fight me."

A few more attack attempts later, I was out of breath and annoyed by my inability to hurt Luca the tiniest bit but then a chance offered itself. He held me against his body and his upper arm was close to my face, so I turned and bit him. He was so startled he actually released me and I tried to jab him with the knife, but he gripped my wrist. "Did you bite me?" he asked as he stared at my teeth marks on his bicep.

"Not hard enough. There isn't even blood," I said.

Luca's shoulders twitched once, then again. He was fighting laughter. Not the effect I'd intended when I bit him but I had to admit I loved the sound of his deep chuckle. "I think you've done enough damage for one day," he said.

***

We grabbed something to eat on our way home, then settled on the rattan sofa on the roof terrace with a glass of wine.

"I'm surprised," I said eventually. Luca and I sat close together, almost touching and his arm was thrown over the backrest behind me but so far he had held back. "I didn't think you'd really try."

"I told you I would. I keep my word."

"I bet this is hard for you." I gestured at the space between us.

"You have no idea. I want to kiss you really fucking bad."

I hesitated. Kissing him had felt good. Luca set the glass down, then he moved a bit closer and touched my waist. "Tell me you don't want me to kiss you."

I parted my lips but nothing came out. Luca's eyes darkened and he leaned toward me, capturing my mouth in a kiss and I lost myself in the sensation of his tongue and lips. Luca didn't push it, never moved his hand from my waist but he'd begun rubbing my skin there lightly and his other hand massaged my scalp. How could I feel that all the way between my legs?

Eventually I lay back on the sofa, Luca propped up above me. I could feel myself getting wet but I didn't have the time or necessary focus to feel embarrassed. Luca's kisses kept me busy. The tingling in my center became difficult to ignore and I tried to alleviate the tension by pressing my legs together.

Luca drew back with a knowing expression. Heat rose into my cheeks.

"I could make you feel good, Aria," he murmured, his hand on my waist tightening. "You want to come, don't you?"

Oh my God, yes. My body was screaming for it. "I'm fine. Thank you."

Luca choked on a laugh. "You are so stubborn." He didn't say it in a mean way. His lips came down on mine again and I could tell he gave it his all, determined to break my resolve and a few times I got close. I was throbbing between my legs but I wouldn't give in, not so soon. I had more control than that.

That night I fell asleep with Luca's arms around me and his erection an insistent presence against my upper thigh. Maybe we could really make this marriage work.

# CHAPTER ELEVEN

When I woke the next morning, I was alone in bed. I sat up, disappointed that Luca hadn't woken me. I slipped out of bed when he came into the bedroom from the hallway, already dressed in black, with a chest holster that held two knives and two guns, and who knew how many more holsters on the rest of his body with more weapons. "Are you leaving already?"

He grimaced. "The Bratva got one of ours. They left him in tiny pieces around one of our clubs."

"Somebody I know?" I asked with dread. Luca shook his head. "Will the police get involved?"

"Not if I can help it." Luca cupped my face. "I'll try to be home early, okay?"

I nodded. He lowered his head, watching me the entire time to see if I would pull back. His lips brushed over mine. I opened my mouth for him and sank into the kiss, but it was over too quick. I watched his back as he left. Then I picked up the phone and called Gianna.

"I thought you'd never call," was the first thing out of her mouth.

I smiled. "I haven't even showered yet, and it's only eight in Chicago. You can't have been awake for long."

"You didn't call yesterday. I was sick with worry. I couldn't sleep because of *you.* I hate that we are so far apart and I can't see for myself if you're okay. Are you okay?"

"Yes, I am." I told her about my conversation with Luca and how we'd spent yesterday together.

"How noble of him to agree to not cheat on you again and actually try to make the marriage work. Give that man flowers."

"He isn't a good man, Gianna. There are no good men in our world. But I think he really wants to try. And I want it too."

"Why don't you ask him if I can come visit for a few days? I don't have school for another two weeks and I'm bored out of my mind without you. We could spend a couple of days at the beach in the Hamptons and go shopping in Manhattan."

"What about Father? Did you ask him?"

"He told me to ask you and Luca."

"I will ask him. I don't think he'll mind. It's not like he's home very often at the moment. Most days I'm alone with Romero."

"Why don't you ask Luca if you can go to college? You've got perfect grades. You would have no trouble getting into Columbia."

"What for? I won't ever be allowed to work. It's too dangerous."

"You could help Luca with his clubs. You could be his secretary or whatever. You'll go crazy if you stay in that penthouse all the time."

"Don't worry, I'll be fine," I said, even though I really wasn't sure. Gianna had a point. "I will talk to Luca about your visit. Now I really need to take a shower and grab something to eat."

"Call me as soon as possible. I need to book a flight."

I smiled. "I will. Stay out of trouble."

"You too."

I hung up. Then I got ready and dressed in a breezy summer dress. It was sunny outside and I wanted to walk through Central Park. When I stepped into the living room, Romero was sitting at the dining table with a cup of coffee in front of him.

"Was Luca very angry with you?" I asked as I walked past him toward the huge open kitchen. Homemade carrot cake set on the counter and I could hear Marianna humming somewhere. She was probably cleaning. Romero got up, took his cup and leaned against the kitchen island. "He wasn't happy. You could have been killed. I'm supposed to protect you."

"What's Luca doing today?"

Romero shook his head.

"What is he doing? I want to know details. Why is he taking so many guns with him?"

"He, Matteo and a few others are going to find the guys who killed our man and then they're going to get revenge."

"That sounds dangerous." A hint of worry filled me. Revenge was never the end of things. The Bratva would take revenge in turn for Luca's revenge. It was a never ending story.

"Luca and Matteo have been doing this for a long time, they are the best, and so are the men with them."

"And instead of being in on the fun, you have to babysit me."

Romero gave a shrug, then he smiled. "It's an honor."

I rolled my eyes. "I'd like to go jogging in Central park."

"Will you try to run away again?"

"Why would I? There's nowhere I can run. And I doubt you'll let me escape again. You look fit enough."

Romero straightened. "Okay." I could tell that he was still suspicious of my motives.

I put on my shorts, a tanktop and my running shoes, then went back out. Romero had changed into sweatpants and a t-shirt. He kept a stash of clothes in one of our guest bedrooms, but he lived in an apartment about ten minutes from here. "Where have you hidden your guns?"

"That's my secret," he said with a rare grin, then he caught himself and put on his professional face.

Romero was fit and could easily keep up with me as we jogged through the many pathways in Central Park for the next hour. It felt wonderful to actually run outside for once instead of always being limited to the treadmill. I felt free and almost as if I belonged among all the people doing ordinary things like walking their dogs or playing baseball. Maybe Luca would run with me one day when the Russians weren't giving him so much trouble anymore. When would that ever be?

*** 

Later that day I sat on the roof terrace, watching the sunset, my legs pulled up against my body. Romero was checking his phone. "Luca will have more time for you soon."

I looked at him. Had I appeared lonely to him? "Did he tell you when he'd be home today?"

"He hasn't written yet," he said slowly.

"That's a bad sign, right?"

Romero didn't say anything, only frowned down at his phone.

I went inside when it became too cold outside, put on my nightgown and curled up on the couch, turning on the TV. I couldn't help but get more worried as the clock edged closer to midnight, but eventually I drifted off.

***

I woke when I was lifted off the couch. My eyes fluttered open and I peered up into Luca's face. It was too dark to make out much. Romero must have extinguished the lights at some point. "Luca?" I murmured.

He didn't say anything. I put a hand against his chest. His shirt was slick with something – water? Blood?

His breathing was even, steps measured. His heartbeat was calm under my palm. But I couldn't read his mood. It was strange. He carried me up the stairs as if I weighed nothing. We reached our bedroom and he put me down on the bed. I could only see his tall shape looming above me.  Why wasn't he saying anything?

I stretched and fumbled for the main switch beside the bed. I brushed it with my fingertips and the lights came on, and I gasped. Luca's shirt was covered in blood. Soaked in it. There was a small cut at Luca's throat and if the rips in his shirt were any indication he probably had more wounds. Then my eyes found his face and I became very still, like a fawn trying to blend in as not to attract the attention of the wolf. I'd thought I'd seen Luca's darkness on a few occasions, had thought I'd glimpsed the monster beneath the civil mask before. Now I realized I hadn't. His expression was void of emotion but his eyes made the hairs on my neck rise.

I licked my lips. "Luca?"

He started unbuttoning his shirt, revealing small cuts and a longer wound below his ribs. His skin was covered with blood. But it couldn't all have come from him, especially not all the blood on the shirt. It worried me that he still hadn't spoke. He shed his shirt and dropped it on the ground. Then he unbuckled his belt.

"Luca," I said. "You are scaring me. What happened?"

He pushed his pants down and stepped out of them. He was barefoot and now only in his briefs as he knelt on the bed and brought one knee between my legs. I began to regret wearing only a nightgown. He slowly moved up until his head hovered over me. Terror gripped my throat, turned my heartbeat into a flutter.

His eyes made me want to bolt, to cry and scream, to escape. Instead I lifted my hand and cupped his cheek. His expression shifted, a chink in the monstrous mask. He leaned into the touch, then he lowered his face and pressed it into the crook of my neck. He breathed in deeply and didn't move for a long time. I tried not to panic. My hand was shaking against his cheek.

"Luca?" I said softly.

He raised his head again. I could see a flicker of the Luca I knew. He slid off the bed and headed for the bathroom. When he was out of sight, I let out a deep breath. Whatever had gone down today must have been horrible. I sat up as I listened to the running shower. In what kind of mood would Luca return into the bedroom? The monster in check, or almost unleashed like a moment ago?

The water stopped and I quickly lay down on my side of the bed and pulled the covers up. A few minutes later, the door opened and Luca walked in with a towel around his waist. It was white, but a few droplets of blood had dripped from his wound and stained the fabric. He didn't walk toward the cupboard to grab boxer shorts as he usually did, instead he came directly toward the bed. When he reached for the towel, I averted my eyes and turned on my other side, my back toward him. He lifted the blanket and the mattress shifted under his weight. He pressed up against me, his hand curled over my hip in an almost bruising grip before he turned me toward him.

My mind screamed at me to stop him. He was completely naked and in a scary mood. He'd spent the day picking up the pieces of one of his men and the remaining day killing his enemies. He grabbed the hem of my nightgown and began pulling it up. I put my hand over his.

"Luca," I whispered.

His eyes met mine. I relaxed slightly. There was still darkness in them but it was more contained. "I want to feel your body against mine tonight. I want to hold you."

I could almost hear the unspoken words: I need you. I swallowed. "Only hold me?"

"I swear," his voice was gruff as if he'd spent hours screaming orders.

I lowered my hand and let him pull my nightgown off. He released a low breath as he gazed at my naked breasts. I had to fight the urge to cover myself. His fingertips brushed the hem of my panties but when I tensed they retreated and he rolled onto his back and lifted me on top of him. I straddled his stomach, my knees on either side of him, my breasts pressed against his chest. I tried to keep my weight off him because I didn't want to hurt his wounds, but he wrapped one arm around my back and pressed me tightly against him. His other hand touched my butt, making me jump. He began moving his thumb across my lower back and butt, and I relaxed slowly. The entire time his eyes were boring into mine and with every passing moment a tiny bit more of the darkness dissipated.

"Doesn't your cut need stitches?"

He bent forward and kissed me sweetly. "Tomorrow." He kept stroking my butt and kissing me slowly as if he wanted to savor every moment. I was completely overwhelmed but it felt good. I loved that he was suddenly so gentle. If he was like that when we were intimate for the first time, then maybe it wouldn't be so bad. My eyelids felt heavy but I couldn't look away from Luca. I touched his throat, an inch below the cut. I wasn't sure why but I leaned forward and pressed a feather-light kiss against the wound. It was small and wouldn't need stitches, not like the one below his ribs. When I drew back, Luca looked almost surprised. His hand on my butt moved lower, cupping my ass cheek. His little finger was almost touching me *there*. He squeezed my cheek and for a moment his finger brushed my opening through the fabric.

I sucked in a breath, shocked by the jolt the small touch had sent through me. Heat gathered between my legs and I could feel myself getting wet. I squirmed in embarrassment, not wanting Luca to realize that a bare brush and his stroking of my butt had caused such a reaction. Maybe I wasn't experienced but I'd been imagining certain things, had caressed myself on many nights. It wasn't that I was frigid. Luca's body turned me on. Maybe I wanted love, but my body wanted something else. The feeling of Luca's strong chest and muscled stomach under me, his gentle kisses, his soft touch, they made me want something more, even if my mind told me it was a bad idea.

Luca's eyes narrowed a fraction as he studied me, like I was a difficult equation he wanted to figure out. Then he lightly graced the crotch of my panties with his fingertips and I knew he could feel it. I *could feel* that the thin fabric was soaked. My cheeks flamed in mortification and I lowered my eyes but I couldn't bring myself to slide off him or even close my legs. His fingertips against my core felt good even if they'd stopped moving.

"Look at me, Aria," Luca said in a rough voice.

I peered into his eyes even as my face felt close to exploding from shame. "Are you embarrassed because of this?" He traced a finger over my wet panties. My butt arched and I exhaled harshly.

I couldn't say anything. My lips were parted as small sounds that weren't quite moans slid out. Luca's moved his finger up and down, gently, teasingly, and small shivers of pleasures slithered through my body. I'd always thought that passion and orgasms came as a forceful wave leaving nothing in their wake, something almost intimidating but this was like a slow trickling; a deliciously sweet tension mounting to something bigger.

I quivered on top of Luca, my fingers clinging to his shoulders. He never sped up his stroking but the pleasure rose with every brush. His eyes bore into mine as he slid two fingers over my opening then between my folds and pressed down on my clit. How could this feel so intense? He wasn't even touching my skin. I gasped and trembled as sparks of pleasure shot through my body. I buried my face against Luca's neck as I clung to him. His finger rubbed my clit through my panties, slower and slower until he simply rested his hand possessively over my folds.

Luca pressed his face into my hair. "God, you're so wet, Aria. If you knew how much I want you right now, you'd run away." He laughed darkly. "I can almost feel your wetness on my cock."

I didn't say anything, only tried to calm my breathing. Luca's heartbeat was strong and fast beneath my cheek. He shifted and his length briefly brushed my inner thigh. He felt hot and hard.

"Do you want me to touch you?" I said in the quietest whisper. I was half-scared and half-excited about seeing him naked and actually touching him. I wanted to lay my claim on him, wanted to make him forget about the women of his past. Luca's hand on my back tightened and he drew in a deep breath, his chest expanding under me.

"No," he growled, and I lifted my head in confusion and a little hurt. Some of it must have showed, because Luca smiled grimly. "I'm not quite myself yet, Aria. There's too much darkness on the surface, too much blood and anger. Today was bad." He shook his head. "When I came home today and found you lying on the sofa, so innocent and vulnerable and mine." Something flickered in his eyes, some of the darkness he'd mentioned. "I'm glad you don't know the thoughts that ran through my head then. You are my wife and I swore to protect you, if necessary even from myself."

"You think you'd lose control?" I whispered.

"I know it."

"Maybe you underestimate yourself." I trailed my fingers over his shoulders. I wasn't sure if I was trying to convince him or myself. He had scared me, there was no denying it. But he had snapped out of it.

"Maybe you trust me too much." He ran a finger over my spine, sending a new wave of tingling toward my core. "When I lay you down on the bed like a sacrificial lamb, you should have run."

"Someone once told me not to run from monsters because they give chase."

The ghost of a smile crossed his face. "Next time, you run. Or if you can't, you ram your knee into my balls."

He wasn't joking. "If I'd done that today, you would have lost control. The only reason why you didn't was because I treated you like my husband, not a monster."

He traced my lips with his thumb, then brushed my cheek. "You are far too beautiful and innocent to be married to someone like me, but I'm too much of a selfish bastard to ever let you go. You are mine. Forever."

"I know," I said, then lowered my cheek back to his chest. Luca extinguished the lights and I fell asleep listening to his heartbeat. I knew a normal person would have run from Luca, but I'd grown up among predators. Decent, normal guys with jobs that didn't involve breaking laws were a foreign species to me. And deep down a primal part of me couldn't imagine being with someone who wasn't an alpha like Luca. It thrilled me to know that a man like him could be gentle with me. It thrilled me that he was mine and I was his.

***

The sky was only just turning gray over New York's skyline when I woke the next morning. I was still lying on Luca's chest, my naked breasts pressed against his hot skin, but I'd slid down his body over night and his stiff length was pressed against my leg. I shifted carefully and peered up into Luca's face. His eyes were closed and he looked so peaceful in sleep, it was hard to belief that the same face had harbored so much violence and darkness last night.

Curiosity gripped me. I'd never seen an erection but I was worried about waking Luca. After what he'd said, I really didn't want to risk him losing control. I tried to peek over my shoulder at Luca's boner, but with the way we were positioned I'd have to break my neck to see it.

Suddenly a buzzing came from the nightstand and Luca sat up so fast I squeaked. He took me with him, one arm steadying me around the waist, the other reaching for his mobile. But the new position had made me slide down his body and now his erection was between my legs, its length pressed up against my core. I was practically riding it like a broom. I'd never been more grateful for my underwear.

I stiffened and so did Luca, the mobile already pressed against his ear. I tried to get into a less problematic position but that only made his cock rub against me. He groaned and I froze. Luca's eyes dilated as his fingers on my waist tightened.

"I'm fine Matteo," he rasped. "I'm *fucking* fine. No. I can handle this. I don't need to see the Doc. Now let me sleep." Luca hung up, put the phone back on the nightstand and stared at me. I was so stiff he could have used me as an ironing board.

He sank back slowly with all the control only lots of sit-ups could give you. I remained in a sitting position, straddling his hips, but quickly draped one arm in front of my breasts. Now that he was lying his erection was no longer touching me. Gathering my courage, I swung my leg over his hips, accidentally brushing Luca's boner.

"Fuck," Luca growled, jerking beneath me. I had to stifle a smile. I knelt beside him, my arm still covering my breasts and then I allowed myself to look. Wow. I had nothing to compare him to, but I couldn't imagine he could be any bigger. He was long and thick, and circumcised. Gianna had won her stupid bet.

"You're going to be the death of me, Aria," Luca said in a low voice.

I turned, embarrassed. I'd been *staring.* There was hunger on Luca's face when I met his eyes. One of his hands rested on his stomach, the other was thrown over his head. His abs were taut with tension, actually every inch of his body seemed that way. Suddenly I was overcome with shyness. Why had I thought it was a good idea to take a look at him? I risked another peek.

"If you keep looking at my cock with that stunned expression, I'm going to combust."

"I'm sorry if my expression bothers you, but this is new for me. I've never seen a naked man. Every first I'll experience will be with you, *so*."

Luca sat up. His voice dropped an octave. "It doesn't bother me. It's fucking hot, and I'll enjoy every first you'll share with me." He stroked my cheek. "You don't even realize how much you turn me on."

With him sitting, our faces were close and Luca pulled me in for a kiss. I pressed my palm against his shoulder, then slowly ran it down his chest to his stomach. Luca paused kissing me. "Last night you asked me if I wanted you to touch me."

"Yeah," I said, my breath catching. "Do you want me to touch you now?"

The fire in his eyes darkened. "Fuck yes. More than anything." He reached out for my arm pressed against my breasts. "Let me see you." He curled his fingers around my wrist but didn't pull. I hesitated. He'd seen them yesterday, but now I felt more exposed. Slowly I eased my arm down. I sat very still as Luca's eyes roamed over me. "I know they're not big."

"You're fucking beautiful, Aria."

I didn't know what to say.

"Do you want to touch me now?" he said in a low voice.

I nodded and licked my lips. I glanced down, then tentatively reached out and ran my finger over his length. He felt soft, hot and firm. Luca let out a harsh breath, the muscles in his arms straining from holding himself up. I brushed the tip, marveling at how soft he was. Luca gritted his teeth.

I felt a strange sense of power over him as I ran my fingertips up and down slowly, fascinated by his silkiness.

Luca quivered under my touch. "Take me in your hand," he said in a low voice.

I wrapped my fingers around his shaft lightly, worried about hurting him. I moved my hand down, then up, surprised at how heavy he felt in my palm. Luca lay back. I knew he was watching me but I couldn't meet his gaze, too mortified by my own courage.

"You can grip harder," he said after a few more of my tentative strokes.

I tightened my fingers.

"Harder. It won't fall off."

I flushed and turned away, dropping my hand. "I didn't want to hurt you." God, this was embarrassing. I couldn't even do this. Maybe Luca should really go back to his whore Grace. She knew what to do.

"Hey," Luca said calmly, pulling me against him. "I was teasing you. It's okay." He kissed me. His mouth moved against mine, unyielding but gentle, and his hand snaked down my arm, my hip and over the curve of my butt until his finger slipped between my legs and grazed over my folds. He slid back and forth lightly before slipping the tip of his finger under my panties. I held my breath at the feel of him against my bare skin. He dipped between my folds, then slid up to my clit, coating it with my wetness. I moaned against his lips before slipping my tongue into his mouth to dance with his. Pleasure swept through me as he twirled his finger over my sensitive nub.

He tore his mouth away from mine, his eyes boring into me. "Want to try again?" he rasped with a nod toward his hard length.

His finger flicked over me again and I gasped, barely able to think straight, much less form a coherent sentence. My body ached with a need I'd never felt before. I slid my hand down his muscled torso, following the fine trail of dark hair to his erection. I curled my hand around it and it jumped under my touch.

Luca's fingers slid faster against my wet flesh. His steady caresses made me pant, but I was far too gone to care. Luca covered my hand around his length with his, showing me how hard to grip him. Then he moved our hands up and down his shaft. I watched in fascination. We moved faster and harder than I would have dared. Luca's fingers between my folds, rubbed me faster too, until I could barely breath and my pulse pounded in my veins. I was about to topple over the edge.

"Luca," I gasped and he flicked my clit, sending me spiraling out of control. Spasms shot through my body as I moaned. My hand pumped Luca's length even faster and with a guttural growl Luca's release washed over him. I shivered against him as I watched him come over our hands and his stomach. My nipples were hard and rubbed against his chest, sending ripples of pleasure through me. His erection throbbing in my palm, it softened slowly. Luca pulled his fingers out from beneath my panties and rested them on my butt.

I closed my eyes, listening to the thundering of his heart. Luca kissed the top of my head, startling me with the loving gesture. My heart burst with new hope. Gradually our breathing slowed. Luca reached out for a tissue box on the nightstand and handed me a tissue, before wiping himself clean. I felt self-conscious as I cleaned his sperm from my hand. I couldn't believe I'd touched him like that. I was still sensitive between my legs and yet I wanted to feel his fingers again. Was it wrong that I enjoyed Luca's touch so much?

He was my husband, but still. My mother had always treated sex like something only men desired. Women simply did their duty. Luca rubbed my arm and I decided not to think about it too much. I'd do what felt right. I released a small breath, but then my eyes focused on the cut below Luca's ribs. Blood was trickling from it.

I sat up. "You're bleeding." I'd forgotten all about it. "Does it hurt?"

Luca looked utterly relaxed. He cast his gaze down to his wound. "Not much. It's nothing. I'm used to it."

I touched the skin below the cut. "It needs stitches. What if it gets infected?"

"Maybe you'll get lucky and become a young widow."

I glared. "That's not funny." Not after what we'd just done. I felt closer to him than ever, and my father would only find me a new husband anyway.

"If it bothers you so much, why don't you grab the first aid kit from the bathroom and bring it to me."

I jumped out of bed and rushed into the bathroom. "Where is it?"

"In the drawer below the sink."

There wasn't only one first aid kit. There were about two dozens kits. I picked one and returned to the bedroom but before I joined Luca in bed, I grabbed my nightgown from the ground and put it on. Luca sat against the headboard, still gloriously naked. I concentrated on his torso, embarrassed by his unabashed nakedness.

Luca stroked my cheek when I settled next to him. "Still too shy to look at me after what happened." He tugged at the hem of my nightgown. "I liked you better without it."

I pursed my lips. "What do you want me to do?" I set the first aid kit between us and opened it.

"Many things," Luca murmured.

I rolled my eyes. "With your cut."

"There are disinfectant wipes. Clean my wound and I'll prepare the needle."

I ripped open one of the packets. The overpowering smell of disinfectant clogged my nose. I pulled the wipe out, unfolded it and dabbed it against the cut. Luca twitched but didn't make a sound. "Does it burn?"

"I'm fine," he said simply. "Wipe harder."

I did, and though he jerked a few times, he never told me to stop. Eventually I threw the wipe into the trash and leaned back. Luca pierced his skin with the needle and began stitching himself up, his hands steady and sure. Watching him made me already feel queasy. I couldn't imagine doing that to myself, but as my eyes wandered over Luca's body and the many scars I realized that it probably wasn't the first time he did this. When Luca was satisfied with his job, he chucked away the needle.

"We need to cover it," I said. I rummaged in the kit for bandages, but Luca shook his head. "It'll heal faster if it's allowed to breathe."

"Really? Are you sure? What if dirt gets in?"

Luca chuckled. "You don't need to worry. This won't be the last time I'll come home injured." Was I worried? Yes. And I didn't like the thought of him taking his health so lightly.

Luca opened his arms. "Come."

"Don't you have to leave?" I glanced at the clock. It was only eight, but on most days Luca had been gone by then.

"Not today. The Bratva is dealt with for the moment. I'll have to be in one of the Familia's clubs in the afternoon."

I smiled slightly. I couldn't help it. I was glad I didn't have to be alone all day again. I snuggled against Luca's side and he wrapped his arm around me.

"I didn't expect you to look so happy," he said quietly.

"I'm lonely." I hated how weak that made me sound, but it was the truth. Luca's fingers on my arm tightened.

"I have a few cousins you could hang out with. I'm sure they'd enjoy going shopping with you."

"Why does everyone think I want to go shopping?"

"Then do something else. Have a coffee, or go to a Spa, or I don't know."

"I still have a Spa certificate that I got at my bridal shower."

"See? If you want I can ask a few of my cousins."

I shook my head. "I'm not too keen on meeting with another one of your cousins after what Cosima did."

"What did she do?" He grew rigid beneath me.

I drew back, looking at Luca. Then I realized I'd never told him how I'd found him in bed with Grace and after all the confusion of the last few days he'd never asked. He'd probably had more than enough on his plate with the Bratva.

"She gave me the letter that led me to you and Grace." Saying her name made my stomach turn again, and unwanted memories resurfaced. I sat up, away from Luca's warmth. I drew my legs up against my chest, overwhelmed by all that had happened.

Luca pushed himself into a sitting position and pressed a kiss against my shoulder. "Cosima gave you a letter that told you to go the apartment?" His voice was tight with barely controlled anger.

I nodded, then swallowed before I dared to speak. "And a key. It's still in my bag."

"That fucking bitch," he growled.

"Who?"

"Both of them. Grace and Cosima. They're friends. Grace must have put Cosima up to this. That cunt."

I flinched away from the fury in his voice. He let out a harsh breath and sneaked an arm around my waist, pulling me against his chest and burying his face in my hair.

"Grace wanted to humiliate me. She looked really happy when I found you."

"I bet," he said. "She's a fucking rat trying to humiliate a queen. She's nothing." Wow, he was furious. And I couldn't help but feel schadenfreude toward Grace.

"How did she react when you told her that you couldn't see her anymore?"

He was silent. I tensed. "You promised you wouldn't see her or other women again." My voice shook and I tried to pull away from him but he held me fast. Had he lied to me? I couldn't believe I'd believed him, couldn't believe I'd let him touch me there, and actually touched him in turn.

"I did, and I won't. But I didn't talk to Grace. Why should I? I don't owe her an explanation, just like I don't owe a fucking explanation to the other sluts I fucked." His body might have been made from stone he was so tense. I wanted to believe him. He grabbed my chin between his thumb and index finger and tilted my face around until I was looking at him. "You are the only one I want. I'll keep my promise, Aria."

"So you won't see her again."

"Oh, I will see her again to tell her what I think about her little stunt."

"Don't."

He frowned.

"I don't want you to talk to her again. Let's just forget her." I could see that he didn't want to forget. "Please."

196

He exhaled, then nodded. "I don't like it, but if that's what you want..."

"It is," I said decidedly. "Let's not even talk about her anymore. Pretend she doesn't exist."

Luca lifted his hand and rubbed his thumb over my lower lip. "Your lips are too fucking kissable." I ducked my head to hide my pleased smile.

"There's something I wanted to talk to you about," I said.

"More bad news?"

"Well, I guess that depends on your viewpoint. I want Gianna to visit me. School doesn't begin for another two weeks and I miss her."

"It's been only a few days since you saw her."

"I know."

"Where would she stay?"

"I don't know. Maybe in our guestroom?" We had three of them on the lower floor of the penthouse.

"Your sister is a major pain in the ass."

I gave him a pleading look.

"How about a deal?" he said in a husky voice.

Nerves fluttered in my stomach. "A deal?"

"Don't look so nervous." Luca smiled sardonically. "I'm not going to ask you to sleep with me so you can see your sister. I'm not that big of an asshole."

"No?" I teased and he slammed his lips against me in a kiss that sent lightning sensations all the way down to my toes.

"No," he said against my lips. "But I'd like to explore your body."

I raised my eyebrows. "Like how?"

"Tonight, I'll try to be home early from the meeting at the club and I want us to soak in the Jacuzzi for a bit and then I want you to lie back and let me touch you and kiss you wherever I want." He licked my ear. "You'll love it."

I parted my lips in surprise. This was moving way faster than I'd thought it would, than I thought it should.

Luca must have seen the uncertainty in my expression because he slipped his hand between my legs and pressed the heel of his palm against my clit over the fabric of my panties. I bucked and let a moan slip out before I could stop myself. God, this was ridiculous. This was what happened when you were forced to live abstinent for so long.

"You like this, Aria. I know you do. Admit it."

He pressed harder and I jerked against him. "Yes," I gasped out. He moved his palm slowly over me, sending spikes of pleasure through my body. "Don't stop."

"I won't," he said, nibbling my throat. "So do you let me have my way with you tonight? I won't do anything you don't want."

I wasn't even sure what I wanted right now. Except for Luca not to stop what he was doing with his hand. I would have promised him anything in that moment. "Yes."

He increased the pressure on my clit and suckled at my throat, then flicked his tongue over my collarbone, and I exploded.

Luca kissed me below my chin before pulling back with a smirk. Once I came down from my high I needed to figure out a way to balance the power between us. He wanted me more than I wanted him. I was sure about it. I needed to take advantage of it.

I rested my forehead against his shoulder. "So can I call Gianna and tell her to buy plane tickets?"

Luca chuckled. "Sure, but remember our deal." His phone buzzed on the nightstand. He picked it up. "For fuck's sake, Matteo, what now?"

I pulled back. Luca got up and began pacing the bedroom, completely naked. "We've got his back. I won't let another fucking restaurant go to the Russians. Yeah. Yeah. I'll be ready in thirty minutes." He flung his phone on the nightstand.

"I'll have to talk to the owner of a restaurant chain."

"Okay," I said, trying to hide my disappointment.

"Call your sister and tell her she can come. And I'll be back in time for dinner, okay? I have a few take-out menus in the kitchen. Order whatever you want." He leaned down and kissed me. "Let Romero take you to a museum or something like that."

Fifteen minutes later, he was gone, and I was left with my doubts. How could I have agreed to his deal? Because I loved the pleasure he gave me. Why not enjoy it? Maybe I would have to live without love, but that didn't mean I would have to be miserable.

Gianna was ecstatic when I called her to tell her she could visit. I didn't tell her about the deal. I couldn't talk about something like that on the phone, or ever. I knew she wouldn't approve of me giving in to Luca so quickly.

***

As promised, Luca was home early. I was incredibly nervous. I'd chosen a beautiful yellow dress and set the table on the roof terrace. Surprise flashed across Luca's face when he found me outside.

"I thought we could eat here?"

He wrapped his arms around me and pulled me in for lingering kiss. Butterflies fluttered in my stomach. "I ordered Indian food."

"I'm hungry for only one thing."

I shivered. "Let's eat." What would Luca do if I told him the deal was off? I took a seat. Luca watched me with intensity. Eventually he sank down on the chair across from me. There was a gentle breeze that caressed my skin and tugged at my hair.

"You look fucking sexy."

I started eating. "Romero took me to the Metropolitan today. It was amazing."

"Good," Luca said with a hint of amusement. Could he see how nervous I was?

"What about the restaurant owner? Did you convince him that the Familia will protect him from the Russians?"

"Of course. He's been under our protection for more than a decade. There's no reason to change that now."

"Sure," I said distractedly, taking a gulp of the white wine.

Luca put down his fork. "Aria?"

"Hm?" I nudged a piece of cauliflower on my plate, not meeting Luca's gaze.

"Aria." His voice sent a chill down my back and I peered up at him. He leaned back in his chair, arms crossed over his strong chest. "You are scared."

"I'm not." He narrowed his eyes. "Maybe a bit, but mostly I'm nervous."

He got up from the chair and came around the table. "Come on." He held out his hand. After a brief moment of hesitation, I took it and let me pull him to my feet. "Let's get into the Jacuzzi, okay? That'll relax you."

I doubted being in a hot tub with him in only swimwear would make me less nervous. I didn't know what to expect and that terrified me.

"Why don't you grab your bikini and I'll set up the Jacuzzi?"

I nodded and went back inside. I picked my favorite white box bikini with pink dots. I pulled my hair into a ponytail, then stared at myself in the bathroom mirror. I wasn't sure why this made me so nervous. This morning Luca's touch had set my skin aflame. He'd promised not to do anything I didn't want.

I took a deep breath and walked into the bedroom. Luca was waiting for me in black shorts; they did nothing to hide his strong body. All muscles and strength. His eyes traveled over me, then he slipped a hand over my hip. "You are perfect," he said in a low voice. With a gentle nudge, he led me out of the bedroom, down the stairs and onto the roof terrace.

I shivered in my bikini. The breeze had picked up and it was definitely too cold to stand outside in nothing but a bikini. Luca lifted me into his arms. I gasped in surprise, my hand coming up against the tattoo over his heart.

My own heart was galloping in my chest. I buried my face in the crook of Luca's neck, trying to relax. Luca's grip on me tightened as he stepped into the Jacuzzi and slowly lowered us into the hot bubbling water. I sat on his lap, my face still hidden against his skin. Luca rubbed his hand up and down my spine. "There's no reason for you to be scared."

"Says the man who crushed a man's throat with his bare hands," I meant to say it teasingly but my voice came out shaky.

"That's got nothing to do with us, Aria. That's business."

"I know. I shouldn't have brought it up."

"What's really the problem?"

"I'm nervous because I feel vulnerable, like I'm at your mercy because of the deal."

"Aria, forget about the deal. Why don't you try to relax and enjoy this?" He nudged my chin up until our lips were almost touching and our eyes were locked.

"Promise you won't force me to do something I don't want to do." I lowered my gaze to his chest. "Promise me that you won't hurt me."

"Why would I hurt you?" Luca asked. "I told you I won't sleep with you unless you want me to."

"So you will hurt me when we sleep together?"

Luca's lips twisted into a wry smile. "Not on purpose, no, but I don't think there's a way around it." He kissed the spot below my ear. "But tonight I want to make you writhe in pleasure. Trust me."

I wanted to, but trust was a dangerous thing in our world. Part of me wanted to hold onto the flicker of hate I'd felt when I'd caught him with Grace. But another bigger part wanted to pretend we hadn't been forced into this union, wanted to pretend that we could love each other.

Luca's tongue trailed over my throat. He stopped over my pounding pulse and sucked my skin into his mouth. I shivered from the sensation. His body was hot and hard against mine and I loved sitting in his lap; though it wasn't exactly comfortable. There wasn't much softness about Luca's body, only firm muscle. He shifted, pressing his erection against my butt as his lips claimed my mouth. The kiss sent small lightning bolts through my body but I needed this to be more than physical. I wanted to know more about the man I'd spend the rest of my life with.

I pulled back, getting a growl from Luca in response. His fingers on my waist tightened, his gray eyes questioning as they settled on my face. I kissed his cheek and slung my arms around his neck. "Can we talk for a bit?"

It was obvious from Luca's expression that talking was the last thing on his mind, but he leaned against the wall of the Jacuzzi. "What do you want to talk about?"

One of his hands slid lower and began caressing my butt. I didn't allow it to distract me from my goal, even if it was *very* distracting. The hungry look in Luca's eyes didn't help either.

"What happened to your mother?" I knew she'd died when Luca had been a young boy but Umberto hadn't said much more, either because he didn't know or because he thought I shouldn't know.

Luca's body turned rigid, eyes hard. "She died." He turned his face away, jaw flexing. "That's not the kind of thing I want to talk about tonight."

His rebuke stung. I wanted to get closer to him, wanted to get to know more sides of him, but it was clear he wouldn't let me. I nodded.

Luca removed his hand from my butt and slowly trailed it over my hip, then lower until he reached my inner thigh. He slipped under my bikini bottoms, rubbing his finger along my folds. I should have pushed him away, but instead I opened my legs a bit wider. Luca nuzzled my neck, then drew back. He hooked the fingers of his other hand under my bikini top and pulled it down. My breast sprang free, gooseflesh covering my skin and my nipple erect from the contact with the cold breeze.

Luca made a sound low in his throat as he stared at my chest. Then he bowed low and sucked my nipple into his mouth and at the same time rubbed his thumb over my clit. I cried out from the sensation. He growled against my skin and released my nipple with an audible pop. His gaze snapped up to me as his tongue lavished my nub. I tried to look away, but he snarled. "No. Look at me."

And I did. I watched my nipple disappear in his mouth once more, watched him as he teased it with his tongue, his hungry gray eyes on me. He bit down gently and my hips bucked against his hand still teasing my folds. Release shuddered through my body. Luca pulled back lightning fast, gripped my hips and lifted me onto the edge of the Jacuzzi.

"Luca, what—" Luca tore my bikini bottoms off me, pretty much ripping them in half. I gasped and tried to close my legs, but Luca positioned himself between them, shoved my legs as far apart as possible and lowered his head.

I gasped again, horrified and stunned and...oh God. Luca ran his tongue all the way from my opening up to my clit.

"Fuck, yes," he growled.

My eyes darted around. What if people saw? Only part of the Jacuzzi was encompassed by a screen, but Luca sucked my outer lips into his mouth and I didn't care anymore.

"Look at me," he ordered against my folds, the feel of his breath against my heated flesh making me shudder. I peered down, my skin burning with embarrassment and arousal as I met his gaze. His eyes locked on mine, he slowly slid his tongue between my folds. I moaned.

"You are mine," he said harshly. He licked me again more firmly but even slower. "Say it."

"I'm yours," I said breathlessly. His thumbs parted me even further, revealing my small pink nub. He released a low breath, a smirk curling his lips. I wanted him to touch me there, wanted nothing more. He leaned forward, eyes on me, and circled his tongue around my nub. I whimpered, my hand shooting out and grabbing Luca's hair. I came violently, shuddering and crying out, writhing against Luca's lips.

He didn't stop. He was relentless. I threw my head back, staring up at the night sky. Luca didn't tell me to look at him this time. But I could hear everything he was doing. How he sucked and licked, how he hummed with approval, how he blew against my heated flesh, then licked again. My entire body was aflame, shaking. I couldn't take much more, but Luca pushed his tongue into me and I came, my muscle clenching around him. I squeezed my eyes shut, my back arching off the cold marble. I was so wet. How could anyone be so wet? The sounds of Luca lapping at me were wrong but they aroused me like nothing ever had.

Luca pulled his tongue out as the last spikes of my orgasm wrecked me. Before I knew what was happening, I felt his finger against my opening and he slid it almost all the way in. The intrusion was foreign and unexpected. I jerked and gasped from the pain. My body became rigid as I tried to catch my breath. I'd never even used tampons because they were too uncomfortable and because my mother worried I might accidentally rupture my hymen.

"Fuck, you're so fucking tight, Aria."

I flattened my palms against the Jacuzzi rim, trying to relax. Water sloshed as Luca moved out of the water to lean over me, his finger still in me. I bit my lip but didn't look at him.

"Hey," he said in a rough voice. I met his gaze. "I should have entered more slowly, but you were so wet."

I nodded but didn't say anything. I couldn't get over the feeling of his finger in me. It didn't move, but it was there, filling me. Luca kissed my lips. His eyes were darker than I'd ever seen them and filled with so much want and hunger that it scared and aroused me at the same time.

"Does it still hurt?" he rasped.

I shifted my hip slightly, trying to find words for the sensation. "It's uncomfortable and it burns a bit." I flushed.

Luca licked my lips, then sucked the lower part into his mouth. "I know I'm an asshole for saying it, but the thought of my cock inside your tight pussy makes me so hard."

My eyes widened but he shook his head. "Don't look so terrified. I told you I wouldn't try it tonight."

"You also told me you wouldn't hurt me." It was more to provoke him than because I was really mad at him. I was slowly getting used to his finger in me, and what he'd done before that had been paradise. I already wanted his lips and tongue back on me.

Something in Luca's expression shifted, but I couldn't read the emotion. "I didn't think it would, Aria," he said softly. "You were so wet and willing. I thought my finger would go in without trouble. I wanted to finger you for your fourth orgasm."

I shivered and a small spike of pleasure built in my core again. I almost wanted Luca to move his finger now. "Did it hurt because you took my you know…" Heat rushed into my cheeks and something flashed in Luca's eyes. "Your virginity? No, principessa. I'm not that deep in and I want to claim that part of you with my cock, not my finger."

Principessa? Warmth settled in my chest. Slowly he pulled his finger out, my muscles clenching around him and sending a strange prickling through my core. He traced the same finger over my lip and dipped it into my mouth. I circled it with my tongue without even knowing why.

Luca groaned. He jerked his finger out and shoved his tongue between my lips. I pressed myself against his chest, my tongue battling with his. "Let's go inside. I want to lick you again."

I exhaled.

"Will you let me put my finger into you again? This time I'll go really slow."

"Yes," I said. He leaped out of the Jacuzzi and helped me to my feet. Then he lifted me into his arms, my legs wrapping around his waist as he carried me inside.

He lowered me to my feet in front of our bed and disappeared in the bathroom only to return with a towel. He helped me out of my bikini top, wrapped the towel around me and started to rub me dry gently. I closed my eyes, enjoying the feel of it. I couldn't believe I'd let Luca do what he'd done. I couldn't believe I wanted him to do it again. Everything was overwhelming. I knew it was too fast, but as Luca had said what was I waiting for? He was my husband.

"Are you cold?"

My eyes peeled open. Luca dropped the towel, leaving me naked. His hands slid up and down my arms. My entire body was covered in goose bumps. "A bit."

Luca made me lie down on the bed before he straightened and slid down his shorts. His erection sprang free, hard and long, and suddenly anxiety gripped me. He'd put his finger into me, maybe now he wanted to do the next step. Maybe I was confused about a few things at the moment, but I knew one thing: I wasn't ready for that.

I still barely knew the man in front of me, and sleeping with him, letting him into me like that was too much, too intimate. Maybe this evening had been his way of manipulating me. Nobody got that far in the mafia without being a master in manipulation. I pressed my legs together and scrambled back. Luca paused, one knee already on the bed.

"Aria?" His fingers curled around my calf and I jerked back and pulled my legs against my chest. He sighed. "What now?"

He sat beside me, his length almost brushing my leg. "Say something."

"This is too fast," I said quietly.

"Because I got naked? You've seen my cock before. You even jerked me off."

My face burned. "I think you're trying to manipulate me. If I gave you the chance, you'd go all the way today."

"You bet I would, but I can't see what manipulation has to do with it," he said with a hint of anger in his voice. "I want you. I never lied to you about that. I'm going to take whatever you are willing to give, and you were willing in the Jacuzzi."

"Not about the finger," I snapped, suddenly getting angry too. "Maybe you'll try the same with sex." I knew it sounded ridiculous.

Luca actually laughed. He leaned very close. "That won't work. My cock won't slide in that easily, believe me, and it will hurt a lot more."

I flinched, remembering what Grace had said at our wedding. *He'll fuck you bloody.* Luca released a harsh breath. "I shouldn't have said that. I didn't mean to scare you."

I watched him over my legs. He ran his knuckles down my side lightly. The hard set of his lips loosened. "Tell me that you enjoyed what I did to you on the roof," Luca murmured, there was a hint of need in his voice, maybe even vulnerability.

"Yes," I said breathlessly. He leaned closer, his lips on my ear. "What did you enjoy the most? My tongue fucking you? Or when I ran my tongue all the way over your pussy? Or when I sucked your clit?"

Oh god. I was getting wet again. Luca's deep voice vibrated through my body. "I don't know."

"Maybe I need to show you again?" Luca pushed against my ankles, which were pressed against me until there was enough room for his hand to slip between them and my upper thighs. He cupped me with his palm. I was about to lie down to make it easier for him, but he shook his head. "No," he rasped. "Stay like that." His fingers began to move against my folds, four of them teasing, circling, rubbing.

I rested my chin on my knees, breathing heavily. Luca kissed my ear and wrapped an arm around my shoulder, pulling me against his side. It was strange, sitting up with my legs pressed against my chest as he touched me, but it felt incredibly good. Luca's erection rubbed against my outer thigh, his breathing hot against my ear.

"Relax," he said in a low voice. There was a gentle pressure against my opening. I peered down between my legs. Luca teased me with his small finger. He dipped the tip in, then circled my opening again before entering me again, sliding a bit deeper every time he did.

"Look at me."

I did, caught up in the intensity of his gray eyes. "You are so wet and soft and tight. You can't imagine how fucking good this feels." His length slid along my outer thigh again. His lips pressed against mine, his tongue demanding entrance. His finger slid into me, this time all the way. It was only his small finger but I was thrilled. He began moving it inside me and I gasped into his mouth, jerking my hips, needing more. He pumped in and out slowly, his thumb rubbing my clit. I could feel pleasure building again and I moved my pelvis in sync with his finger. He pulled away his hand, eliciting a sound of protest from me.

Luca laughed, a deep rumbling in his chest. He knelt in front of me and pushed my legs apart, then he looked up at me. He traced his index finger over my folds, then rubbed my opening with it. Never looking away from my face, he pushed the tip in, my muscles clenched and I released a low breath. It didn't hurt and I relaxed. Slowly he started sliding in and out, moving a bit deeper every time like he'd done with his small finger. His mouth closed over my clit.

I whimpered, my legs falling wider apart. My pleasure was mounting scarily fast as Luca worked me with his finger and lips. With a cry, I tumbled over, my legs shaking, hips bucking. My fingers clutched the blanket as I shattered into pieces. Luca removed his finger, kissed my bellybutton, then lay down beside me, his erection red and glistening. I reached out, spreading the droplet of liquid that had trickled out all over his tip.

Luca growled, his abs flexing. "I want your mouth on me," he said in a low voice. I froze, my hand on him stilling. It seemed only fair after what he'd just done, but I had no clue how to actually go down on him. Blow job was a pretty confusing name, because I knew I wasn't supposed to blow his erection, but sadly I wasn't exactly sure what to do in detail. And what if I didn't like it?

I remembered his words about Grace, that she knew how to suck a cock. Not that I wanted to be anything like Grace. I had no intention about becoming Luca's whore, but I didn't want to fail completely either. I was overthinking this.

"Is this because you don't want to, or because you don't know how?" Luca asked calmly, but I could tell he had trouble making his voice sound that way. He'd given me several orgasms. He was probably bursting. "You can jerk me off like last time," he said when I stayed silent. His hand brushed a strand of blond hair away from my face, his gray eyes questioning.

"No, I mean, I think I want to do it."

212

"You think?" Amusement tinged Luca's voice. "But?"

"What if I don't like it?"

Luca shrugged but it was obvious from his expression that he didn't like the idea. "Then you don't. I won't force you."

I nodded and brought my face a bit closer to his erection, which hadn't softened at all during our conversation. Luca tensed in anticipation, his fingertips against my scalp twitching. Embarrassed, I admitted. "I don't know what to do."

His erection jerked in response. I couldn't help but laugh, and Luca grinned his predator grin. "You like to torture me with your innocence, don't you?"

I blew against his tip, making him groan. "I don't think that's why it's called blow job, right?"

He actually laughed a real laugh, and the sound filled my stomach with butterflies. "You're going to be the death of me, principessa."

"Don't laugh," I said with a smile. "I don't want to do something wrong."

"Do you want me to tell you what to do?" Excitement blazed in his eyes.

I nodded.

"Okay," he said hoarsely. "Close your lips around the tip and be careful with your teeth. I don't mind it a bit rougher, but don't chew on it."

I snorted, then nerves made me go quiet. Luca's fingers slipped through my hair until they came to rest on the back of my head. He didn't push me, but from the way they tensed I could tell he wanted to. I took the tip into my mouth. He was thick and I had to be careful not to grace him with my teeth. His tip was slightly salty, but not in a bad way.

"Now swirl your tongue around it. Yes, just like that." He watched me, his jaw clenched. "Take a bit more of me into your mouth and move your head up and down. Now suck as you move. Yes, fuck." His hips bucked when I was as far as I could take him, driving his erection even further inside. I gagged and pulled back, coughing.

He stroked my hair. "Fuck, sorry." He rubbed his thumb over my lips. "I'll try to stay still."

Instead of taking him back into my mouth, I licked him from his base to the tip. He groaned. "Is that okay?" I whispered before doing it again.

"Fuck yes."

I took my time licking every inch of him, but especially his tip. I loved the feel of it against my tongue.

"This feels really fucking good, but I really want to come." I glanced up uncertainly. I could come when he stroked and licked me gently. Did he need it more rough? Would he need it rough during sex too? Grace's stupid words jumped into my head again, but I pushed them aside. I wouldn't let that whore ruin this for me. "What do you need me to do?" I whispered.

"Suck me harder and keep looking at me with your fucking beautiful eyes."

I fixed my gaze on him and took him into my mouth until he hit the back of my throat, then bobbed my head up and down fast and hard, my lips tight around him. Luca moaned, his hips rocking lightly. His eyes burnt into me, his teeth gritted. "If you don't want to swallow, you need to get away…"

I jerked away, releasing him with a pop and a moment later he spilled his seed on his stomach and legs. Luca closed his eyes as his erection twitched. His hand was still in my hair, gently stroking my neck and scalp. Slowly he eased it down, but I gripped his hand and pressed my cheek into it, needing his closeness after what we'd done. His eyes flew open with an unreadable look in them. His thumb brushed my cheekbone gently. We stayed like that for a couple of heartbeats, then Luca sat up, taking in the mess on his upper thighs and abs. "I need a fucking shower." Luca reached for a tissue and cleaned off the sperm before swinging his legs out and standing.

I nodded, strangely disappointed that he'd slip out of bed so quickly. I felt suddenly self-conscious about what I'd done.

Luca held out his hand. "Come on. I don't want to shower alone."

I scrambled off the bed, put my hand in his and followed him into the bathroom.

As the hot water poured down on us, Luca began lathering my body with soap and I closed my eyes, enjoying the feel of his hands on me. He pressed up to my back, one arm coming around my stomach. "So was it okay for you?" he asked quietly.

He was probably worried I wouldn't go down on him again, if it wasn't. "Yeah."

He kissed my throat. He did that a lot. It felt so gentle, loving and intimate, but I knew it wasn't meant like that. "I'm glad, because I really enjoy being in your mouth."

I flushed with embarrassment and a strange sense of accomplishment. Ridiculous. "Are you angry that I didn't, you know, swallow? I bet the women you've been with so far always did."

"No, I'm not angry. I won't lie, I'd love to come in your mouth but if you don't want that, it's okay."

We stepped out of the shower and dried off before we crawled back into bed. I rested my head on Luca's chest. He turned off the lights, bathing us in darkness. "When your father told you to marry me, what was your reaction?" I murmured. I'd been wondering about it for a while.

Luca's fingers on my hips paused. "I'd expected it. I knew I'd have to marry for tactical reasons. As future Capo, you can't let emotions or desires rule any part of your life."

I was glad for the darkness so Luca couldn't see my face. He sounded so detached and emotionless. His touches and kisses made me want to believe that maybe he was starting to care for me, but now I wasn't so sure anymore.

"And what about you?" he asked.

"I was terrified."

"You were only fifteen. Of course, you were terrified."

"I was still terrified on the day of our marriage. I'm still not entirely sure you don't terrify me."

Luca was silent. "I told you, you have no reason to fear me. I'll protect and take care of you. I'll give you anything you want and need."

Except for one thing: love.

"But the Familia always comes first," I said lightly. "If you had to kill me to protect the business, you would."

Luca became rigid, but he didn't deny it. My father always said there's only room for one true love in the life of a made man and that's the mafia.

# CHAPTER TWELVE

Gianna managed to get a ticket for a flight two days later. I was brimming with excitement that day. It hadn't been long since I'd last seen her, but it felt like eternity. It was already getting dark outside when Luca and I pulled up at JFK. I wished Gianna could have gotten a morning or afternoon flight instead.

Since my comment that Luca would kill me in order to protect the Familia, he'd been emotionally withdrawn, not that he'd been an open book even before that. The only way we interacted was at night when Luca pleasured me with his hands and mouth, and I him in turn. Maybe without Gianna's impending visit, I'd have tried to talk to him or even pleaded him to show me where he worked, instead I'd given him the space he obviously wanted. Luca parked the car and we got out. He didn't try to take my hand. I didn't think he was the type of man who held hands, but he touched my lower back as we entered the arrival area of the airport.

"Are you sure you'll be okay with Gianna living with us for the next few days?"

"Yes. And I promised your father to protect her. It's easier when she's living in our apartment."

"She will provoke you," I said.

"I can handle a little girl."

"She's not that little. She's barely younger than me."

"I can handle her."

"Luca," I said firmly. "Gianna knows how to push people's buttons. If you aren't absolutely sure that you can control yourself, I won't let her near you."

Luca's eyes blazed. He'd been on edge all day. "Don't worry. I won't kill her *or you* in the next few days."

I took a step back. Where did that come from? Was he angry because of what I'd said? It was the truth; we both knew it.

"Aria!"

I whirled around. Gianna rushed toward me, dropping her trolley on the way. We collided almost painfully, but I clutched her to myself tightly. "I'm so glad you're here," I whispered.

She nodded, then pulled back, searching my face. "No visible bruises," she said loudly, her gaze darting behind me toward Luca. "You only hit places that are covered by clothes?"

I gripped her hand and gave her a warning look.

"Get your luggage," Luca ordered. "I don't want to stand here all night."

Gianna glared at him but retrieved her trolley and returned to us. "A gentleman would have got it for me."

"A gentleman, yes," Luca said with a tight smile.

We walked back to our car, my arm linked with Gianna's. Luca walked a few steps ahead and got behind the steering wheel without a word.

"What's the matter with him? He's even more of an asshole than I remember."

"I think the Russians are giving him trouble."

"Aren't they always?" Gianna put her trolley into the trunk of the car before we both sat in the backseat.

Luca raised his eyebrows at me. "I'm not your driver. Get in the front with me."

I was taken aback but his harshness but I did as he said and sat shotgun. Gianna's face was scrunched up with anger. "You shouldn't talk to her like that."

"She's my wife. I can do and say to her what I want."

I frowned. Luca turned to me, meeting my gaze. I couldn't place the look in his eyes. He turned back to the street.

"How are Lily and Fabi?"

"Annoying as hell. Especially Lily. She doesn't stop talking about Romero. She's in love with him."

I laughed, and even Luca's lips twitched. I wasn't sure why but I reached out and put my hand on his leg. His eyes snapped toward me briefly, then he covered my hand with his until he needed it to shift gears again. Gianna's eyes were attentive as they watched. She'd bombard me with questions the moment we were alone, no doubt.

***

When we stepped into the apartment, the smell of roast lamb and rosemary wafted over to us.

"I told Marianna to prepare a nice dinner," Luca said. Gianna's red eyebrows shot up in surprise.

"Thank you," I said.

Luca nodded. "Show your sister to her room and then we can eat." He was still withdrawn and stiff. I watched him head around the corner toward the kitchen area.

I showed Gianna her guestroom, but she quickly pulled me inside and closed the door. "Are you okay?"

"Yes. I told you on the phone. I'm fine."

"I prefer to hear you say it when I can see your face."

"I'm not lying to you, Gianna."

She gripped my hand. "Did he force you to sleep with him?"

"No, he didn't. And I haven't."

Her eyes widened. "But something happened between the two of you. I want details."

I pulled away. "We need to have dinner now. Marianna will be mad if the food gets cold. We can talk tomorrow when Luca's busy with business."

"Tomorrow," Gianna said firmly.

I opened the door and led her toward the dining area. Her eyes took everything in, then became slits when she saw who else would be having dinner with us: Matteo. He and Luca stood beside the table, discussing something, but stepped apart when they noticed us.

"What's he doing here?" Gianna said, her nose wrinkled.

Flashing his shark grin, Matteo walked toward her and gripped her hand to kiss it. "Nice to see you again, Gianna."

Gianna snatched her hand away. "Don't touch me."

She needed to stop provoking him; he liked it way too much. Luca and I sat beside each other and Matteo beside Gianna. I wasn't sure that was the best decision. I glanced at Luca, but his cautious gaze rested on his brother and my sister.

Marianna bustled in, serving roast lamb, rosemary potatoes and green beans. We ate in silence for a while until Gianna couldn't keep her tongue anymore. "Why did you crush that guy's throat?"

I put my fork down, expecting Luca to explode but he only leaned back in his chair and crossed his arms over his chest.

Gianna huffed. "Come on. It can't be that big of a secret. You got your nickname for it."

Matteo grinned. "The Vice is a nice name."

Luca shook his head. "I hate it."

"You earned it," Matteo said. "Now tell them the story or I will."

I'd been curious about it for a while. Nobody from the Chicago mob wanted to give me details and I hadn't dared to ask Romero yet.

"I was seventeen," Luca began. "Our father has many brothers and sisters, and one of my cousins climbed the ranks in the mafia alongside me. He was several years older and wanted to become Capo. He knew my father would choose me, so he invited me to his house and tried to stab me in the back. The knife only graced my arm and when I got the chance I wrapped my hands around his throat and choked him."

"Why didn't you shoot him?" Gianna asked.

"He was family and it used to be tradition that we put down our weapons when we entered the home of a family member," Luca said coldly. "Not anymore, of course."

"The betrayal made Luca so angry, he completely crushed our cousin's throat. He choked on his blood because the bones in his neck cut through his artery. It was a mess. I'd never seen anything like it." Matteo looked like a kid on Christmas morning. It was more than a little disturbing.

Luca glared down at his plate, hands clutching his thighs. No wonder he didn't like to trust people. To be betrayed by family must have been horrible.

"That's why Luca always sleeps with an eye open. He never even spends the night with a woman without a gun under the pillow or somewhere at his body."

Luca shot his brother a glower.

Matteo raised his hands. "It's not like Aria doesn't know you screwed around with other women."

I didn't think that was the reason for Luca's reaction.

"So are you wearing a gun now?" Gianna asked. "We're all family after all."

"Luca always wears a gun." Matteo leaned toward Gianna. "Don't take it personally. I don't think even I have seen him without a gun since that day. It's Luca's tic."

Luca didn't wear a gun when we were alone. He wore one when Romero or Marianna were there, even when Matteo was there, but when Luca and I shared a bed, there wasn't a gun under his pillow or anywhere else. *That's probably because he could overpower you with his hands bound behind his back.* Still it seemed like an unnecessary risk.

Luca spent the rest of dinner, tense and silent, but Gianna's and Matteo's arguments filled the silence. I wasn't sure who got off more on their fights.

When we were done eating, I got up to clean the table. Marianna had already left and I didn't want to leave the dirty dishes waiting for her when she came back tomorrow. Luca surprised me when he rose as well and carried the serving platters and plates over to the dishwasher. I yawned, exhausted.

"Let's go to bed," Luca said quietly.

I glanced at Gianna. There was so much I wanted to talk to her about, but it was late and tomorrow was another day. "Not before Matteo leaves. I won't leave him and my sister alone."

Luca nodded grimly. "You are right. She shouldn't be alone with him." He went over to Matteo and put a hand on his shoulder before leaning down and saying something into his ear. Matteo's face darkened with anger but he rose smoothly, gave Gianna his shark grin and then walked out of the apartment without another word.

Gianna came toward me. "He's obsessed with me."

Worry clawed at my insides. "Then stop teasing him. He likes it."

"I don't care what he likes."

Luca leaned beside me against the counter, his arm sneaking around my waist to Gianna's obvious displeasure. "Matteo is a hunter. He loves the chase. You better not make him want to chase you."

I worried it might already be too late for that warning. Gianna rolled her eyes. "He can hunt me all he wants. He won't get me." She looked at me. "You don't intend to go to bed now, right?"

"I'm really tired," I said guiltily.

Gianna's shoulders slumped. "Yeah, me too. But tomorrow I want you all to myself." She gave Luca a pointed look before heading off toward her room. She paused in her doorway. "If I hear screams, no gun under a pillow will save you, Luca." With that, she closed her door.

Luca brushed my ear with his lips. "Will you scream for me tonight?" He licked my skin and I shivered.

"Not with my sister under the same roof," I said, even as a tingling between my legs betrayed me.

"We'll see about that," Luca growled, then gently bit my throat. I moaned, but quickly bit my lip to stifle the sound. Luca took my hand and pulled me upstairs. With every step that we got closer to the bedroom, the pressure between my legs increased. I couldn't believe how eager my body was for his touch, for the release he brought me. It was the only time I forgot everything about my life, the only time I was free of the shackles in our world.

Luca slammed the door shut behind us and I hoped it wouldn't draw Gianna's attention. But I didn't have much time for worry because Luca pulled my dress off, then he lifted me into his arms, only to lay me down in the middle of the bed. Luca pressed a kiss against my lace panties, inhaling, before he kissed my stomach and my ribs, then my breasts through the lace of my bra.

"Mine," he growled against my skin, making me tremble with arousal. He slid his hands under my back and unclasped my bra and slowly pulled it off. My nipples were hard. "I fucking love your nipples. They're pink and small and perfect."

I pressed my legs together, but Luca gripped my panties and slipped them down. He ran a finger over my folds, smirking. His hungry gaze returned to my breasts and he bent his head and trailed his tongue from one nipple to the other. I moaned softly. He took his time with my breasts and when he slowly moved lower I was already panting. His lips found my folds, teasing and gentle, then suddenly his tongue slid out hard and fast, and I covered my mouth with my palm, stifling my gasps and cries.

"No," Luca snarled. He gripped both of my wrists in his hand and pressed them against my stomach, trapping them there.

My eyes widened. "Gianna will hear."

He smirked and sucked my clit hard and fast, then gentle and soft. I whimpered and moaned, my body trembling from the effort to keep quiet. "Oh god," I gasped as Luca slipped his finger achingly slow into me, then eased in and out in rhythm with his sucks on my clit. I buried my face in the pillow. Luca's grip on my wrists tightened and pleasure ripped through me. I cried out into the pillow, my back arching, legs quavering.

Luca moved up my body until he bent over me, knees between my spread legs. "When will you let me take you?" he whispered harshly against my throat.

I turned to stone. Luca raised his head, eyes meeting mine. "Fuck. Why do you have to look so fucking scared when I ask you that question?"

"I'm sorry," I said quietly. "I just need more time."

Luca nodded, but there was a deep need in his eyes that seemed to grow every day.

I ran my hands over his chest, feeling his gun holster beneath the shirt. He sat back and I leaned forward, beginning to unbutton his shirt, revealing his toned torso and the black holster with his gun and knife. Luca took off his shirt and I opened the holster, helping him out of it. He thrust it to the ground. Matteo's words came back to me and I ran my hands over Luca naked chest.

I pressed a kiss against Luca's tattoo, then against the healing wound over his ribs. I brushed Luca's nipples with my fingertips and he groaned in response. He quickly got out of his pants. I lowered my lips to his erection but paused an inch from his tip. "If you're not quiet, I'll stop."

Luca's eyes flashed. He put his hand on my head. "Maybe I won't allow you to stop."

"Maybe I'll bite."

Luca chuckled. "Have your way with me, I won't make a sound. Don't want to offend your sister's virgin ears."

"What about my virgin ears?" I kissed his tip.

"You shouldn't still be one," Luca said in a low voice. I took his erection into my mouth to distract him. He made a sound deep in his throat, then quieted as I took care of him.

I pulled back again before he came.

After he'd cleaned himself, Luca spooned me.

"I'm sorry for what your cousin did," I said into the darkness.

"I should have known better than to trust anyone. Trust is a luxury people in my position can't afford."

You can trust me, I wanted to say because he could. No matter how much I tried to fight it, I had fallen for him. "Life without trust is lonely."

"Yes, it is." He kissed the back of my neck, then we fell silent.

***

Luca was asleep when I woke, his body wrapped around mine, his hardness pressing against my lower back. I untangled myself and slipped into the bathroom. It wasn't late yet, but Gianna was an early riser and I couldn't wait to spend the day with her. I took a long shower, feeling more awake already. I got out of the shower and wrapped a towel around myself, then went back into the bedroom. Luca sat on the edge of the bed but got up when I entered. His erection jutted out. I gave him a teasing smile as he curled his fingers over my hipbones. "Hard again?"

He growled. "I'm always hard for you. One day my balls are going to explode."

I could hear movement somewhere in the apartment, then a curse. Gianna was awake. "I should go to her."

"Oh no, you won't," Luca rasped. He kissed me possessively and I stood on my tiptoes to make it easier for him. One kiss couldn't hurt, but the way Luca was grinding himself against me I knew he wanted more than a kiss. He turned me around and pulled me flush against his chest so his erection pressed into my back.

I gasped. We were facing the floor length mirror across from the bed. Luca gripped the towel and pulled it down, leaving me naked. He kissed my throat, eyes on me through the mirror. His strong hands traveled up my sides and cupped my breasts. He captured my nipples between his forefinger and thumb, and twirled them. My lips parted and a soft moan escaped.

I could hear Gianna coming up the stairs toward our floor. Oh god.

Luca pinched my nipples, then tugged. I closed my eyes at the delicious sensation that swept through me. He peppered my throat and collarbone with kisses and licks while his hand slid down the valley between my breasts, over my stomach and between my thighs. Gianna stopped outside of our bedroom. Luca flicked his thumb over my clit and I bit down on my lip to stop myself from moaning.

"Aria? Are you awake?"

"Your sister is a fucking nuisance," Luca muttered in my ear, then licked the skin below before sucking it. His index finger slid between my folds, then entered me. I exhaled. "But you're so fucking wet, principessa." A new wave of wetness pooled between my legs. "Yes," Luca growled into my ear. His eyes bored into me in the mirror and I couldn't look away. His finger slipped in and out of me, spreading my wetness all over my folds.

I couldn't believe he was making me watch him fingering me. I couldn't believe how much it turned me on. His fingers pinched my nipple again, harder this time and I could feel it all the way in my clit. I whimpered.

"Aria?" Gianna hammered against the door. God, she wouldn't stop. I tried to pull away. This was wrong. I couldn't do this with my sister outside of the door. Luca smirked, his grip on me tightening. His second hand moved down and rubbed my clit while his other kept slipping in and out of me. I was spiraling out of control. His lips crashed down on mine, swallowing my moans as pleasure washed over me. My legs spasmed and I rocked myself against Luca's hands as I came hard. Luca didn't stop moving his hands, even as I tried to step away. Instead he pushed against my shoulders until I leaned forward, my hands coming up to support me against the mirror. My eyes grew wide when he knelt behind me, palming my butt and then spreading me. And then his tongue was there, sliding over my folds. He licked the entire length of me. I tensed when his tip slid along my back entrance and he quickly returned his mouth to my clit. I lost all sense of myself, even as I heard Gianna's insistent knocking and her occasional calls. All that mattered was Luca's tongue as it drove me higher and higher. This had to be wrong, but it felt too good. I bit the inside of my cheek and as pain and pleasure mingled my second orgasm crashed over me. My legs gave way and I fell to my knees beside Luca, panting and gasping, and hoping Gianna couldn't hear it.

I glared at Luca, but he smirked, hunger on his face. He stood, and his erection twitched. I watched as he began stroking himself in front of my face. I knew what he wanted. I parted my lips and he slid his tip in. The saltiness of his pre-cum spread on my tongue. I couldn't believe I was blowing Luca with Gianna close by, but the wrongness of it turned me on even more. What was wrong with me? Luca

230

caressed my cheek as his other hand cupped the back of my head. His eyes never left me as he slowly slid in and out of my mouth. I wasn't sure why I liked it, but I did.

"You're so beautiful, Aria," he murmured, pushing a bit deeper into my mouth. I swirled my tongue around his tip and he exhaled sharply, so I did it again.

Gianna's step receded down the stairs but I kept sucking Luca, slow and sensually. Luca's hand guided me, a light pressure against my head. I sucked him faster, increasing the pressure of my lips. "Cup my balls."

I did. I loved how soft they felt in my palm. Luca rocked his hips faster. "I want to come in your mouth, principessa," he said harshly. I wasn't sure if that was something I'd like, but Luca didn't mind tasting me down there, so I should at least give it a try. I nodded and sucked him deeper into my mouth. Luca growled, his hips bucking faster. After a few more thrusts, he came in my mouth. I swallowed. It tasted strange and was more than I'd thought it would be but it wasn't exactly bad.

Luca still stroked my cheek as he softened in my mouth. He pulled back, his penis sliding out from between my lips. I swallowed again. Luca grabbed my arm and lifted me to my feet, his mouth crashing down on mine in a fierce kiss. He didn't mind tasting himself on me. "I hope you remember this all day."

***

Luca left shortly after breakfast and Gianna immediately pulled me out onto the roof terrace, away from Romero's attentive ears.

"What's going on? You've been acting strange all morning. Why didn't you answer when I called you this morning?"

I looked away, a blush spreading on my cheeks. Gianna's eyes shot open. "What did he do?"

"He went down on me," I admitted.

"You let him?"

I laughed. "Yes." More heat rose into my cheeks at the sound of eagerness in my voice.

Gianna leaned forward. "You like it?"

"I love it."

Gianna bit her lip. "I hate thinking about you with him, but you really seem to enjoy it. I guess it has its advantages that Luca fucked every society girl in New York."

I didn't want to think about it.

"So how does it feel?"

"As if I'm shattering. It's overwhelming and amazing, and I don't know how to describe it."

"But you didn't sleep with him?"

I shook my head. "Not yet, but I don't think Luca wants to wait much longer."

"Fuck him. He can screw himself." She narrowed her eyes. "Did he make you blow him?"

"He didn't make me. I wanted to do it."

Gianna looked doubtful. "And? Tell me more. You know I have to vicariously live through you. I'm so fucking tired of being under surveillance all day. I want a boyfriend. I want to have sex and have orgasms."

I snorted. "I doubt Father will allow it."

"I don't intend to ask him," Gianna said with a shrug. "I'm here now. Nobody's stopping me from having fun, right?"

My eyes widened. "Father would kill me if I let you hook up with guys while you were here."

"He doesn't have to know, does he?" She shrugged again. "It's not like I would tell him."

I gaped, then laughed. "Well, unless you want to seduce Romero or Matteo your options are kind of limited."

"Ugh, no. I don't want either of them. I want a normal guy. A guy who doesn't know who I am."

"Well, I don't know how we could find a guy for you."

Gianna grinned. "How about we hit a club?"

"Romero won't let me out of his sight after I ran away from him once. There's no way we can escape him and go off to a club."

Gianna contemplated this. I worried about the crazy plan she might come up with. I actually liked the idea of going out for a night of dancing. I'd always imagined how it would be to spend a night on the dance floor and let loose.

"Romero can come with us. He's guarding you, not me. Maybe I can slip away."

"And then what? A quickie in a restroom stall? Do you really want to experience all your firsts like that?"

Gianna glared. "At least, I'd experience them on my own terms. It would be my choice. You don't have a choice at all. Luca and Father took them all away. I don't get how you can be so calm about it. How can you not hate Luca?"

Sometimes I wondered that myself. "I should hate him."

Gianna's face crumbled. "But you don't. Fuck, Aria, do you actually care about him? Love him?"

"Would you really prefer I hate him and be miserable?"

"He treats you like a prisoner. You don't really believe Romero is just for your protection, right? He keeps an eye on you, so no other guy gets a piece of you."

I knew that. "Let's go shopping."

"Really? That's so trophy wife of you."

"Shut up," I said teasingly, wanting to light the mood. "Shopping for hot outfits for tonight. We can hit one of Luca's clubs."

Gianna grinned. "I want to wear something that gives guys a fucking boner from looking at me."

***

Romero had waited outside the store while we went shopping. He'd probably checked beforehand if there was a back entrance we could use to escape. I hadn't told him about our plan to head out to a club yet. It was better if I sprang it on him at the last moment.

Gianna whistled as I turned around so she could admire my outfit. "Holy shit. You are sex on legs. Or maybe death on legs, because Luca will probably kill every guy that looks at you the wrong way."

I rolled my eyes. "Luca won't kill anyone for looking."

"Wanna bet on that?"

No, I wouldn't. I'd never worn anything that sexy in public. The black leather pants hugged my body so tightly, they looked like a second skin. The sheer black sleeveless blouse I'd tugged into my waistband, revealed my sparkly push-up bra below.

"You don't look too shabby either," I said.

Gianna jumped up from my bed. "You think?" She flashed me a seductive smile. She really looked smoking hot in her black tights and black leather hot pants.

"You're jailbait." Good thing we didn't have to worry about getting carded. I linked our arms and led her out of the bedroom and down the staircase. Romero was sitting on the sofa, cleaning his knife. His eyes darted up and he stilled completely. His gaze wandered over our bodies. He'd never openly stared at me.

"Are you checking us out?" I couldn't help but tease him. He was always so controlled. This small flicker of humanness was a relief.

He stood abruptly, sheathing the knife into its holder. His eyes were again firmly focused on my face. "What's going on?" There was a hint of strain in his voice.

I walked up to him and he actually tensed as if he thought I would jump in. That almost made me laugh. "Gianna and I want to go to Marquee." That was one of the hottest clubs in town.

Romero shook his head. "That belongs to the Bratva."

"Oh, what's hottest club that belongs to the Familia then?"

Romero didn't say anything at first. He reached into his pocket and pulled out his phone, probably to call Luca. Something snapped in me then. I couldn't believe he needed to ask Luca permission. I gave Gianna a look and nodded toward Romero who had started typing. She sidled up to him and actually squeezed his butt. He jumped and I used the moment to snatch his phone from him. He took a threatening step toward me, eyes blazing with anger, then he froze. "Aria," he said. "Give it back."

I slipped the phone into my waistband. The pants were tight enough that there wasn't a risk of it slipping down.

Gianna stepped away from Romero, grinning. "Why don't you shove your hand down Aria's pants and get it. I'll take a pic and send it to Luca."

Romero's eyes lingered on the shape of his phone in my pants, but I knew he wouldn't try to get it. "This isn't funny."

"No it isn't, you're right," I said sharply. "I'm an adult. If I tell you to take me to a club, I don't want you to ask my husband for permission. I'm not a child, nor am I his property."

"You are Luca's," Romero said calmly.

I stepped up to him, so close that I had to tilt my head back. "Gianna and I are going to a club. So unless you want to keep me at gunpoint, you'll drive us there or let us leave alone."

Romero's jaw tightened. The look in his eyes made me realize why he was my bodyguard. For the first time I was reminded that

236

Romero was a killer. "I'll drive you. But you will go to Sphere. It's Luca's."

"Is it any good?" Gianna asked.

"It's hotter than the fucking Marquee." Romero was really pissed.

"Take us there then." He put on his jacket and led us to the elevator. "Luca won't like it," he said.

***

Gianna and I sat in the back as Romero steered the car through traffic. I pulled the phone out and checked what Romero had been writing.

**A wants to hit a club. Permission?**

He had managed to send it off before I'd snatched it, but Luca's reply had come afterward.

**No**

My blood boiled. Gianna huffed. "I can't fucking believe his nerve."

Romero glanced at us through the rearview mirror. "Did Luca reply?"

"Yeah," I said. "He said you should stay close at all times."

Romero bought my lie and actually relaxed. Gianna winked. Luca would go through the roof, but I really couldn't bring myself to care. Romero parked the car in a side alley and led us around the building. A long line of partygoers waited in front of the entrance but Romero ushered us past it.

"Hey you stupid fucker, there's a line," a guy shouted. Romero stopped, a cold anger replacing his usual calm.

"Go ahead," Romero said to us before he turned around to the guy. Gianna gripped my hand and dragged me toward the two bouncers at the front. They were as tall and muscled as Luca.

"You don't look old enough to hit a club," the dark-skinned man said.

"Is that a problem?" Gianna asked with a flirty smile.

The man's eyes moved to something behind me. "Romero," he said with a hint of confusion.

"She belongs to the boss, Jorge. This is Aria Vitiello and her sister Gianna Scuderi of the Chicago Outfit."

Both men stared at me, then stepped back respectfully. "We didn't know she was coming tonight. The boss didn't say anything," Jorge said.

Romero grimaced, but didn't say anything. Instead he led Gianna and me inside, past the cloakroom tinged in bluish light and a bar area. Behind it the doors opened to a dark dance floor. Blue and white light flashed and hip hop beats blasted toward us. Gianna tugged at my hand, wanting to go in that direction.

"We should go to Luca first," Romero said.

"He's here?" I asked surprised.

Romero nodded. "The club has several backrooms and a basement where we handle some business."

"Why don't you go tell him I'm here while Gianna and I hit the dance floor."

238

Romero gave me a look. "No chance in hell."

"That's your problem then. Gianna and I are going dancing." Romero grasped my wrist. I tensed. "Let me go right this second," I hissed and he did, his chest heaving. Gianna and I walked into the club. The beat vibrated under our feet as if the floor had come to life. The club was crowded with writhing bodies. Romero shadowed my sister and me as we squeezed through the throng of dancers toward another bar area.

"Two gin tonic," I said. The barman frowned briefly before noticing Romero, then he prepared our drinks and handed them to us. Romero leaned over the bar and said something to the man, who nodded and walked around the bar. I knew what it meant. I took a deep gulp of my drink, then set it down and moved onto the dance floor.

I let the music claim my body and started writhing to the beat. Gianna grinned widely, throwing her head back. She looked happier than I'd seen her in a long time. She moved her hips and butt, shaking and rotating her hips. I stepped closer and mimicked her motions. Our eyes locked as we lost all sense of everything around us, as we let the beat carry away who we were. I wasn't sure where Romero was and I didn't care. This felt like freedom.

Men were watching us. I didn't return their hungry gazes. It wouldn't be fair to lead them on. Gianna didn't share my restraint. She smiled and flirted, batted her eyelashes and ran her hands through her hair. A few men started dancing around us. Gianna pressed up to one of them, hands on his chest. Another man raised his eyebrows at me, but I shook my head. He opened his mouth then closed it and backed away.

I didn't need to look back. I kept dancing. I knew who was behind me, knew from the looks of respect from the men around me, from the looks of admiration from the women. I rotated my hips, thrust my butt out, raised my arms. Firm hands came down on my hips. For a second I worried they belonged to some suicidal idiot, but they were the strong big hands I knew. I arched, pressing my butt against a crotch. I smiled. I was wrenched against a muscled body and Luca's hot breath brushed my ear. "Who are you dancing for?"

I tilted my head to stare into his blazing gray eyes. "You. Only you."

Luca's expression was hungry, but there was still a hint of anger too. "What are you doing here?"

"Dancing."

He narrowed his eyes. "I told Romero 'no'"

"I'm not your possession Luca. Don't treat me like one."

His fingers on my waist tightened. "You are mine Aria, and I protect what's mine."

"I don't mind being protected, but I do mind being imprisoned." I turned in Luca's arms, catching a glimpse of Gianna in a heated argument with Matteo. "Dance with me," I shouted.

And Luca did. I knew from photos on the internet that he'd often been to clubs in the past and it became obvious when he moved his body. A man as tall and muscled as him shouldn't be able to move so smoothly. His eyes never left mine, his hands possessive on my waist.

Luca bent his head toward me to whisper in my ear. "You look fucking hot, Aria. Every man in the club wants you and I want to kill them all."

"I'm only yours," I said fiercely, and God help me it was the truth, not just because of the ring on my finger that marked me as his. Luca's lips crashed down on mine, fierce and demanding and possessive, and I opened up for him, letting him claim me in front of everyone.

"I'm so fucking hard," Luca growled against my lips and I could feel his erection against my stomach. "Fuck. I have a call set up with one of our distributors in five minutes." I didn't ask what they were distributing. I didn't want to know.

"It's okay," I said. "Come back when you have time. I'm going to grab a drink."

"Go to the VIP area."

I shook my head. "I want to pretend I'm an ordinary girl tonight."

"Nobody who looks at you will think you are ordinary." His eyes travelled the length of my body and I shivered. Then he took a step back, regret obvious on his face. "Cesare and Romero will keep an eye on you." I was about to nod when I noticed a familiar face in the VIP area, watching me. Grace.

My breath caught. She sat on another man's lap so she wasn't here for Luca but the look in her eyes said it all. She wasn't over him. Luca followed my gaze and cursed. "She's not here because of me."

"Yes, she is."

"I can't throw her out. She comes here all the time to party. I haven't seen her since that night. I usually stay in the back."

I nodded, a lump forming in my throat. Luca took my chin between his thumb and index finger, forcing me to meet his eyes. "There's only you, Aria." He glanced at his watch, then pulled back. "I really need to go now. I'll be back as soon as I can." He turned and strode through the crowd that parted for him. Matteo followed after him and Gianna stepped up beside me. "That asshole."

"Who?" I said distractedly. Grace had disappeared from the VIP area.

"Matteo. The guy has the nerve to tell me not to dance with other men. What is he? My owner. Fuck him." She paused. "Are you okay?"

"Yeah," I whispered. "Let's go to the bar." Romero and Cesare fell into step behind us but I turned around to them, feeling on edge. "Can you watch us from afar? You're driving me crazy." Without a word they separated and took positions in corners of the club. I released a breath and settled on a barstool.

I ordered two new Gin & Tonics and took a deep gulp from the cool liquid, trying to relax. Gianna jiggled her leg. "You can go dancing," I told her, but she shook her head and bobbed her head to the music. "In a few minutes. You look pale."

"I'm okay," I said, my eyes searching the club for a sign of Grace, but she seemed to have vanished into thin air. There were too many people on the dance floor to find her anyway.

"I really need to go to the restroom," Gianna said after a while. Her Gin & Tonic was almost gone.

"I need to sit for a few more minutes."

Gianna gave me a worried look but then she slipped away and Cesare followed at a safe distance.

I put my head in my palm, taking a deep breath. An arm bumped against mine, startling me. I drew back as a man with long blond hair leaned against the counter beside me. He reached past me for a straw. His jacket brushed my breast and I leaned even further back, and glanced away, uncomfortable with the look he was giving me.

"What's your name?" he shouted.

I tried to ignore him. Something about him was seriously giving me the creeps. I took a sip from my drink and tried to pretend I was busy searching for someone. The man kept leering at me with an ugly smile on his unshaven face. "Are you waiting for someone?"

I turned away, really trying to ignore him and not make a big deal out of this. If I started freaking out, Romero would come over and make a scene. Maybe he was already on his way. My vision started to blur and my stomach gave a lurch. I took another sip from my drink but it didn't help. I slid off the stool but my legs were shaky and I felt dizzy. I grabbed the counter behind me. Suddenly, the man's mouth was at my ear, his stale-cigarette breath on my face. "I'm going to fuck your tight ass. I'll make you scream, bitch." His grip on my arm was crushing as he tried to drag me away from the bar. My eyes found Romero who was steering toward me, hand under his jacket where his gun and knife were. Impatient by our slow progress, my attacker wrapped an arm around me like a loving boyfriend ready to help his drunk girlfriend out of the club. "I'll fuck you like an animal. I'll fuck you bloody, cunt," he rasped into my ear. I stared at him, my limbs feeling heavy, my mouth like it was filled with cotton. I'd heard those exact words not too long ago.

I forced my lips into a smile. "You are a dead man."

Confusion flickered across the man's face a second before it contorted in agony. He released me and my legs gave away, but Cesare caught me, his arm replacing that of the man. My eyes darted around for Gianna. She hovered beside Cesare, face drawn in worry. Romero was close behind my attacker, his knife buried in the man's upper thigh. "You will follow us. If you try to run, you'll die."

"Take her drink," Cesare said to Gianna. "But don't drink."

Cesare half carried me toward the back of the club and down a flight of stairs. He shouldered open a door and we walked into a sort of office. Matteo rose from his chair. "What's going on?"

"Probably roofies," Romero said, giving the man he was holding a good shake.

"I'll get Luca," Matteo said with a twisted smile. He walked through another door and a moment later Luca stalked into the room, as tall and impressive as ever. I hung in Cesare's grasp, my face half pressed against his chest. Luca's eyes narrowed, then flitted between me and my attacker.

"What happened?" he snarled.

Suddenly he was in front of me, lifting me into his arm. My head lolled against his chest as I gazed up at him. He put me down on the couch. Gianna knelt beside me, gripping my hand. "What's happening to her?" she cried.

"Roofies," Romero said again. "This sick fuck was trying to drag her outside."

Luca drew himself up before my attacker. "You put Roofies in my wife's drink, Rick?"

Luca knew that man? Confusion flickered in my hazy mind.

"Wife! I didn't know she was yours. I didn't. I swear!" The man's lower lip was trembling.

Luca pushed away Romero's hand and curled his fingers around the handle of the knife still buried in Rick's leg. He twisted and the man screamed. Romero held him upright by the arms. "What did you plan to do to her once you had her outside?"

"Nothing!" the man cried.

"Nothing? So if my men hadn't stopped you, you would have just dropped her off at a hospital?" Luca's voice was pleasant, calm, his face devoid of emotion.

Gianna's grip on my hand was painful. I swallowed and cleared my throat. "I'll fuck your tight ass," I whispered.

Luca's head whirled around, then he was at my side, his face so close to mine, I could have kissed him. Maybe it was the Roofies but I really wanted to kiss him senseless in that moment, wanted to rip his shirt off, wanted to...

"What did you say, Aria?"

"I'll fuck your tight ass. I'll make you scream, bitch. I'll fuck you bloody, cunt. That's what he said to me." Luca stared into my eyes, a

245

muscle in his jaw working. Before he could move, Gianna had leaped to her feet and flew at Rick. She hit his face and kicked his groin, and struggled ferociously against Matteo's grip as he dragged her away from Rick.

"You will die!" she screamed.

Luca straightened and she stopped moving.

"Let me go," she hissed.

"You promise to behave?" Matteo asked with an amused smile.

She nodded, her stare fixed on Rick. Matteo dropped his arms and she straightened her clothes. "They will make you bleed," she said coldly. "And I hope they will rape your ugly ass with that broomstick over there."

"Gianna," I rasped. She came over to me and sank down on the edge of the couch, taking my hand again.

Matteo didn't take his eyes off her. "I'll make him pay, Gianna."

"No," Luca said firmly. Rick looked ready to burst from relief. "He's my responsibility." Matteo and Luca exchanged a long look, then Matteo nodded.

Luca brought his face close to Rick's. "You wanted to fuck my wife? Wanted to make her scream?" His voice tore through my growing dizziness and sent a shiver down my back. I was glad it wasn't directed at me. I'd been scared of Luca before, but never had he sounded anything like this. Rick shook his head frantically. "No, please."

Luca wrapped his hand around Rick's throat and lifted him until he stood on his tiptoes and his face was turning red. Then he tossed him away and Rick collided with the wall and crumpled to the floor.

"I hope you're hungry," Luca snarled. "Because I'm going to feed you your cock."

"Take the girls to the car, Romero," Matteo ordered as Luca unsheathed his knife. Romero lifted me into his arms and walked out the backdoor, Gianna close behind. Dizziness cloaked my brain and I pressed my face into Romero's jacket. He stiffened.

Gianna snorted. "Do you think Luca will cut off your dick too because she leaned against you while she was sick?"

"Luca is my boss and Aria is his."

Gianna muttered something under her breath but I couldn't make out the words.

"Open the door for me," Romero said and then I was lying on cool leather. Gianna lifted my head and put it in her lap. Her fingers untangled my hair and she rested her forehead against mine. "That guy gets what he deserves."

I closed my eyes. I had condemned a man to his death with my words. My first murder. "Your bodyguard doesn't even dare to wait in a car with us. Luca is a beast."

"Romero keeps watch," I whispered.

"Sure." I must have dozed off because suddenly the door was ripped open and Luca spoke. "How is she?"

"Holy fuck," Gianna said, voice shrill. "You're covered in blood."

I opened my eyes, but had trouble focusing.

"Only my shirt," Luca said, annoyance clear in his voice. There was rustling.

"You have no shame," Gianna said.

"I'm taking off my shirt, not my fucking pants. Do you ever shut your mouth?"

"Here, Boss."

Blurrily I saw Luca putting on a new shirt. "Burn that one and take care of everything, Romero. I'll drive."

A hand brushed my cheek and Luca's face hovered over me. Then he was gone, the door closed and he slipped behind the driver seat. The car started moving and my stomach churned.

Gianna leaned forward, her head between the seats. "You are quite a hunk, you know that? If you weren't married to my sister and not such an asshole I might consider giving you a go."

"Gianna," I groaned. When she was scared or nervous or angry, she never stopped talking, and the longer she talked the more offensive she got. And around Luca she was constantly angry.

"What, cat got your tongue? I hear you usually jump everything that doesn't have a dick," Gianna said.

Luca still didn't say anything. I wished I could see his face to find out how close to exploding he was. He'd killed a man not long ago; Gianna should really shut up.

Gianna sat back, but I knew she wasn't done yet. She wouldn't give up until she got a rise out of him. He pulled into the underground garage of our apartment building. "We're there," Gianna whispered into my ear. I wished she would talk as reasonably to Luca as she did to me.

The car door swung open and Luca hoisted me into his arms. He carried me toward the private elevator and stepped in. The bright halogen lights hurt my eyes but I kept them open to watch Gianna and Luca in the mirror. She leaned beside him and her expression didn't bode well. "Have you ever had a threesome?"

Luca didn't move a muscle. He was looking down at me but I kept my attention on the mirror, trying to send Gianna a silent message to close her mouth. "How many women have you raped before my sister?"

Luca's head shot up, eyes burning as he stared at Gianna. I pressed my palm gently against his chest and he glanced down at me. The tension remained. "Can't you do something else with your mouth than yap?"

Gianna straightened. "Like what? Give you a blowjob?"

Luca laughed. "Girl, you've never even seen a dick. Just keep your lips shut."

"Gianna," I croaked in warning.

At last, we arrived on the top floor and Luca stepped out into our penthouse. He headed for the stairs to our bedroom when Gianna blocked his way. "Where are you taking her?"

"To bed," Luca said, trying to sidestep my sister but she followed his movements.

"She's high on Roofies. That's probably the chance you've been waiting for. I won't let her alone with you."

Luca became very still like a wolf on the verge of attacking. "I'm going to say it only once and you better obey: get out of my way and go to bed."

"Or what?"

"Gianna, please," I pleaded. She searched my face, then she nodded once and quickly kissed my cheek. "Get better."

Luca walked past her, carried me up the stairs and then into the master bedroom. The sickness that had been a distant pressure in my stomach turned into an insistent throbbing. "I'm going to be sick."

Luca carried me into the bathroom and held me over the toilet as I retched. When I was done, I said, "I'm sorry."

"What for?" He helped me stand, though the only thing keeping me upright was his steely grip on my waist.

"For throwing up."

Luca shook his head and handed me a wet towel. My hands shook as I wiped my face with it. "It's good that you got some of that shit out of your system. Fucking Roofies. It's the only way for ugly fucks like Rick to get their dicks into a pussy."

He led me back into the bedroom and toward the bed. "Can you undress?"

"Yeah." The moment he let go, I fell backward and landed on the mattress. Laughter bubbled out of me, then a new wave of dizziness hit me and I groaned. He leaned over me, his face slightly blurry.

"I'm going to get you out of your clothes. They stink of smoke and vomit." I wasn't sure why he was telling me. It wasn't as if he hadn't seen me naked before. He grabbed the hem of my shirt and

250

pulled it over my head. I watched him as he unzipped my leather pants and slid them down my legs, his knuckles brushing my skin, leaving goosebumps in their wake. He unhooked my glittery bra and threw it to the ground before he straightened and stared down at me. He turned abruptly and disappeared from my view. Dots danced in and out of my vision and I was on the brink of another laughing fit when Luca returned and helped me into one of his shirts. He was only in his briefs. He slid his arms under my knees and shoulderblades, and moved me up until my head rested on the pillow, then he got into bed beside me.

"You're impressive, you know?" I babbled.

Luca scanned my face, then pressed a palm against my forehead. I giggled and reached out, wanting to touch his tattoo but misjudging the distance and brushing my fingertips across his abdomen and then lower. He hissed, snatched my hand away and pressed it against my stomach. "Aria, you're drugged. Try to sleep."

"Maybe I don't want to sleep." I wriggled in his grip.

"Yes, you do."

I yawned. "Will you hold me?"

Luca didn't say anything but he extinguished the lights and wrapped his arms around me from behind. "You better lie on your side in case you feel sick again."

"Did you kill him?"

There was a pause. "Yes."

"Now there's blood on my hands."

"You didn't kill him."

"But you killed him because of me."

"I'm a killer, Aria. It had nothing to do with you." It had everything to do with me, but I was too tired to argue.

I listened to his breathing for a few heartbeats. "You know, sometimes I wish I could hate you, but I can't. I think I love you. I never thought I could. And sometimes I wonder how it would be if you made love to me."

Luca pressed his lips against my neck. "Sleep."

"But you don't love me," I mumbled. "You don't want to make love to me. You want to fuck me because you own me." His arm tightened around me. "Sometimes I wish you had taken me in our wedding night, then at least I wouldn't still wish for something that will never be. You want to fuck me like you fucked Grace, like an animal. That's why she told me you would fuck me bloody, right?"

My tongue felt heavy and my eyelids stuck together. I was talking nonsense, a garble of words I shouldn't say.

"When did she say that? Aria, when?"

Luca's sharp voice couldn't rip through the fog blanketing my thoughts and blackness claimed me.

# CHAPTER THIRTEEN

A wave of sickness wrenched me from sleep. I stumbled toward the bathroom and threw up again, kneeling on the cold marble floor, too exhausted to get up. I shuddered. Luca reached over me and flushed the toilet before stroking my hair back from my forehead. "Not that hot anymore, am I?" I laughed hoarsely.

"That shouldn't have happened. I should have kept you safe."

"You did." I gripped the toilet seat and staggered to my feet. Luca's hands grasped my waist.

"Maybe a bath will help."

"I think I'll drown if I lie in the bathtub now."

Luca turned the water on in the tub while still holding me with one hand. The sky was turning gray over New York. "We can take a bath together."

I tried a teasing smile. "You just want to grab a feel."

"I won't touch you while you are on Roofies."

"A Capo with morals?"

Luca's face was serious. "I'm not Capo yet. And I have morals. Not many but a couple."

"I'm only teasing," I whispered as I leaned my forehead against his naked chest. He rubbed my back and the motion sent a sweet tingling down into my core. I drew back and carefully walked over to the washbasin to brush my teeth and wash my face.

Luca shut the water off when the tub was almost full. Then he helped me out of my panties and got out of his boxer-shorts before he lifted me into the tub. I ducked my face under the water for a moment, hoping it would clear the remaining fog from my head. Luca slid in behind me and pulled me back against his chest. His erection pressed against my thigh. I turned so I was facing Luca and his length slid between my legs and brushed my entrance. I stiffened. Luca would only have to push his hips upward to enter me. He groaned, gritted his teeth, then he reached between us and pushed his erection back so it rested against my thigh again and pulled me flat on his torso.

"Some men would have taken advantage of the situation," I murmured.

Luca's jaw clenched. "I'm that kind of man, Aria. Don't kid yourself into believing I'm a good man. I'm neither noble nor a gentleman. I'm a cruel bastard."

"Not to me." I pressed my nose against the crook of his neck, breathing in his familiar, musky scent.

Luca kissed the top of my head. "It's better if you hate me. There's less chance of you getting hurt that way."

What had I told him last night when I was out of it? Had I told him I'd fallen in love with him? I couldn't remember. "But I don't hate you."

Luca kissed my head again. I wished he'd say something. I wished he'd say that he...

"You mentioned something Grace said to you." His voice was casual but tension gripped his body. "Something about fucking you bloody."

"Oh, yeah. She said you'd hurt me, fuck me like an animal, fuck me bloody when she talked to me during our wedding reception. Scared me out of my mind." Then I frowned. "I think that guy last night almost said the same thing."

"Before I killed him he said one of the women who bought dope from him told him you were a skank who needed to be told a lesson. She gave him cash."

I lifted my head. "Do you think it was Grace?"

Luca's eyes were like a stormy sky. "I'm sure it was her. The description fits and who else would have an interest in attacking you."

"What are you going to do?"

"I can't kill her, even if I want to cut her fucking throat, but that would cause too much trouble with her father and brother. I'll have to talk to them, though. Tell them they need to put her on a fucking leash or there won't be any more money from us."

"What if they refuse?"

"They won't. Grace has been fucking things up for a long time. They'll probably ship her off to Europe or Asia for rehab or some shit like that."

I kissed him but the tension didn't leave Luca's body. "I can't stop thinking about what would have happened if Romero and Cesare hadn't been there, if that fucker had gotten you out of the club. The

255

thought of his dirty hands on you makes me want to kill him again. The thought that he might have…" He shook his head.

I knew it wasn't because Luca had emotions for me. He was possessive. He couldn't bear the thought that someone might have gotten his hands on me, that someone might have taken what Luca considered his. Resignation filled me. "When Gianna leaves in a few days, you can have me," I whispered against his throat. Luca's hands stilled on my back. He didn't ask me if I was sure. I hadn't expected him to. Luca had said it himself; he wasn't a good man.

***

Gianna and I had spent the last few days trying different cafés and restaurants, talking and laughing and shopping, but today Gianna had to go back to Chicago. My arms around her were tight as we stood in the departure hall of JFK. Gianna needed to go through security soon but I didn't want to let her go. Not only because I'd miss her terribly but also because I was anxious about my promise to Luca.

I braced myself and took a step back from Gianna. "Visit again soon, okay?"

She nodded, her lips pressed together. "You call me every day, don't forget."

"I won't," I promised. She backed away slowly, then turned and headed for the line at security. I waited until she walked through and disappeared from view.

Luca stood a few steps behind me. I rushed over to him and pressed my face against him. He stroked my back. "I thought we could grab dinner and then have a relaxing evening." He sounded hungry and excited, but not for food.

"Sounds good," I said with a small smile. Something shifted in Luca's face but then it was gone.

***

I hadn't eaten much; my stomach was already churning. I didn't want to take any risks. Luca pretended not to notice. He ate what I didn't. When we stepped back into our penthouse, I headed for the liquor cabinet, looking for some liquid courage, but Luca gripped my wrist and pulled me against him. "Don't."

He lifted me into his arms and carried me upstairs into our bedroom. When he set me down on the edge of the bed, my eyes found his crotch. He was already hard. Nerves twisted my insides. He wanted me. I wouldn't deny him, not tonight.

Luca climbed on the bed and I lay back, my palms flat against the blanket. His lips found mine, his tongue dipping in and I relaxed under his skillful mouth. This was good, familiar, comforting. My leg muscles loosened. Luca ripped his mouth away from me and sucked my nipple into his mouth through the fabric of my dress. I cupped his head, letting his experienced ministrations carry away my fear. There was an urgency to his kisses and touches that I'd never felt before.

He tugged at my dress and slid it down my body, leaving me in only my panties. He took a moment to admire my body before he moved down and buried his face between my legs, his tongue sliding between my folds over my panties. With a growl, he gripped them and ripped them off, then tossed them away. His mouth was hot and demanding, but too quickly he stopped and thrust a finger into me. Then he stood abruptly and slipped out of his shirt before he removed his holder and pants. His body was taut with tension and his erection harder than I'd ever seen it. The raw hunger on his face sent a spike of fear through me. "You're mine."

And then Luca loomed over me, his knees parting my legs and his tip nudged against my entrance. My muscles seized up and I dug my nails into his shoulders and squeezed my eyes shut. This was too fast. He seemed barely in control. I pressed my face into the crook of his neck, trying to let his smell calm me.

Luca didn't move, his erection still only lightly touching my entrance.

"Aria," he said in low voice. "Look at me." I did. His gaze was hunger mixed with something gentler. I tried to focus on the gentle. For a long time we gazed at each other. He closed his eyes and lowered himself so his body was flush with mine. "I'm an asshole," he rasped. He kissed my cheek and my temple.

Confusion filled me. "Why?" God, was that small voice mine? Luca was my husband and I sounded as if I was terrified.

I *was* terrified, but I should have hidden it better.

"You are scared and I lose control like that. I should know better. I should prepare you properly and instead I almost shove my cock into you."

I didn't know what to say. I shifted and Luca's erection rubbed over my entrance, making me gasp. Luca released a harsh breath, squeezing his eyes shut. When he opened them again, the hunger was contained. He slid down until his head hovered over my breasts and his abs pressed against my folds. I exhaled at the friction and Luca's muscles flexed. I could tell he was still on edge.

"You are my wife," he said fiercely as if to remind himself. Then his fingers closed around my nipples and he tugged at them. I moaned, bucking my pelvis, making my core rub against Luca's abs again.

"Stop squirming," Luca ordered, almost pleadingly. He tugged again, this time I forced myself to stay still but a moan escaped my lips. Luca's expression was concentration and restrain as he tugged and twisted, twirled and rubbed. I arched my back, practically pushing my breasts into his face and he gladly took me up on my invitation and sucked my nipple into his mouth. I closed my eyes as he suckled one breasts while his fingers pinched my other. He shifted and ghosted his fingers over my ribs, my hips, my sides before his tongue followed the same trail. He bit the skin over my hipbones, then soothed the spot with his tongue. My entire body was on fire, desperate for release.

His fingers began massaging my thighs, parting me further as he moved lower. He kissed my mound, then my inner thigh before biting gently. I gasped and rocked my hips. He slid his hand under my butt and lifted me a few inches, then he kissed my folds. I whimpered at the soft touch. He kissed me again, his lips moving against my folds, then he pulled back. My eyes peeled open. He watched me, then he kissed my opening and I could feel wetness pool out of me. Luca thumbs spread my lips for him and he licked his tongue over my wetness.

I shuddered and felt another trickle. Luca gently lapped at me, not once touching my clit. He sucked my folds, licked them, circled his tongue around my entrance but never touched me where I needed his touch.

"Luca, please." I bucked my hips again.

Luca nudged my clit with his tongue and I cried out. "You want this?"

"Yes."

"Soon," he growled and eased a finger into me, fucking me with it slowly as his tongue slid around my opening, coating me with his saliva. His tongue moved up, finally circling my clit. I relaxed with a moan. Luca took my clit into his mouth and suckled, bringing me closer and closer to the edge.

"Tell me when you come," Luca said against my wet flesh.

He fingered me faster and pressed his tongue against my clit.

"I'm com--"

Luca pulled his finger out, then entered me again with two fingers. I gasped in discomfort but my orgasm ripped through me, pain mingling with pleasure as my body tried to get used to the fullness. Luca kissed my inner thigh, then groaned. "You're so fucking tight, Aria. Your muscles are squeezing the life out of my fingers."

My pulse was slowing and I glanced at Luca. He was watching me, two fingers buried in me. He slid them out a couple of inches and I winced but he slowly found a rhythm as he slid in and out.

"Relax," Luca murmured, and I tried. "I need to widen you, principessa." Luca traced his tongue over my folds and clit again. I hummed in pleasure. The discomfort in my core lessened with every stroke from Luca's tongue and I could feel myself approaching another release. Luca must have felt it too. He pulled his fingers out and moved up until he was propped up over me. He lined himself up and shifted my legs and hips until he found the angle he wanted, then his tip brushed my entrance. And just like that I froze up again. I wanted to cry in frustration. Why couldn't my body work with me?

Luca kissed my chin, then my lips. "Aria." My eyes finally met his. His expression reflected some kind of inner struggle. I wrapped my arms around him, my palms coming to rest on his flexing back. Resolve claimed his expression.

He shifted his hips and the pressure increased. I tensed even further and Luca let out a harsh breath. "Relax," he said as he cupped my cheek and kissed my lips. "I'm not even in yet." His hand caressed my side down to my thigh. He cupped it and opened me a bit wider. Then he pushed in slowly. I tightened my hold on him, pressing my lips together. It hurt. God, it hurt like hell. He would never fit. I whimpered when the tearing sensation got too much and tensed even further. Luca halted in his movement, jaw clenched. He brought one of his hands up and cupped my breast, rubbing and twisting my nipple.

"You are so beautiful," he murmured into my ear. "So perfect, principessa." His words and his teasing of my breast made me relax slightly and he pushed in a bit further. I tensed again. Luca kissed my mouth. "Almost there." He slid his hand down my body, fingers ghosting over my belly until he brushed my folds. He rubbed my clit slowly and I exhaled. Through the pain and discomfort I could feel small bolts of pleasure. Luca took his time teasing my clit and kissing me. His lips were hot and gentle, and his finger sent tingling sensations through my body. Slowly, my muscles loosened around his cock.

Rocking his hips forward, he pushed all the way in and I gasped, my back arching off the bed. I squeezed my eyes shut, breathing through my nose to get through the pain. I felt too full as if I was going to rip apart. I buried my face against Luca's throat, and started to count, trying to distract myself. 'It gets better', that's what the women said at my bridal shower, but when?

Luca moved, slowly and just an inch, but it hurt too much. "Please don't move," I gasped, then I pressed my lips together in shame. Other women had gone through this and they had lied back and suffered through it. Why couldn't I? Luca's body became taut like a bowstring. He touched my cheek as he pulled back, forcing me to look at him.

"Does it hurt that much?" His voice was pure restrain, eyes dark with an emotion I couldn't place.

Get a grip, Aria. "No, not that much." My voice caught on the last word because Luca had twitched. "It's okay, Luca. Just move. I won't

262

be mad at you. You don't have to hold back for me. Just get it over with."

"Do you think I want to use you like that? I can see how fucking painful this is. I've done many horrible things in my life but I won't add that to my list."

"Why? You hurt people all the time. Only because we're married you don't have to pretend to care for my feelings."

His eyes flashed. "What makes you think I have to pretend?"

My lips parted. I didn't dare to hope, didn't dare to read too much into his words, but God, did I want to.

"Tell me what to do," he said harshly.

"Can you hold me close for a while? But don't move."

"I won't," he promised, then kissed my lips. He gritted his teeth as he lowered himself completely. We were incredibly close, not even a sheet of paper would have fit between us. Luca curled one arm under my shoulders and pressed me against his chest, and then we kissed, our lips gliding over each other, our tongues tangling, soft and teasing. Luca caressed my side and my ribs before sneaking a hand between us and drawing small circles on my nipple. Slowly my body became slack under his soft caress and the taste of his mouth on mine. The pain between my legs became a dull ache and my core loosened around Luca, my body growing accustomed to his size. Luca didn't seem to notice or he chose to ignore it, instead he kept kissing me. His fingernail scraped my nipple and a flicker of pleasure spiked between my legs. I drew back, my lips raw and hot from our kiss. Luca's eyes were hooded.

"Can you still…?" I asked.

He shifted and I could feel how hard he was. He hadn't softened at all. My eyes widened in surprise.

"I told you I'm not a good man. Even though I know you're hurting, I still have a boner because I'm inside you."

"Because you want me."

"I've never wanted anything more in my life," Luca admitted.

"Can we go slow?"

"Of course, principessa." Still holding me close, he withdrew a few inches watching my face. The look of concern on his face released a knot in my chest.

I exhaled. It still hurt but not nearly as much as before and behind the pain was the hint of something better. Luca eased back into me and found a slow and gentle rhythm. I soaked in the feel of Luca's strong body pressed against me, the sharp lines of his face. His eyes never left my face. He didn't seem to mind the slow pace. The tension in his shoulders and neck was the only sign of how difficult this was for him. He changed the angle and a spark of pleasure shot through me. I gasped. Luca halted. "Did that hurt?"

"No, it felt good," I said with a shaky smile. Luca smiled and repeated the motion, sending another tingle through me. He lowered his lips to mine. I wasn't sure how long he kept up the slow rhythm, but I was getting sore and I knew I wouldn't come. I wasn't even close, despite the occasional flickers of pleasure. Dull pain still covered too much of it. I didn't know how to say what I needed to say.

He must have seen something on my face because he said. "Are you okay?"

I bit my lip. "How long until you…?"

"Not long, if I go a bit faster." He scanned my face and I nodded. He propped himself up on his elbows and thrust faster and a bit harder, and I pressed my lips together and buried my face against his shoulder, clutching his back. The pain was back, but I wanted Luca to come. "Aria?" Luca rasped.

"Keep going. Please. I want you to come."

He growled and kept thrusting. His pants came faster. He thrust deeper than before and I bit down on his shoulder to keep from whimpering in pain. Luca tensed with a groan, then he shuddered and I could feel him expand even further in me, filling me up until I was sure I'd come apart. He stopped moving, his lips against my throat. I could feel him softening in me and I almost breathed a sigh in relief. I held onto Luca, relishing in the feel of his quick heartbeat and the sound of his harsh breathing.

Luca pulled out and lay down beside me, pulling me into his arms. He brushed back my hair from my sweaty face. I felt something trickling out of me and shifted uncomfortably.

"I'll get a washcloth." Luca got out of bed to head for the bathroom. I felt cold without him. I stretched my legs but winced. I sat up and my eyes widened. There was blood smeared on my thighs and the bed, mingled with Luca's semen. Luca knelt on the bed beside me. He must have cleaned himself because there wasn't any blood on him.

"There's much more blood than the fake scene you created during our wedding night." My voice was shaky.

Luca nudged my legs apart and pressed the warm wet washcloth against me. I sucked in a breath. Luca kissed my knee. "You were a lot tighter than I thought," he said quietly. He pulled the washcloth away and I flushed, but he discarded it on the floor without another glance before he pressed his hand against my abdomen. "How bad is it?"

I put my head back on the pillow. "Not that bad. How can I complain when you're covered in scars from knife and bullet wounds?"

"We're not talking about me. I want to know how you feel, Aria. On a scale of one to ten, how much does it hurt?"

"Now? Five?"

Luca tensed. He lowered himself beside me, curled an arm around me and scanned my face. "And during?"

I avoided his eyes. "If ten is for the worst pain I've ever felt, then eight."

"The truth."

"Ten," I whispered.

Luca clenched his jaw. "Next time will be better."

"I don't think I can again so soon."

"I didn't mean now," he said firmly, kissing my temple. "You'll be sore for a while."

"On a scale of one to ten, how fast and hard did you go? The truth," I mimicked his words.

266

"Two."

"Two?" I must have looked pretty horrified because Luca rubbed my stomach lightly. "We have time. I will go as gentle as you need me to."

"I can't believe Luca – The Vice - Vitiello said 'gentle'," I said teasingly to light the mood.

Luca smirked. He cupped my face and leaned close. "It'll be our secret."

Emotions crowded in my chest. "Thanks for being gentle. I never thought you would be."

Luca laughed, a raw sound. "Believe me, nobody's more surprised about this than me."

I rolled onto my side, wincing, and snuggled against Luca's shoulder. "You never were gentle to someone?"

"No," he said bitterly. "Our father taught Matteo and me that any kind of gentleness was a weakness. And there was never any room in my life for it."

Even if the words wanted to get stuck in my throat, I said. "What about the girls you were with?"

"They were a means to an end. I wanted to fuck, so I looked for a girl and fucked her. It was hard and fast, definitely not gentle. I mostly fucked them from behind so I didn't have to look them in the eyes and pretend I gave a shit about them."

He sounded cold and cruel.

I kissed his tattoo, wanting to banish that part of him again. His arms around me tightened. "The only person who could have taught me how to be gentle was my mother." I held my breath. Would he tell me about her now? "But she killed herself when I was nine."

"I'm sorry." I wanted to ask what happened but I didn't want to push him and make him retreat behind his cold mask. Instead I cupped his cheek. He looked startled by the gesture but didn't pull away. I licked my lip, trying to suppress my curiosity.

"Does it still hurt?" he asked suddenly. For a moment, I didn't know what he was talking about. He brushed a hand across my abdomen. "Yeah, but talking helps."

"How does it help?"

"It distracts me." I gathered my courage. "Can you tell me more about your mother?"

"My father hit her. He raped her. I was young but I understood what was going on. She couldn't bear my father anymore, so she decided to slice her wrists and overdose on dope."

"She shouldn't have let you and Matteo alone."

"I found her."

I jerked up and stared. "You found your mother after she'd cut her wrists?"

"That was actually the first body I saw. Of course it wasn't the last." He shrugged as if it didn't matter. "The floor was covered with her blood and I slipped on it and fell. My clothes were soaked with her blood." His voice was calm, detached. "I ran out of the bathroom screaming and crying. My father found me and slapped me. Told me to be a man and clean myself up. I did. I never cried again."

"This is horrible. You must have been terrified. You were only a boy."

He was silent. "It made me tough. At one point every boy has to lose his innocence. The mafia isn't a place for the weak."

I knew that. I'd seen how Father had tried to shape Fabiano in the last few years and it always broke my heart when my little brother had to act like a man instead of the young boy that he was. "Emotions aren't a weakness."

"Yes, they are. Enemies always aim where they can hurt you most."

"And where would the Bratva aim if they wanted to hurt you?"

Luca extinguished the lights. "They won't ever find out."

That wasn't the answer I'd hoped for but I was too tired to ponder about it. Instead I closed my eyes and let sleep claim me.

# CHAPTER FOURTEEN

Going to the toilet burnt like hell, and walking wasn't exactly comfortable either. I winced as I stepped back into the bedroom where Luca lay with his head propped up on his arm. He watched me. "Sore?"

I nodded, blushing. "Yeah. I'm sorry."

"Why are you sorry?"

I lay down beside him. "I thought you might want to do it again, but I don't think I can."

Luca traced his fingertips over my ribs. "I know. I didn't expect you to be ready so soon." He rubbed my stomach, then inched a bit lower. "I could lick you if you are up for it."

My core tightened and I really wanted to say yes. "I don't think that's a good idea."

Luca nodded and settled back against the pillows. The blanket crowded around his hips, revealing his muscled torso and the scars there.

I moved closer and propped myself up above him. I traced Luca's scars, wondering what kind of stories hid behind each of them. I wanted to know all of them, wanted to figure out Luca scar by scar like a puzzle. Where did he get the long scar on his shoulder and the bullet wound below his ribs? Luca was doing his own exploring with his eyes, wandering over my breasts and face. He ran his thumb over my nipples. "Your breasts are fucking perfect." His touch was more possessive than sexual, but I could feel it all the way between my legs anyway.

Trying to distract myself, I paused with my fingertips against a mostly faded scar on his abs. "Where did you get this scar?"

"I was eleven." My eyes grew wide. I was pretty sure where the story was going. "The Familia wasn't as united as it is now. A few men thought they could grab power by killing my father and his sons. It was the middle of the night when I heard screaming and shooting. Before I could get out of bed, a man stepped into the room and pointed his gun at me. I knew I'd die as I stared into the barrel. I wasn't as scared as I thought I'd be. He would have killed me, if Matteo hadn't jumped him from behind when he pulled the trigger. The bullet went a lot lower than it was supposed to and hit my middle. It hurt like a motherfucker. I was screaming and probably would have passed out if the man hadn't turned on Matteo to kill him. I had a gun stashed in the drawer of my nightstand, took it out and put a bullet in the man's head before he could kill Matteo."

"That was your first murder, right?" I whispered.

Luca's eyes, which had been lost in another time, focused on me. "Yeah. The first of many."

"When did you kill again?"

"That same night." He smiled humorlessly. "After that first man, I told Matteo to hide in my closet. He protested but I was bigger and locked him in. By then I'd lost quite a bit of blood but I was high on adrenaline and could still hear shooting downstairs, so I headed for the noise with my gun. My father was in a shooting match with two attackers. I came down the stairs but nobody paid me any attention, and then I shot one of them from behind. My father took the other down with a shot in the shoulder."

"Why didn't he kill him?"

"He wanted to question him to find out if there were other traitors in the Familia left."

"So what did he do with the guy while he took you to the hospital?"

Luca gave me a wry look. I gasped. "Don't tell me he didn't take you."

"He called the Doc of the Familia, told me to put pressure on the wound and went ahead and started torturing the guy for information."

I couldn't believe a father would let his child suffer through pain and risk its life, so he could gather information.

"You could have died. Some things need to be treated in a hospital. How could he do that?"

"The Familia comes first. We never take injured to a hospital. They ask too many questions and the police get involved and it's an admittance of weakness. And my father had to make sure the traitor spoke before he got a chance to kill himself."

"So you agree with what he did? You would have watched someone you love bleed to death so you could protect the Familia and your power."

"My father doesn't love me. Matteo and I are his guarantee for power and a way to keep on the family name. Love has nothing to do with it."

"I hate this life. I hate the mafia. Sometimes I wished there was a way to escape."

Luca's face became still. "From me?"

"No," I said, surprising myself. "From this world. Have you never wanted to live a normal life?"

"No. This is who I am, who I was born to be, Aria. It's the only life I know, the only life I want. For me to confirm to a normal life would be like an eagle in a small cage in a zoo." He paused. "Your marriage to me shackles you to the mafia. Blood and death will be your life as long as I live."

"Then so be it. I'll go where you go no matter how dark the path."

For a moment, Luca held his breath, then he gripped the back of my head and kissed me fiercely.

\*\*\*

I'd thought Luca would want to sleep with me again soon after our first time, but he didn't push me. Even though I tried to hide it, he could tell that I was sore for a few days after. He pleasured me with his tongue a few times, never even entering me with his finger, and I made him come with my mouth in turn.

I wasn't sure if he was waiting for an okay from me but when he came home one night a week after he'd taken my virginity, looking exhausted and angry, I wanted to make him feel better. After he'd showered, he stumbled toward the bed in only his boxers, his eyes filled with darkness.

"Bad day?" I whispered as he flung himself on the bed beside me. He lay on his back and stared up at the ceiling with empty eyes.

"Luca?"

"I lost three of my men today."

"What happened?"

"The Bratva attacked one of our warehouses." His lips thinned, chest heaving. "We'll make them pay. Our retribution will make them bleed."

"What can I do?" I said softly, my hand stroking his chest.

"I need you."

"Okay." I slid my nightgown over my head and pushed down my panties. I knelt beside Luca. He got rid of his boxers and his erection sprang free. Gripping my hips, he made me straddle his stomach. Nerves twisted my stomach. I'd hoped that for my second time Luca would still be on top. The thought of lowering myself on his length after how much it had hurt last time terrified me, but if Luca needed me, then I could do it. I cried out in surprise when Luca gripped my butt and hoisted me toward his face, so I was hovering over his mouth. He pressed me down and I screamed out in pleasure, my hands coming up to press against the headboard. This was more intense than anything Luca had ever done to me.

His tongue slipped into me deeply and he massaged my butt with firm fingertips. I peered down into Luca's eyes as he closed his mouth over my clit. I rocked my hips, pressing myself against his mouth. He growled. The vibration sent pleasure through me and I started rotating my hips, riding Luca's face. I closed my eyes, let my head fall back as Luca fucked me with his tongue again, humming all the while. And then I shattered, rocking against Luca's mouth and screaming his name. Somewhere deep inside a part of me wanted to be embarrassed but I was too aroused.

When my orgasm subsided, I tried to pull away from Luca's lips but he held me fast, his eyes burning into me as he licked me with slow strokes. It was too much, but he was relentless. With soft caresses and nudges from his tongue he slowly built my pleasure up again. My pants came quicker and I didn't try to escape anymore, instead I let Luca move my hips back and forth as he licked me. I was seconds away from my second orgasm. Without warning he pulled back and in one fluid motion he flicked me on my back and knelt between my legs, his erection pressed against my entrance.

I tensed up but Luca didn't enter. He bowed his head so he could suck my nipple into his mouth and rubbed the tip of his erection back and forth over my clit. I mewed helplessly at the sensation. I'd been so close to coming before and could feel myself getting there again. Then he dipped only the tip into my opening. I gasped at the brief pain but he retreated quickly and slid his slick tip over my clit again. He did this over and over again until I was panting and so wet I could hear it, then he released my nipple with a pop and brought his face up to mine. His tip slipped into my opening but this time he didn't retreat.

Slowly he slid into me all the way, never taking his eyes off me. I bit my lip to stifle a sound. It wasn't as painful as last time but still uncomfortable. I felt too stretched, too full. Luca cupped the back of my head and began moving. My breath hitched despite the slow pace but Luca didn't falter. He slid in and out at an excruciatingly slow and gentle rhythm until my breath stopped catching in my throat. He sped up but I clawed his arms and he slowed again. He lowered his mouth to my ear, his voice low and husky as he spoke. "I loved the taste of you, principessa. I loved how you rode my fucking mouth. I loved my tongue in you. I love your pussy and your tits, and I love that you're all mine." Luca kept up his steady thrusting as he whispered into my ear. And I forgot about the dull pain, and moaned. Nothing was sexier than Luca talking dirty to me in his deep baritone.

Luca kept talking and through the discomfort I could feel an orgasm building. Luca sneaked his hand between us and found my clit, rubbing frantically as he thrust into me. He sped up a bit, and I whimpered from both pain and pleasure. Luca didn't slow. He was panting, his skin slick with sweat as he fought for control. I could see on his face how his grip on it was fading but he didn't lose it. I moaned as he slid deeper into me than before. Pleasure radiated through my body.

"Come for me, Aria," he rasped, increasing the pressure on my clit. Another spike of pleasure mixed with pain slammed through me and I fell apart, gasping and moaning as my orgasm rocked my body. Luca growled and thrust harder. I clung to him, fingers digging into his shoulders as he approached his own peak. With a guttural groan, Luca tensed above me and I could feel him release into me. I moaned at how full and stretched I felt. Luca kept thrusting until I could feel him soften. He pulled out but stayed on top of me, his weight supported on his forearms. "Was I too rough?" he asked thickly.

"No, it was okay." I didn't dare ask how much harder he could go.

He kissed the corner of my mouth, then my lower lip until he dipped his tongue into me for a delicious kiss. We kissed for a long time, our slick bodies pressed against each other. I wasn't sure how long we lay like that, kissing, but eventually I could feel Luca getting hard again.

My eyes grew wide in surprise. "So soon? I thought men needed time to rest."

Luca laughed, a deep sexy sound. "Not with your naked body beneath me." He kneaded my butt. "How sore are you?"

Too sore, but the way he rubbed his erection lightly against my folds I couldn't say it. "Not too sore."

Luca gave me a look that made it clear he recognized the lie but he rolled on his back, taking me with him. I straddled his abs. He must have seen how nervous I was because he stroked my sides gently. "Take your time. You are in control."

He rocked his hips, rubbing his length over my butt cheeks.

"I want you in control," I admitted.

Luca's eyes darkened. "Don't say something like that to a man like me." But he gripped my hips and positioned me above his erection. From this vantage point he looked even bigger. He rubbed his tip in small circles over my clit as his other hand trailed up toward my breast and cupped it. He lined himself up with my opening before grabbing my hips and slowly guiding me down. When he was almost all the way in, I paused, catching my breath. I lay my palms flat against his chest as I tried to get used to the new position. He felt bigger and my muscles clenched tightly around his erection. Luca gritted his teeth. He ran his hands up my torso and cupped my breasts again, twirling my nipples between his fingers. I moaned and made small rocking motions with my hips. Luca pressed his thumb against my clit and flicked, then as I moaned he pushed me all the way down to the base of his erection.

I cried out in surprise more than pain and froze, exhaling slowly to get over the feeling of utter fullness.

"Aria," Luca rasped. I met his gaze. A hint of uncertainty flickered in his eyes.

I forced my lips into a smile. "Give me a moment."

He nodded, his hands resting lightly on my waist as he watched me. I released another breath, then shifted my hips experimentally. There was a twinge but there was also pleasure. "Help me?" I whispered, gazing at him through my lashes.

He clasped my waist, his fingers splaying across my butt and guided me into a slow rhythm of rocking and rotating. It was exhilarating to feel the strength of his body beneath my hands, to feel his pectoral muscles flex under my fingertips but even better was the look in his eyes as he watched me on top of him. The hunger and admiration mixed with another emotion I didn't dare to guess. Luca's chest heaved under my palms, his breath coming faster as he started thrusting upwards, driving himself into me harder and faster. His

278

thumb flicked back and forth over my clit as he drove into me. I cried out. Luca gripped my hips in a bruising grip and thrust faster. I threw my head back, riding through my orgasm as I felt Luca tense beneath me and release into me with a low moan.

I shivered helplessly on top of him as I came down from my high. I slumped forward on Luca's chest and pressed my lips to his. His heart pounded against my breasts. He slung his arms around my back and pressed me against him tightly.

"I won't lose you," he growled, startling me.

"You won't."

"The Bratva is closing in. How can I protect you?"

Why would the Bratva have any interest in me? "You will find a way."

# CHAPTER FIFTEEN

A couple of weeks had passed and sex got better every time we did it. I had a feeling Luca was still holding back quite a bit but I didn't mind. Sometimes I wondered if maybe he needed the gentle lovemaking as much as I did after all the stress he went through with the Bratva.

Lovemaking? No matter how much I tried to ignore my feelings, I knew I loved Luca. Maybe it was natural to fall in love with the person you were married to, the person you shared intimacy with. I wasn't sure why I had fallen for Luca despite my best intentions before our marriage not to let him into my heart, I only knew that I had. I knew what men like Luca thought of love. I hadn't told him about my feelings, even though a few times the words had been on the tip of my tongue after we'd lain in each other's arms, sweaty and sated after sex. I knew Luca wouldn't say it back and I didn't want to make myself vulnerable like that.

I watched the sun set over New York from my position in the lounge chair on the roof terrace. Romero was inside, reading a sports magazine on the sofa. A few times I'd considered asking Luca to stop Romero's constant presence. Nothing could happen to me in our penthouse but then I couldn't go through with it. I would have felt more alone without Romero in the apartment, even if we didn't talk all that much. Marianna only came in around lunch time to clean and prepare lunch and dinner, and Luca was gone most days. I still hadn't met any of the women from the Familia for coffee. After Cosima's betrayal I really wasn't keen on meeting more of Luca's family anyway.

My phone vibrated on the small table. I snatched it up, seeing Gianna's name flash on the screen. Happiness burst in my chest. We had only talked this morning, but it wasn't unusual for my sister to call more than once per day and I didn't mind.

The moment I heard her voice, I sat up, my heart pounding in my chest like crazy.

"Aria," she whispered, her voice thick with tears.

"Gianna, what happened? What's going on? Are you hurt?"

"Father's giving me to Matteo."

I didn't understand, couldn't. "What do you mean he's giving you to Matteo?" My voice shook and tears already burnt in my eyes as I listened to Gianna's heart-wrenching sobs.

"Salvatore Vitiello spoke to Father and told him that Matteo wanted to marry me. And Father agreed!"

I couldn't breathe. I'd worried that Matteo wouldn't let Gianna get away with her rudeness toward him. He was a man who didn't like to be refused, but how could Father have agreed? "Did Father say why? I don't understand. I'm already in New York. He didn't need to marry you off to the Familia too."

I stood, couldn't sit still anymore. I started pacing the roof, trying to calm my racing pulse with low breaths.

"I don't know why. Maybe Father wants to punish me for saying what I think. He knows how much I despise our men, and how much I hate Matteo. He wants to see me suffer."

I wanted to disagree but I wasn't sure Gianna was wrong. Father thought women needed to be put in their place and what better way to do that with Gianna than bind her to a man like Matteo. Behind his grins lurked something dark and angry, and I had a feeling Gianna wouldn't have the sense not to provoke him until he lost it.

"Oh, Gianna. I'm so sorry. Maybe I can tell Luca and he can change Matteo's mind."

"Aria, don't be naïve. Luca knew all along. He's Matteo's brother and the future Capo. Something like that isn't decided without him being involved."

I knew she was right, but I didn't want to accept it. Why hadn't Luca told me about this? "When did they make the decision?"

"A few weeks ago, even before I came to visit."

My heart clenched. Luca had slept with me, had made me trust him and love him and hadn't bothered to tell me that my sister was being sold to his brother.

"I can't believe him!" I whispered harshly. Romero was watching me through the windows, already getting up from the sofa. "I'm going to kill him. He knows how much I love you. He knows I wouldn't have allowed it. I would have done anything to prevent the agreement."

Gianna was silent on the other end. "Don't get in trouble because of me. It's too late anyway. New York and Chicago shook hands on it. It's a made deal, and Matteo won't let me out of his clutches."

"I want to help you, but I don't know how."

"I love you, Aria. The only thing that stops me from cutting my wrists right now is the knowledge that my marriage to Matteo means I'll live in New York with you."

Fear crushed my heart. "Gianna, you are the strongest person I know. Promise me you won't do anything stupid. If you hurt yourself, I couldn't live with myself."

"You are much stronger than me, Aria. I have a big mouth and flashy bravado, but you are resilient. You married Luca, you live with a man like him. I don't think I could have done it. I don't think I can."

"We'll figure it out, Gianna."

The elevator doors opened and Luca stepped into our apartment. His eyes darted from Romero to me, his brows drawing together.

"He's here. I'll call you tomorrow." I hung up as fury burnt through me. I hadn't thought I could ever hate Luca again, not even for a moment but in this second I wanted to hurt him. I stormed inside, my hands balled to fists as I headed toward Luca. He didn't move a muscle, only watched me with calm scrutiny. That calm more than anything else fueled my rage. I wasn't sure what he thought I was going to do, but it wasn't attack that was obvious from his reaction. My fists hammered his chest as hard as I could. Shock flashed across Luca's face, his entire body exploding with tension. From the corner of my eye I saw Romero take a step in our direction, obviously unsure if he was supposed to do something. He was my bodyguard but Luca was his boss. Of course, Luca didn't have trouble handling me. After a moment, he gripped both of my wrists in his hand. I hated that he could overpower me so easily. "Aria, what—"

He didn't get to finish because I rammed my knee upward and only his quick reflexes prevented me from hitting my goal. The sound of Gianna's sobs rang in my mind, made me lose whatever rationality I had.

"Get out," Luca ordered sharply. Romero did without protest. Luca's blazing eyes met mine but I was past being scared. I would die for Gianna. I tried another kick and graced Luca's groin this time. He snarled and pushed me down on the sofa, my legs pinned down by his knees and my arms pushed above my head. "For god's sake, Aria. What's gotten into you?"

I glared. "I know about Gianna and Matteo," I spat, and then I lost it completely and I started crying, big gasping sobs raking my body. Luca released my wrists and sat back so I could move my legs. He regarded me like I was a creature he would never understand.

"That's what this is about?" He sounded incredulous.

"Of course you don't understand, because you never loved anyone more than your own life. You can't possibly understand how it is to feel your own heart breaking at the thought of the person you love getting hurt. I would die for the people I love."

His eyes were hard and cold as he stood. "You are right. I don't understand." The cold mask was back. I hadn't seen it directed at me in weeks.

I wiped my eyes and stood as well. "Why didn't you tell me? You've known for weeks."

"Because I knew you wouldn't like it."

I shook my head. "You knew I'd be mad at you and you didn't want to ruin your chances of fucking me." I didn't even blush, even though I never used the word.

Luca became rigid. "Of course I wanted to fuck you. But I got the impression you enjoyed our *fucking sessions*."

I wanted to hurt him. He was so cold. Of course it had always been about taking what was his, about claiming my body. He didn't give a shit about me, or anyone. "And you worried I wasn't a good enough actress to fool everyone after our little trick in our wedding night. I even fooled you." I let out an ugly laugh. "I made you believe I actually enjoyed it."

Something flickered in Luca's eyes, something that made me want to take back my words for a moment, but then his mouth pulled into a cruel smile. "Don't lie to me. I've fucked enough whores to know an orgasm when I see one."

I flinched as if he'd hit me. Had he just compared me to his whores? I said the ugliest thing I could think of. "Some woman even experience an orgasm when they're being raped. It's not because they're enjoying it. It's their body's way of coping."

For a long time Luca didn't say anything. His nostrils flared and his chest heaved and his hands were clenched to fists. He looked like he wanted to kill me on the spot. Then the scariest thing happened, the anger slipped off his face. His expression became emotionless, his eyes as smooth and impenetrable as steel. "Your sister should be happy that Matteo wants her. Few men can stand her gab."

"God that's the reason, isn't it?" I said in disgust. "It's because she told him that he'd never get her hot body that day in the hotel. He didn't like it. He couldn't bear that she was immune to his creepy charm."

"She shouldn't have challenged him. Matteo is a determined hunter. He gets what he wants." Still not a flicker of emotion, not even in Luca's voice. It was like he was made from ice.

"He gets what he wants? It's not hunting if he forces her into marriage by asking my father for her hand. That is cowardice."

"It doesn't matter. They're getting married." He turned his back to me, as if he was dismissing me.

Luca didn't get it. He couldn't. He didn't know Gianna as well as I did. She wouldn't go into this union quietly like I had. I stormed toward the elevator. "Aria, what the fuck are you doing?"

I was in the elevator before Luca could reach it and was on my way one floor down. I stepped out into Matteo's apartment. It was basically a mirror image of our own, except that it wasn't a duplex. Matteo had sat in an armchair, listening to some kind of crappy rap music when he saw me. He rose, eying me cautiously as he came toward me. "What are you doing here?"

I pushed my palms against his chest when he stopped in front of me. "Take your proposal back. Tell my father you don't want Gianna."

Matteo laughed. "Why would I? I want her. I always get what I was want. Gianna shouldn't have played games with the big boys."

I lost it and slapped him across the face. My stupid Italian temperament. I usually reigned it in, better than my other siblings at least, but not today. He gripped my arm, shoved me back so my spine collided painfully with the wall, and trapped me between it and his body. I gasped. "You are lucky that you are my brother's wife."

The elevator bling-ed as it stopped and opened. "Let her go," Luca growled, stepping out. Matteo back away at once and gave me a cold smile.

Luca walked up to me, eyes scanning my body before facing his brother. "You won't do that again."

"Then teach her manners. I won't let her hit me again." Teach her manners? His marriage to Gianna would end in an utter catastrophe.

Luca's voice dropped an octave. "You won't touch my wife again, Matteo. You are my brother and I'd take a bullet for you, but if you do that again, you'll have to live with the consequences." They faced each other and for a moment I worried they'd pull knives and fight each other. That wasn't what I'd intended. I knew how much Luca cared about his brother, more than he cared about me anyway. Matteo was the only person Luca trusted. For a while I'd thought I might be that person, but if that were the case, today would have gone very differently. I knew his protecting me was a power game and not about emotions. By touching me, Matteo had shown disrespect toward Luca and of course Luca couldn't let that slide.

"I won't hit you again, Matteo," I ground out, though the words tasted foul in my mouth. "I shouldn't have done it."

Both men turned to me in surprise. Matteo relaxed his stance. Luca didn't.

"I'm sorry if I hurt or scared you," Matteo said. I couldn't tell if he meant it or not. He had the emotionless mask down just like his brother.

"You didn't."

Luca smirked, then he stepped up to me and pulled me against him possessively. Our eyes met and as if he remembered our earlier words his smirk disappeared and his lips tightened. He didn't release me but his hold on me loosened.

I turned away from him, not able to bear his expression any longer, and faced Matteo. "Don't marry, Gianna," I tried again, and Luca's grip on my waist tightened in warning. I ignored him. "She doesn't want to marry you."

"You didn't want to marry Luca either and here you are," Matteo said with his shark grin.

"Gianna isn't like me. She won't come to terms with an arranged marriage."

Luca dropped his hand from my waist.

"She will become my wife the moment she turns eighteen. No power in this universe will stop me from making her mine."

"You disgust me. You all do," I said. With that I stepped back into the elevator. Luca didn't follow. He didn't even watch me to see if I was returning to our apartment. He knew I wouldn't go anywhere. Even if I still wanted to run, I couldn't. My heart belonged to him even if he didn't have a heart that he could give me in turn.

# CHAPTER SIXTEEN

I twisted and turned, not able to fall asleep. I wasn't used to being alone in bed. Even though, Luca and I had barely spoken in the last three days since our fight and hadn't had sex, we'd always ended up in each other's arms during the night. Of course, the moment we woke we moved apart. I missed Luca's closeness. I missed talking to him, missed his kisses, his touch, his hot tongue between my legs. I sighed as I became wet. I wouldn't give in. How much longer could Luca go without sex anyway?

What if he wasn't? What if he fucked Grace again? She was supposedly in England but who knew if that was the truth. Or maybe he'd found a new woman to fuck. My eyes found the clock. It was almost two in the night. A heavy weight settled on my chest. Was Luca giving up on our marriage that easily?

Why not? He'd gotten what he wanted. He'd claimed my body. It wasn't like I was the only person who could give him what he wanted.

A bang sounded downstairs, followed by deep voices. Romero was one of them, the other was Luca. I slipped out of bed and quickly rushed out of the bedroom in my nightgown. I froze on the staircase. The lights were out but the moon and the surrounding skyscrapers provided enough light for me to see what was going on. Luca had Romero in a chokehold. I took another step down and Luca's eyes shot toward me, furious and wild. The monster was back. His arms were covered in blood. Romero stopped struggling when he realized Luca was too strong.

"I would never betray the Familia," Romero choked out, then coughed. "I'm loyal. I'd die for you. If I were a traitor, Aria wouldn't be here, safe and unscathed. She'd be in the hands of the Bratva."

Luca loosened his hold and Romero fell to his knees, gasping for breath. I walked down the remaining steps, ignoring Romero shaking his head at me. What was going on? Luca had never been this unhinged.

"Out now," he snarled at Romero. When Romero didn't move, Luca grabbed him by the collar and dragged him into the elevator. Before the doors slid shut, Romero's worried gaze settled on me. Luca jabbed a code into the panel beside the elevator that deactivated it and stopped people from coming into our apartment, then he turned to me. Not only his arms but his shirt too were covered in blood. I didn't see any bullet holes in his shirt or pants.

"Are you okay?" I said, but even my whisper felt too loud in the silence.

I approached Luca slowly as his eyes followed my movement like a tiger would watch the antelope. A strange flicker of excitement filled me. Despite what I'd witnessed, I knew Luca wouldn't really hurt me. When I'd almost reached him, Luca stalked toward me and crashed his lips against mine. I gasped and he thrust his tongue into my mouth. His hands ripped at my nightgown, tearing it from my body. When it fluttered to the ground, he tore my thin lace panties off. His hungry gaze traveled over me, then he wrenched me toward him and bit into my throat, then my nipple. I gasped in pain and arousal. I should have run as Luca had told me a long time ago, but this side of him actually turned me on, and my arousal spoke louder than my fear, even when Luca pushed me toward the sofa and bent me over the backrest. His hand held my neck as his other hand slid between my folds. He pushed two fingers into me and found me wet and aching. I released a harsh breath as my walls clamped tightly around his fingers. He pulled them out. I heard him open his belt and unzip his pants, and I shivered with fear and excitement. Luca bit into my butt cheek then my lower back and shoulder blade before he shoved his entire length into me without warning.

I cried out, but Luca didn't hesitate, he pressed his chest against my back while he held me captive with one arm around my chest, and then he started pounding into me hard and fast. I bit down on my lip. It hurt but it felt also good. Every time he pushed into me, he hit a spot deep in me that sent sparks of pleasure through me. Luca reached down, his hot breath against my neck, and rubbed his fingers over my clit. I cried and gasped and whimpered. I could feel the tension building. The sound of Luca's pants and growls turned me on even more. His fingers twisted my nipple almost painfully and he bit down on the crook of my neck, and stars erupted before my vision as I exploded. I screamed Luca's name over and over again as I trembled in the wake of my orgasm but he didn't slow. He drove into me hard and fast, his fingers on my clit relentless as his breathing grew labored, and then I came again, shattered into thousand tiny pieces of pleasure. My legs crumbled but Luca pinned me against the backrest with his body. With a growl, he gripped my hips and fucked me even harder. I'd be bruised and sore tomorrow, but I couldn't bring myself to care. When he shuddered against me and bit the other side of my throat, I hung limply over the sofa. Too sated and exhausted to do anything as he came in me.

I thought it was over, but Luca lifted me off the backrest and lowered me to the ground. He shoved my legs as wide apart as they would go. I was oversensitive and couldn't possibly come again, but Luca's eyes pinned me with their intensity. He grasped my wrists and pushed my arms up above my head, then he rubbed two fingers along my folds, back and forth, before circling my opening and sliding them in inch by inch. My eyes rolled back in my head as he fingered me in a torturously slow way. My walls clamped around his fingers and I heard sounds coming from the back of my throat I didn't recognize. He didn't touch my clit, just fucked me with his fingers with an intense look on his face.

"Is this a fucking lie?" he asked roughly as he curled his fingers in me and made me gasp in pleasure. "Tell me Aria. Tell me you enjoy this as much as I do." The despair in his voice startled me.

He curled his fingers again and I whimpered. "Yes, Luca. I enjoy this."

He flicked my clit with his thumb and I arched off the ground, but he pulled his thumb away despite my mew of protest and kept fingering me. "So you lied? Why?"

He was driving me insane with need. I wanted him to touch my clit, wanted him to finger me faster, wanted him to fuck me. "Yes, I lied!" I squirmed in his hold, wanting to free my hands to reach for his cock. He was already growing hard and I wanted to convince him to stop my torture, but he was too strong and too relentless.

"Why?" he growled. He paused his fingers and I wanted to scream in frustration.

"I lied because I hate that I love you, because I hate that you can hurt me without ever laying a finger on me, because I hate myself for loving you even though you won't ever love me back." Luca released my wrists, eyes dark and questioning.

I didn't want to talk. I reached for his erection and gave it a hard squeeze. "Now fuck me."

He grabbed my legs and pulled me toward him, my feet pressed up against his shoulders, and then he slid into me in one hard stroke and I came around him, my muscles clenching around his cock so tightly that he grunted. He fucked me even harder and I scratched my fingers over the wooden floor as my eyes shut tightly. I was coming apart from pleasure and emotions. My back rubbed against the hard floor, I was sore and my legs were stiff but I came again when Luca hit his release, and then I passed out.

***

My entire body hurt. I groaned when I shifted and realized I was lying in our bed. Luca must have carried me upstairs last night. My eyes fluttered open and found Luca watching me with a strange look on his face.

"What did I do?" he asked in a harsh whisper.

I frowned, then looked down at myself. The blankets were pulled back, revealing the entire length of my body and the proof of last night's actions. There were finger-shaped bruises on my hips and wrists. My throat and shoulders were tender where Luca had marked me and my inner thighs were red from the friction. I looked like a mess. I sat up and winced from the sharp soreness between my legs. Yet I couldn't find it in me to regret anything. I didn't always want it this rough, but once in a while it was a nice change of pace.

"Aria, please tell me. Did I...?"

I searched his eyes, trying to figure out what he was talking about. Self-hatred flashed on his face and then I realized what he thought. "You don't remember?"

"I remember bits and pieces. I remember holding you down." His voice caught. He wasn't touching me. In fact he perched on the edge of the bed as far from me as possible. He looked exhausted and broken. "You didn't hurt me."

His eyes flickered to the bruises. "Don't lie to me."

I knelt and moved toward him even when he stiffened. "You were a bit rougher than usual but I wanted it. I enjoyed it."

Luca didn't say anything but I could tell he didn't believe me.

"No, really, Luca." I kissed his cheek and lowered my voice. "I came at least four times. I don't exactly remember everything. I passed out from sensatory overload." Relief washed away some of the darkness in Luca's eyes but I was surprised that he didn't tease me for my comment.

"I don't understand what got into you. You even attacked Romero."

"My father is dead."

I jerked. "What? How?"

"Last night. He had dinner at a small restaurant in Brooklyn when a sniper put a bullet into his head."

"What about your step-mother?"

"She wasn't there. He was with his mistress. She was shot too, probably because the Bratva thought she was his wife. Someone must have told them where to find him. Only very few people knew he went there. He was in disguise. Nobody could have recognized him. There has to be a traitor among us."

# CHAPTER SEVENTEEN

The sky over New York was hung with heavy clouds but it didn't rain. It fit the occasion. For the funeral of Salvatore Vitiello, the elite of New York, the Familia as well as the most important members of the Chicago Outfit had gathered on the cemetery. The perimeter around it had been closed off and most of the soldiers of the New York mafia were keeping guard to make sure the Bratva didn't disturb the funeral. A gathering of the most important members from both New York and Chicago at this time was a risk, but paying respect to the Capo dei Capi was more important.

Luca stood tall and stoic beside his father's grave. He was now the new Capo and he couldn't show a flicker of weakness, not even after the death of his father. Luca and his father hadn't been close in the traditional sense, but losing your parent, no matter how cruel and cold he'd been, always ripped a hole into you. I could tell that many of the older men in the Familia watched Luca with a calculating look in their eyes.

Luca didn't give any indication that he noticed but that was definitely an act. So soon after he'd come into power was the most dangerous time. I hadn't known Salvatore Vitiello very well and I wasn't sorry about that. For me the funeral meant only one thing: I got the chance to see my family again.

Gianna, Fabi and Lily stood with Father and Mother among the guests from the Chicago Outfit. They'd arrived this morning and I couldn't wait to spend some time with them. Every guest shook Luca's hand, clapped his shoulder and said a few words of comfort, most of them lies. How many of these men were waiting for a chance to rip the power from Luca's hands?

When it was my father's turn, I had to stop myself from attacking him for agreeing to marry Gianna off to Matteo. Instead I gritted my teeth and gave him a cold smile. Gianna pointedly avoided Matteo's eyes. She'd lost weight and it broke my heart to see her so hopeless.

I was glad when the funeral was over. The men had a meeting scheduled for the evening to discuss the rising threat of the Russians. In our world there wasn't time to mourn the dead for long. Chicago and New York needed to figure out a way to stop the Bratva before another Capo lost his life. And that would be either Luca, or Dante Cavallaro.

***

Luca wanted me out of New York, so he sent me to the Vitiello mansion in the Hamptons. Gianna, Lily and Fabi were allowed to accompany me for the night before they'd have to leave for Chicago tomorrow evening. I had a feeling Father hoped I would talk some sense into Gianna about her arranged marriage with Matteo. The engagement party was planned for the beginning of November, so Gianna didn't have all that long to come to terms with it. Mother stayed with Father in Manhattan, but they sent Umberto with us. He, Cesare and Romero were supposed to keep us safe.

We arrived at the mansion around dinnertime and the staff had already prepared a meal for us. My heart swelled with happiness as Lily, Fabi, Gianna and I settled around the long dining table, but it was dimmed by the fact that our three bodyguards discussed the Russian threat in hushed voices and by Gianna's refusal to eat more than two bites. I didn't want to discuss her betrothal to Matteo with everyone there. Later when they'd gone to bed, Gianna and I would have enough time for that.

Fabi was the only one who kept the conversation on our side of the table going as he told me excitedly about the collection of knives Father had given him. Lily was busy sneaking admiring glances at Romero who was completely oblivious to her pining.

After dinner, we moved on to the loggia overlooking the ocean. The night sky out here twinkled with stars. In New York you rarely got a glimpse at them. Cesare had gone off to do God knows what, probably check the security system, and Umberto and Romero had settled in the living room; from there they could watch us without overhearing our conversation. Fabi lay curled up beside Lily, fast asleep, while she was typing something on her phone while checking out Romero occasionally.

"Do you want to talk?" I whispered to Gianna who sat beside me, legs pressed up against her chest. She shook her head. It felt as if a rift had grown between us since she'd gotten the news about her betrothal and I didn't know why. "Gianna, please."

"There's nothing to talk about."

"Maybe it's not as bad as you think." She gave me an incredulous look but I kept talking. "When I found out I had to marry Luca, I was terrified, but I've come to terms with it. Luca and I are getting along better than I thought possible."

Gianna glared. "I'm not like you, Aria. You're eager to please him, to do anything he says. I'm not like that. I won't submit to anyone."

I flinched. Gianna had never lashed out at me like that.

She jumped up. I tried to catch her arm but she shook me off. "Leave me alone. I can't talk to you right now." She whirled around and stormed off toward the beach. I stood, unsure if I should follow her, but I knew she wouldn't listen to me when she was like that. Umberto stepped outside. I raised a hand. "No, give her a few minutes to herself. She's upset."

Umberto nodded, then his eyes darted to Fabi. "I should take him to bed."

I was about to nod when an ear-splitting alarm broke the silence, but it stopped a few seconds later. Fabi's eyes were wide as he clung to Lily, both were looking at me as if I knew what was going on. Romero stormed toward us, two guns drawn, when a red dot appeared on Umberto's forehead. I cried out but it was too late. There was a shot and Umberto's head flung back, blood splattering everywhere. Lily started screaming, and I still couldn't move. I stared at the dead eyes of Umberto. A man I'd known all my life.

Romero flung himself at me and we landed on the ground as a second bullet blasted the glass door, sending shards flying.

"What's going on?" I screamed, hysteria rocking my body.

"The Bratva," was all Romero said as he dragged me toward the living room. I struggled against him. Lily and Fabi cowered beside a lounge chair, still in shooting range of the sniper. "Get them!"

But Romero ignored my command and he was too strong for me. He shoved me against a wall inside the living room, his grip biting into my skin, his eyes hard and wild. "Stay here. Don't move."

"Lily and Fabi," I gasped.

He nodded, then ducked and rushed back outside. I was shaking all over. Romero returned with my sister and brother, who clung to him desperately. I wrapped my arms around them tightly the moment they were at my side. And then my world tilted.

"Gianna," I whispered.

Romero didn't hear me. He was shouting into his phone. "Where? How many?" His face paled. "Fuck." He turned to me, and his expression made my stomach drop. "The Russians are on the property. Too many for us. I'll take you to the panic room in the basement where we'll wait until backup arrives."

He gripped my arm but I pulled away. "Take Fabi and Lily there. I need to warn Gianna."

"You are my responsibility," Romero hissed. Somewhere in the house glass shattered. Shots rang out.

"I don't care. I won't come with you. You will do as I say. Take them to the panic room. If something happens to Lily or Fabi, I will kill myself and nothing you or Luca or any other power in this world can do will change that. I want you to protect them. Keep them safe. That's all that matters to me."

"You should come with us."

I shook my head. "I have to find Gianna."

"Luca will be here soon."

I knew that wasn't true. "Go now!"

We stared at each other, then finally he turned to my siblings. "Stay down and follow my orders."

Male voices screamed something in Russian, then more shots were fired. Cesare wouldn't be able to keep them at bay for long if the number of voices were any indication.

Romero shoved a gun at me. I grabbed it, then I ducked and ran outside. Umberto's blood covered the stone tiles but I didn't look at his body. I hurried down the slope toward the bay when I noticed the vibrating of my phone. I pulled it out and pressed it to my ear as I scanned the beach for Gianna.

"Aria?" Luca's worried voice sounded. "Are you safe?"

"They killed Umberto," was the first thing out of my mouth.

"Where are you?"

"Searching for Gianna."

"Aria, where's Romero? Why isn't he taking you to the panic room?"

"I have to find Gianna."

"Aria," Luca sounded desperate. "The Bratva wants you. Get into the panic room. I'm taking the helicopter. I'll be there in twenty minutes. I'm already on the way."

Luca would need more than twenty minutes even with a helicopter and he wouldn't be able to take as many of his men with him, so there was no saying how long it would take him to fight his way into the mansion. There was the possibility that he would fail.

Gianna came running toward me, eyes wide.

"I can't talk anymore," I whispered.

"Aria—"

"What's happening?" Gianna asked, as she stumbled against me.

"The Bratva." I pulled her toward the dock where the boat was anchored. It would be safer to hide there than to go back inside and look for the panic room. The boards of the dock groaned under our weight as we walked toward the boat. But then Lily's scream pierced the night and I froze. Gianna and I exchanged a glance. Without a word, we turned around and hurried back toward the house.

My heart hammered in my chest when we arrived on the loggia. The living room was deserted. I knelt beside Umberto and took his knives even as I shuddered. I handed one of them to Gianna and put the switchblade into my back pocket.

"Come on," I whispered. I wasn't even sure what Gianna and I were going to do once we got inside. I'd shot a gun once and I had handled a knife only when I'd sparred with Luca, that didn't bode well in a fight against Russian mobsters. Yet I knew I wouldn't be able to live with myself if I didn't find Lily and Fabi.

Gianna and I crept inside. It was dark. Someone must have turned the lights off in the entire house. I held my breath but it was terrifyingly quiet. I approached the door that led into the lobby when an arm shot out and wrapped around my waist. I cried out, struggled, tried to angle the gun toward my attacker, but he twisted my wrist. Pain shot through my arm and the gun tumbled from my fingers. Gianna gasped behind me. I kicked out. A deep voice snarled at me in Russian. Oh God. My foot collided with his shin. He pushed me away but before I could catch my balance, his fist collided with my lips. My vision turned black and I dropped to my knees as blood filled my mouth and trickled over my chin, the warm salty taste making bile rise into my throat.

Fingers twisted into my hair and I was wrenched to my feet, crying out from the pain in my scalp. My attacker didn't care. He dragged me into the lobby by my hair. I could see Gianna in the arms of another tall man. She was unconscious, a bruise already forming on her forehead.

I was thrown to the ground in front of jeans-clad legs and quickly peered up into a pockmarked face and cold blue eyes. "What's your name, whore?" he asked in heavily accented English. Didn't he recognize me? I supposed I looked different with blood all over my face. I stared back at him defiantly. He kicked me in the stomach and I toppled over, gasping for breath. "What's your name?"

My eyes darted to a body to my right. Cesare. He was making gurgling noises, clutching at a bleeding wound in his stomach. I didn't see Lily, Fabi or Romero anywhere and I hoped they'd made it to the panic room. At least, they would survive.

A hand gripped my chin and wrenched my head up. "Will you tell me your name or do I have to make Igor hurt her?" He nodded toward Gianna who lay on her side on the marble floor, blinking dazedly.

"Aria," I said quietly.

"As in Aria Vitiello?" The man asked with a cruel smile.

I nodded. There was no use denying it. He said something in Russian and the men guffawed. My skin crawled from the way they were looking at me.

"Where are the others? Your shadow and the children?"

It took me a moment to realize whom he meant with shadow. "I don't know," I said.

Igor kicked Gianna. She screamed. Her eyes met mine and I could see she didn't want me to say anything, but how could I watch them hurt her?

Voices and shooting carried over to us from outside. The leader of the Russians grabbed me and pulled my back flush against his chest before pressing a blade against my throat.

Fear paralyzed my body as I listened to the sound of fighting. I was dragged backwards closer to the living room. Igor was yanking Gianna by her hair. She didn't seem capable of standing. Another Russian mobster was flung back as a bullet tore through his throat. "We have your wife Vitiello. If you want to see her in one piece you better stop fighting and drop your weapons."

Luca walked in, a gun in each hand. Matteo was a step behind him.

"So this is your wife, Vitiello?" the man said, his breath hot against my neck. I squirmed in his hold but he held me in a death grip. The blade sliced into my skin and I became still.

Luca's face was a mask of fury as he stared at my capturer. Matteo twisted the knives in his hands over and over again, his eyes flickering to Gianna's trembling form on the ground. Cesare had stopped gurgling. This night could very well end with all of us drowning in our own blood.

"Let her go, Vitali," Luca snarled.

Vitali grabbed my throat. "I don't think so."

I could barely breathe in his hold, but all I could think about was that I could lose everyone I loved tonight. I hoped they'd kill me first. I couldn't bear the thought of watching everyone die.

"You took something that belongs to us, Vitiello, and now I have something that belongs to you." Vitali licked my cheek and I almost threw up. "I want to know where it is."

Luca took a step forward, then froze as Vitali raised the knife to my throat again. "Put your guns down or I'll cut her throat."

Vitali was stupid when he thought Luca would do that, but then I watched in horror as Luca dropped his guns on the floor.

"Your wife tastes delicious. I wonder if she tastes this delicious everywhere." He turned me around so I was facing him. His foul breath hit my face. From the corner of my eye, I could see Luca watching me, but I wished he'd look away. I didn't want him to see this. Vitali's lips came closer. I was sure I'd throw up.

I tried to lean back but he laughed nastily and gripped my hip but I barely noticed, because my shifting had made the switchblade dig into my butt. As Vitali trailed his tongue over my chin, I slipped my hand into my back pocket, pulled the knife out, released the blade and rammed it into his thigh.

He cried out, stumbling back and then all hell broke loose. Luca practically flew through the room and pulled me against him as he sliced Vitali's throat open from one ear to the other. The man's head tilted back, blood spurting out, then he toppled over. Bullets tore through the air, and there was screaming. The ground was slippery with blood and only Luca's firm grasp on my arm kept me upright. He must have dropped the knife at some point because he was shooting bullet after bullet out of a sleek black gun with a silencer. I picked up a gun lying in a pool of blood. It was slippery in my hand but its weight felt good. Suddenly Romero was there too. My eyes tried to find Gianna but she was gone from her spot on the floor.

Luca shot another enemy and reached down for the gun of the dead guy as his own was out of bullets, when one of the Russian mobsters to our right pointed his gun at Luca. I cried out in warning and at the same time stumbled forward and aimed my gun at the guy and fired. I didn't even think about it. I'd sworn to myself I wouldn't watch anyone I loved die tonight even if meant I had to die first.

The bullet hit my shoulder and my world exploded with pain. My shot hit the guy in the head and he dropped to the ground dead. Luca ripped me to the side, but my vision turned black.

When I came to my senses again, Luca was cradling me in his arms. It was silent around us except for someone's whimpers. It took me a moment to realize they were my own and then the pain sliced through me and I wished I'd stayed unconscious but I needed to know if everyone was alright. "You okay?" I croaked.

Luca trembled against me. "Yes," he gritted out. "But you aren't." He was pressing down on my shoulder. That probably explained the pain. The back and front of my shirt were slick with a warm liquid.

"What about Gianna, Lily and Fabi?" I whispered even as darkness wanted to claim me again.

"Fine," Gianna called from somewhere. She sounded far away, or maybe that was my imagination. Luca slid his hands under me and stood. I cried out in pain, tears leaking out of my eyes. The lobby was crowded with our men.

"I'll take you to the hospital," Luca said.

"Luca," Matteo said in warning. "Let the Doc handle it. He's been taking care of our business for years."

"No," Luca snarled. "Aria needs proper care. She's lost too much blood." I could see a few of Luca's men glancing our way before pretending they were busy again. He was their Capo. He couldn't show weakness, not even for me.

"I can do a blood transfusion," came a deep, soothing voice. The Doc. He was over sixty with snow-white hair and a kind face.

Luca's grip on me tightened. I clutched at his arm. "It's okay, Luca. Let him take care of me. I don't want you to take me to a hospital. It's too dangerous."

Luca's eyes showed hesitation, then slowly he nodded. "Follow me!" He carried me toward the staircase but I lost consciousness again.

***

I woke in a soft bed, feeling battered and foggy. My eyes peeled open. Gianna lay beside me, sleeping. It was light outside, so several hours must have passed. There was a huge bruise on her forehead, but I supposed I looked worse. We were alone and disappointment filled me. I tried to sit up and was rewarded with a fierce throbbing in my shoulder. Glancing down, I found my upper arm and shoulder wrapped with bandages.

Gianna stirred, then she gave me a relieved smile. "You're awake."

"Yeah," I whispered. My mouth felt as if it was filled with cotton.

"Luca has been guarding your bed almost all night, but Matteo forced him to come out and help him with the Russian mobsters they caught."

"They caught some?"

"Yeah, they're trying to extract information from them."

My lips twisted, but I couldn't bring myself to feel sorry for them. "How are you?"

"Better than you," Gianna said, then she closed her eyes. "I'm sorry I lashed out at you yesterday. I would have hated myself forever if that had been the last thing I said to you."

I shook my head. "It's okay."

She hopped off the bed. "I better tell Luca you're awake, or he'll rip my head off."

She disappeared and a couple of minutes later, Luca stepped in. He stood in the doorway, his expression unreadable as he let his gaze wander over me. Then he stepped up to the bed and pressed a kiss against my forehead. "Do you need morphine?"

My shoulder felt like it was on fire. "Yeah."

Luca turned toward the nightstand and picked up a syringe. He took my arm and slid the needle into the crook of my arm. When he was done, he threw the syringe into the trash but didn't let go of my hand. I linked our fingers. "Did we lose someone?"

"A few. Cesare and a couple soldiers," he said, then he paused. "And Umberto."

"I know. I saw him get shot." My stomach churned violently. It still felt surreal. I'd have to write Umberto's wife a letter, but I needed a clear head for that.

"What did that guy Vitali mean when he said you had something that belonged to him?"

Luca's lips thinned. "We intercepted one of their drug deliveries. But that's not important now."

"What is important then?"

"That I almost lost you. That I saw you get shot," Luca said in an odd voice, but his expression gave nothing away. "You are lucky the bullet only hit your shoulder. The Doc says it'll heal completely and you will be able to use your arm like before."

I tried a smile, but the morphine was making me sluggish. I blinked, trying to stay awake. Luca leaned down. "Don't do that ever again."

"What?" I breathed.

"Taking a bullet for me."

# CHAPTER EIGHTEEN

Taking a shower was a struggle. I had to cover my bandages with a waterproof cap, which was a major hassle, but the feel of the warm water washing away the blood and sweat was worth it. Gianna, Lily and Fabi had left less than one hour ago. Father had insisted they leave. Not that they were much safer in Chicago. The Bratva was closing in on the Outfit as well. At least, I'd had them with me a day longer than planned. They'd kept me entertained as I lay in bed while Luca had to take care of everything. As Capo he couldn't abandon his soldiers. He needed to show them he had a plan of action.

I was already feeling so much better. Maybe that was the lingering effect of the painkillers I'd taken two hours ago. I stepped out of the shower and awkwardly put on my panties. I could move both of my arms, but the Doc had said I should use my left arm as little as possible. Putting on the nightgown proved more difficult. I'd managed to slip one strap over my injured shoulder when I stepped back into the bedroom where I found Luca sitting on the bed. He got up immediately.

"Done with business?" I asked.

He nodded. He came toward me and slid the second strap into place, then he led me toward the bed and made me sit down. We hadn't been able to talk alone since our first conversation and then I'd been high on morphine.

"I'm fine," I said again because he looked like he needed to hear it. He didn't say anything for a long time before he suddenly knelt before me and pressed his face against my stomach. "I could have lost you two days ago."

I shivered. "But you didn't."

He peered up at me. "Why did you do this? Why did you take a bullet for me?"

"Do you really not know why?" I whispered.

He became very still, but didn't say anything.

"I love you, Luca." I knew saying out loud was a risk, but I'd thought I'd die a couple days ago, so this was nothing.

Luca brought his face up to mine and cupped my cheeks. "You love me." He said it as if I'd told him the skies were green, or that the sun revolved around the earth, or that fire was cold to the touch. As if what I'd said didn't make sense, as if it didn't fit into his view of the world. "You shouldn't love me, Aria. I'm not someone who should be loved. People fear me, they hate me, they respect me, they admire me, but they don't love me. I'm a killer. I'm good at killing. Better probably than at anything else, and I don't regret it. Fuck, sometimes I even enjoy it. That's a man you want to love?"

"It's not a matter of want, Luca. It's not like I could choose to stop loving you."

He nodded, as if that explained a lot. "And you hate that you love me. I remember you saying it before."

"No. Not anymore. I know you aren't a good man. I've always known it, and I don't care. I know I should. I know I should lie awake at night hating myself for being okay with my husband being the boss of one of the most brutal and deadliest crime organizations in the States. But I don't. What does that make me?" I paused, staring down at my hands, the hands that had cradled a gun two days ago, at the finger that had pulled the trigger without hesitation, without a twitch or tremor. "And I killed a man and I don't feel sorry. Not one bit. I would do it again." I glanced up at Luca. "What does that make me, Luca? I'm a killer like you."

"You did what you had to. He deserved to die."

"There's not one of us who doesn't deserve death. We probably deserve it more than most."

"You are good, Aria. You are innocent. I forced you into this."

"You didn't Luca. I was born into this world. I chose to stay in this world." The words of my wedding day popped into my mind. "Being born into our world means being born with blood on your hands. With every breath we take sin is engraved deeper into our skin."

"You don't have a choice. There's no way to escape our world. You didn't have a choice in marrying me either. If you'd let that bullet kill me, you would have at least escaped our marriage."

"There are few good things in our world, Luca, and if you find one you cling to it with all your might. You are one of those good things in my life."

"I'm not good," Luca said almost desperately.

"You're not a good man, no. But you are good for me. I feel safe in your arms. I don't know why, don't even know why I love you, but I do, and that won't change."

Luca closed his eyes, looking almost resigned. "Love is a risk in our world, and a weakness a Capo can't afford."

"I know," I said even as my throat corded up.

Luca's eyes shot open, fierce and blazing with emotion. "But I don't care because loving you is the only pure thing in my life."

Tears brimmed in my eyes. "You love me?"

"Yes, even if I shouldn't. If my enemies knew how much you meant to me, they'd do anything to get their hands on you, to hurt me through you, to control me by threatening you. The Bratva will try again, and others will too. When I became a made man, I swore to put the Familia first, and I reinforced that same oath when I became a Capo dei Capi even though I knew I was lying. My first choice should always be the Familia."

I held my breath, unable to utter a word. The look he gave me almost broke me into pieces.

"But you are my first choice, Aria. I'll burn down the world if I have to. I'll kill and maim and blackmail. I'll do anything for you. Maybe love is a risk, but it's a risk I'm willing to take and as you said, it's not a choice. I never thought I would, never thought I could love someone like that but I fell in love with you. I fought it. It's the first battle I didn't mind losing."

I slung my arms around him, crying, then whimpered from the twinge in my shoulder. Luca pulled back. "You need to rest. Your body needs to heal." He made me lie down but I held onto his arms. "I don't want to rest. I want to make love to you."

Luca looked pained. "I'm going to hurt you. Your stitches could rip open."

I trailed my hands down over his chest, his taut stomach until I brushed the bulge in his boxers. "He agrees with me."

"He always does, but he's not the voice of reason, believe me."

I giggled, then winced as pain shot down my arm.

Luca still hovered over me but he shook his head. "That's what I mean."

"Please," I whispered. "I want to make love to you. I've wanted this for a long time."

"I've always made love to you, Aria."

I swallowed, and began stroking Luca's erection through the thin fabric. He didn't draw back. "Don't you want this?"

"Of course I want it. We almost lost each other. I want nothing more than to be as close to you as possible."

"Then make love to me. Slow and gentle."

"Slow and gentle," Luca said in a low voice and I knew I had him. He moved down to the edge of the bed and began massaging my feet and calves. I opened my legs wide. My nightgown rode up, baring my thin white panties to Luca. His eyes traveled up and I knew he could see how much I wanted and needed this. Luca groaned against my ankle, then trailed his fingers up my leg, only dusting the skin until he brushed my center with his fingertips. My panties stuck to my slick heat. "You make slow and gentle really hard on me. If you weren't hurt, I'd bury myself in you and make you scream my name."

"If I wasn't hurt, I'd want you to do it."

Luca flicked his tongue across my ankle, then gently sucked the skin into his mouth. "Mine."

Then he covered my calves and thighs with kisses, saying the word 'mine' over and over again as he made his way up toward my center. He slid my panties down, then settled between my legs and kissed my outer lips. "Mine," he whispered against my heated flesh. I arched and immediately jerked in pain.

"I want you to relax completely. No tensing your muscles, or your shoulder will hurt," he said, his lips brushing against me as he spoke and making me wet with arousal.

"I always tense up when I come," I said teasingly. "And I really really want to come."

"You will, but no tensing."

I didn't say that I thought it was impossible. Luca could probably see it on my face and his expression said that he accepted the challenge.

I should challenge him more often. As he began to pleasure me with ghost touches and kisses and licks that made my toes curl with need, I felt my muscles loosen and my mind drift into a cocoon of bliss. My quiet moans and the soft sound of Luca's mouth working my folds mingled with the silence of the room. A knot slowly formed deep in my core, and every brush of Luca's tongue tightened it, and then deliciously slowly the knot unraveled and my orgasm flowed through my body like honey, and I released a long breath as Luca kept my orgasm going for what seemed like forever with feathery touches. I watched him get up through a haze that had nothing to do with painkillers. He slipped out of his boxers as I lay like a boneless heap on the bed. My body was humming as if every cell had been infused with sweet pleasure. He stretched above me, his tip at my entrance. Then he slid into me ever so slowly, stretching me. I let out a long moan when he filled me completely.

"Mine," he said quietly.

I stared into his eyes as he withdrew inch by inch until only his tip was in me before sliding back in. "Yours," I whispered.

The path stretching before us was one of darkness, a life of blood and death and danger, a future of always watching my back, of knowing every day could be Luca's last, of fearing that one day I might have to watch him receive a lethal injection. But this was my world and Luca was *my* man, and I would go this path with him until the bitter end.

As he made love to me, I touched my hand to the tattoo over his heart, felt his heart beating against my palm. I smiled. "Mine."

"Always," Luca said.

# Books in the Born in Blood Mafia Chronicles:

## Bound by Honor

(Aria & Luca)

## Bound by Duty

(Valentina & Dante)

## Bound by Hatred

(Gianna & Matteo)

## Other Books by Cora Reilly

Voyeur Extraordinaire

Lover Extraordinaire (February 2015)

<>

Not Meant To Be Broken

# About the Author

Cora Reilly is the author of erotic romance and New Adult novels. She lives in one of the ugliest cities of the world with too many pets and only one husband. She's a lover of good vegetarian food, wine and books, and she wants nothing more than to travel the world.

CPSIA information can be obtained
at www.ICGtesting.com
Printed in the USA
LVHW081425110319
610216LV00014B/315/P